T0277559

Where No One Should Live

Where
No One
Should Live

A Novel

Sandra Cavallo Miller

UNIVERSITY OF NEVADA PRESS | *Reno & Las Vegas*

University of Nevada Press | Reno, Nevada 89557 USA
www.unpress.nevada.edu
Copyright © 2021 by Sandra Cavallo Miller
All rights reserved
Cover photograph © iStock/CSA Archive
Jacket design by Iris Saltus

LIBRARY OF CONGRESS CATALOGING-IN-PUBLICATION DATA
Names: Miller, Sandra Cavallo, author.
Title: Where no one should live / Sandra Cavallo Miller.
Description: Reno : University of Nevada Press, [2021] |
Summary: "Public health physician Dr. Maya Summer faces a myriad of medical challenges
  as she comes to grips with her uneasy past. Helped by faculty physician Alex Reddish, who
  withstands his own identity trials, she uncovers the grave truth behind a series of illnesses
  as she and Reddish draw close to one another" —Provided by publisher.
Identifiers: LCCN 2021008770 | ISBN 9781647790165 (cloth) | ISBN 9781647790172 (ebook)
Subjects: LCSH: Physicians—Fiction. | Interpersonal relations—Fiction.
Classification: LCC PS3613.I55293 W485 2021 | DDC 813/.6—dc23
LC record available at https://lccn.loc.gov/2021008770

FIRST PRINTING

Manufactured in the United States of America

Dedicated to the steadfast legions of public health physicians and workers who spend their careers studying science and keeping us safe.

The heat slowly climbed, and the afternoons began to bake. First ninety degrees, then ninety-five. The fingertips of saguaro cactus erupted with creamy white blossoms, and Phoenix residents did their best to enjoy this last taste of spring before June struck.

For Dr. Maya Summer at Arizona Public Health, it was already too late. The mosquitoes were rising along with the temperature.

"Just give me another week, you little villains," she muttered to the mosquitoes. Maya switched between two computers on her large desk, one screen filled with spreadsheets, the other displaying grisly images of crushed motorcycles.

Her breath caught as she surveyed the carnage in those sterile numbers and twisted fenders, imagining the heartache and pain. The ruined bodies, the grieving families. Although Arizona once imposed helmets, voters withdrew that law in the seventies. Maya's personal mission, an uphill battle, meant convincing citizens to reverse the decision and make motorcycle helmets mandatory again. And meanwhile, more urgent issues kept derailing her.

Like now. A message flashed in one corner of the screen "Dr. Summer— please reply now to schedule TV interview."

Maya sighed. She already taped a small sign on her door to discourage interruptions "Hopelessly behind. Knock only for emergencies. BIG emergencies."

Because of that sign, Sheila had emailed her instead of knocking. But Maya knew Sheila would soon knock anyway, her red-framed glasses perched low on her nose, her lips a grim line. Just give me an hour, Maya pleaded silently, scanning the statistics, hurriedly tapping her analysis into a document.

A sharp double rap on the door and the latch opened, someone entering behind her.

"I'm really sorry, Sheila," Maya said over her shoulder, contrite, typing faster. "I just need to wrap this up and—"

Mel Black slouched past her, clearing his throat and dropping his bent frame into a chair. Maya stopped working, abandoning her task. One of her favorite people, Mel was always welcome.

"Not a very friendly note out there on your door," he complained, half closing one eye as he peered at her. "You in a bad mood or something?"

Maya tried to match his frown, but her smile spread—something about Dr. Melvin Black, with his morose expression and forlorn eyes, brooding under unruly gray brows, just made her feel better. In his late sixties, he had a face like the side of a mountain, furrowed and hard, eroded from a lifetime of working his cattle ranch. Or at least he chased a few cows, when he wasn't attending patients in his rural clinic north of Phoenix. Then four years ago his wife died of cancer, and he announced he was tired of clinical medicine. Within months, he sold his practice and turned the ranch over to his brother, moving himself to the city and tackling the roller coaster of public health. Thoughtful and meticulous, he had a surprising aptitude for it, despite his prolific scorn.

"No, Mel. I'm just trying to get some work done without constant interruptions." Maya looked pointedly at him.

He snorted, ignoring her implication. "Good luck with that."

Maya waited, but Mel seemed in no hurry to explain his presence. He looked past her at the shattered motorcycle on her screen.

"Mel. You need something?" Her fingers strummed the desk.

"I thought you were working on mosquitoes. What's with the wrecks?" He leaned back and crossed his denim-clad legs, a walnut gleam of cowboy boots. Mel always wore jeans and a corduroy blazer; he added a turquoise bolo tie if he felt like dressing up.

"Helmets. Just trying to save a few lives." Maya clicked through both computers, minimizing the windows. She would never finish that now, not today.

Maya rarely acknowledged the roots of her fervor about this. Personal misfortune only muddied the water. It wouldn't help and might make things worse, so she suppressed that uneasy memory. Needless sentiment, old news.

She saw Sheila pause at the door, a fierce scowl, then slowly move on. Waiting for Mel to leave so she could pounce. "And yes, I'm working on mosquitoes. And the nuclear power plant. And contaminated well water. And the rising air pollution. And blood donor screening. And—"

"Easy." Mel held up a tired hand. "Do you think maybe you take on too much at once? Do you ever say *no*? As in, *hell no*?"

Maya lifted one shoulder. "No. I like being busy."

"Well, just be careful. Some of those biker guys might get mean, might come after you."

"They already have. That is, verbally." Her lips tightened as she recalled the latest round of online threats. Suggesting she might have an accident. Might find something missing. Might need a lesson.

"You talk to security?"

"It's okay, don't worry." She veered from the subject. "How's your task force going?"

"My brand new opiate task force? It's peachy, as you can imagine. The most fun I've ever had. I think they assigned me there just so I'd quit. So they wouldn't have to fire me." Glum, his eyes drooped.

"You won't quit. Besides, I heard your new guidelines look really good."

"Eh. No one will ever agree to them. Maybe I *should* quit. I'm too old for this crap."

His face sagged and he looked suddenly weary, truly exhausted, and Maya reminded herself that his path to this job had not exactly been painless.

"Are you okay, Mel?"

"Just above water." He stared into space and rubbed his mouth with a gnarled hand.

"I think I'm worried about you," Maya said, kind but serious. "Should I be?"

He chuckled, put his hands on his thighs and leaned forward, about to rise. "Hell, no. Maybe someone could've worried about me thirty or forty years ago. Too late now."

Her eyes narrowed. "Are you dodging me?"

"You youngsters are all alike, busy busy busy. Fixing this, fixing that. You should relax and have more fun with your life. You still seeing that guy? It's been a while, hasn't it?" His eyes now lively, probing.

"Whitaker? Yes, just over a year now. I'll see him tonight, if he gets done in time." Mel had a way of throwing her off balance. "I'm pretty flexible. Luckily."

"Not sure if that's your brightest move, Maya. Dating a busy cardiologist. What's he like?"

"He's very smart."

Mel frowned. "That's not what I asked."

"Okay," she nodded, tried not to grin. "How about the fact that he's very good looking?"

"I didn't ask that, either." He shook his head. "Ought to be a law against doctors dating doctors. Doomed from the start."

"Mel. Lighten up."

"I am. You don't want to see me when I'm down." He pushed himself up with a grunt. "And by the way, your staff out there is having a small meltdown. You really need to see what they want."

Mel ambled out the door and Sheila swooped in.

"Dr. Summer, we have to take care of this. Now."

Maya knew she was in trouble. Unless Sheila was distressed, she always called Maya by her first name. Sheila railed on, her short brassy hair in spiky disarray except for the dyed green curl that hooked around one ear.

"That TV station is driving me to the brink. You simply must talk with them, do that interview. Today."

"Today?" Maya blinked. She liked to prepare for interviews and usually studied up the night before, at home, armed with her computer and notebooks. Now she glanced at a pile of reports that needed attention, new data from the well water studies. Some with good news, some alarming, all clamoring for her scrutiny. But she felt bad about ignoring Sheila, who helped her a hundred times every day, and knew she owed her this one.

"Yes, today. That's what I've been trying to tell you." Sheila's glasses slid to the tip of her nose, about to fly off, an exasperated glare shooting over the rims.

"We can't do it tomorrow?"

"You're not here tomorrow—it's your day at the clinic." Another sharp look. "I swear, Maya, you'd think I was the thirty-something and you were almost seventy."

"All right, all right. I just forgot for a second." Maya usually spent Thursdays at the family medical clinic, seeing patients and supervising doctors-in-training. "Only tell me it isn't KTAN. Their reporters are always so aggressive."

"Of course it's KTAN. They're threatening to say how we must be hiding something since we won't set up an interview." Her chin jerked indignantly and the glasses tumbled from her face, caught by a thin silver chain around her neck.

Maya nodded, resigned, searching for an ounce of determination to carry her through. "Don't worry, Sheila, I'll take care of it. What's it about? And how much prep time do I have?"

"Their station is only a few miles away, so you've probably got thirty minutes before the crew sets up. They'll fly in like vultures the minute I call them. But it's just about mosquitoes and Zika, so no big deal. You can do that in your sleep." Sheila must have seen something in Maya's face, because she softened. "Really, Maya. Don't stress. You always do fine."

Sheila zipped out and Maya retreated to her computers. She could comfortably deliver a splendid lecture to an audience of hundreds, complete with slides and graphics. But being interrogated in front of a camera, by intense reporters with sharp questions for sound bites, unsettled her. While most stations were courteous, and extremely helpful in spreading vital information, reporters from KTAN were notoriously not. They prided themselves on "getting to the guts" of stories, whether the guts were there or not.

Stupid mosquitoes, she thought crossly. Those tiny, whiny, weightless creatures, little wisps floating through the air, barely visible, barely felt. Yet they contained circulatory systems that moved fluids through their hair-like bodies, respiratory systems for oxygen, reproductive organs for mating and giving birth. They had teeny eyes and complicated mouths that could thrust a thin proboscis through your skin, striking blood and injecting a minute drop of anticoagulant saliva to keep the blood from clotting while sucking it up like a straw.

And that was the problem. That bit of saliva sometimes carried a stray organism from the mosquito's last meal, and suddenly that little organism found itself inside a new animal, a human, in a warm cozy place where it could thrive.

"Ready?" Sheila thrust her head in the doorway, baring her long teeth in a forced smile.

"Not really. Do I look okay?" Too late to check the latest CDC data now, Maya realized she should have spruced up instead of losing herself in a daydream of insects. It was a bad old habit, that withdrawing, something she had never completely eliminated after the accident.

"Yes. No, wait." Sheila hustled around the desk, fussed with Maya's hair. "You're all flyaway. Don't you have any hairspray?"

"You know me better than that." Maya smiled but felt her mood deteriorate, a slow landslide.

"Lord love a duck, Maya. Don't move." Sheila rushed out and immediately rushed back, a spray can in hand, enveloping Maya in a chemical-scented cloud and patting her hair into place. "There. Better. Come on."

The media room stood by the front lobby, a bright glassed-in square where a cameraman jockeyed his equipment and a neatly groomed reporter studied his reflection, licked his finger, and stroked an eyebrow into place. Maya introduced herself, extending her hand. Everyone just needs reassurance, she thought. It would probably be a ten-second blurb on the evening news. Six seconds, if she was lucky.

The reporter, whose name she immediately forgot, seemed blunt and unlikable. His name was something alliterative, like Bluff Blunderson, although that couldn't possibly be right. He threw questions like darts, often cutting her off halfway through her response.

No, she replied patiently, it's unlikely that we'll see Zika in Phoenix this summer. Yes, Zika-positive mosquitoes had appeared along the coast of Central America, but the mosquitoes in Arizona remained negative so far. No, she said ruefully, the health department never gave guarantees—the roaming habits of mosquitoes and the viruses they carried were not an exact science. She almost said *we can't keep them behind a border wall*, but caught herself. Not a moment for humor.

Instead, she reviewed the symptoms of Zika. Only a quarter of infected humans developed fever, aches, and rash. But even without symptoms, a person could still pass Zika on. The virus just needed a handy mosquito to bite one infected person, then carry through saliva to another. Or it could pass in semen, through sex. Bluff wanted more, so she explained the damage to a growing fetus: possible microcephaly and altered brain development. How everyone should try to avoid mosquito bites and drain any standing water, even small amounts around their homes, where the insects might lay their eggs. Abandoned swimming pools posed a major problem.

"But not all mosquitoes carry Zika, correct?" Bluff challenged.

"You're absolutely right. Just the *Aedes aegypti* mosquito, which lives in Arizona. And the *Culex* mosquito lives here too, which carries West Nile virus. That's the one we really need to dodge right now." Maya wondered if she should have said that, wished she could snatch back those words. Interviewing felt like walking a tightrope: say enough to help, but not too much. Don't say *worry* or *afraid*.

The reporter jumped on it, a gleam in his eye. "West Nile? How close is that to reaching Arizona?"

"It's here now, has been for years. We had thirty cases last year, that we know of." His eyes widened and she tried to take it down a notch. "Most people don't have symptoms, or just mild symptoms. In some states, it's much worse."

"So you mean there's this other virus that no one knows about—" He looked alarmed and held up his hand when Maya began to protest. "—and no one's talking about it? Is it as bad as Zika?"

Maya fixed him with her look. "First of all, we talk about it all the time. It doesn't get publicity like Zika for some reason. Maybe you could help change that." Her expression hopeful. "People get West Nile virus through mosquitoes from infected birds, like crows and ravens, not from other people, like Zika. And like I said, most patients don't get sick at all, but a few get very ill. We had five deaths last year. That's why we always recommend mosquito protection."

"*Deaths?*"

The interview went in circles after that. He gave his signature sign-off, glaring into the camera and proclaiming "We get to the guts of the story." Afterward, he seemed preoccupied and barely thanked her.

Maya withdrew to her office, dispirited, and picked up the reports on contaminated well water, sorting them into piles. What an untidy day, she thought, frustrated by how little she had accomplished.

Sheila drifted in and plopped down in a chair.

"I hate that TV station. They always act like we're lying. Or making things up." She rubbed her temples, and for a moment her face wilted, her creased skin showing every day of her sixty-seven years. Then she brightened. "You did great, though."

"I don't think so. I'm afraid how they'll slice that up for the news tonight." Maya appreciated Sheila's reassurance, but shook her head. She disliked watching herself on television; maybe she would skip it this time and not torment herself about whether she said "um" too often or frowned excessively. She thought her frown made her look angry, but she couldn't completely control it. When she concentrated, she frowned.

Sheila tugged at the green curl by her ear, an unconscious habit. Then she stood and took the files from Maya, pushed them to the corner of the desk.

"Come on," she said. "It's happy hour with free nachos down the street. We've both earned our keep for today."

Maya checked her watch. Five-twenty, and Whitaker wouldn't be done with his cases for at least an hour, maybe two. Maybe not until nine o'clock if problems arose, and then he would beg off from their plans. She pictured him in the cardiac lab, scrubbed and masked, his sharp eyes examining a narrow artery, intently absorbed in the delicate task.

Maybe Mel was right and doctors shouldn't date doctors.

"I've got time," Maya agreed, suddenly hungry. The sky through her window turned tangerine, cooling as the sun sank. A tall saguaro stood there, the white blossoms starting to wilt and drop as the season heated up. *Carnegiea gigantea*, enticing nocturnal bats to spread the tiny seeds… an unlikely beginning for a forty-foot one-ton behemoth plant that drank very little water and pointed long prickly limbs at the sun. Maya loved her office with that large window, as if the sky and saguaro watched her work, companions. "Let's go, then."

She unexpectedly recalled those lines of poetry. *Let us go then, you and I…the evening spread out against the sky, like a patient etherized upon the table.* Like Whit's patients on the table, tiny plastic tubes threaded through their hearts.

Some kind of omen, when T. S. Eliot appeared in her head.

3

Alex Reddish loved his teaching job, almost all the time.

The interns were fairly seasoned now, accustomed to the clinic flow. Since starting last summer, they had improved their skills at juggling patients' blood pressures and backaches and family stressors, knew what problems to handle immediately and what to delay until the next visit. When to talk about depression, when to counsel, and when to intervene with medication. How to suture lacerations and how to interpret an EKG, that cryptic sketch of heart muscle. The ways to differentiate between migraine headaches and tumor headaches, and a thousand other scenarios. Most of the interns, anyway.

No wonder becoming a family physician took three extra years of training. The first-year residents—the interns—got close supervision. They discussed every patient with Alex or another attending physician, who dissected their notes for logic and diligence to details. They must develop proper diagnoses, give sound advice, and recommend appropriate follow-up. Alex gave feedback and monitored progress, and residents gradually became more autonomous.

And now his advisee Veronica Sampson wanted to talk with him. About to begin her third and final year of residency, Veronica hoped to review her performance reports. She stopped by a few minutes ago, near his spot in the attending office.

"Dr. Reddish." She slipped into a chair by the desk, leaned forward confidentially. Although she clipped back her tawny hair, it spilled down her shoulders, dense and wavy like a lion's mane. She slid her hand onto his forearm. "I'm just dying to see my latest reviews. Can we meet when you're done?"

Alex regarded her, her wide brown eyes flecked with gold, the slender gold chain around her neck, dangling a tiny star that sparkled and made you look at her throat. He wasn't fond of gold. Gold felt opulent, oppressive, old money…it reminded him too much of his mother. He preferred the clean shine of silver.

He paused before answering, not because she was attractive and commanded attention, but because he always did that. Waiting a moment came second nature, even when he knew precisely the words he would say. As if he needed one more tick of time, which he did not. He appreciated how this habit made others uneasy, the last thing he intended, but he still almost always paused. No doubt a leftover habit from playing chess all those years. It wasn't exactly a hesitation, more like a suspension, as his fingers lingered over the piece before committing and touching down. Not a reassessment, just a thoughtful double-check.

Really, he told himself—quit doing that. People get uncomfortable. Just react spontaneously, like a normal human.

"Of course." He clicked the clinic schedule on the computer, a wide grid of patient slots and physicians on duty. Everyone seemed reasonably on time except Jim Barrow, an hour behind. No surprise. Alex shrugged at Veronica. "But I'm not sure when I'll be done."

"Well, let's pencil it in." A smile, her suede lips some shade of mauve. She gave his arm a little squeeze. "If you're feeling okay. I heard you caught that virus. Me too. I felt terrible."

"Yeah, that was bad."

On Monday, half the staff and physicians succumbed to gastroenteritis, everyone suddenly weak and vomiting. Alex still felt slightly off. They had to cut back on patient visits for two days because so many doctors and nurses were incapacitated.

It had been a difficult year, more incidental illnesses than usual. The clinic heightened hygiene protocols and promoted liberal use of face masks and gloves, although no one could tell if it made much difference. With the year only half over, some employees had no sick leave left. Of course, Alex thought, when your job is working with diseases, you risk getting ill.

"Are you all right now, Veronica?" Alex rolled his chair back and casually moved his arm from under her hand. He saw Jim Barrow waiting awkwardly in the doorway, gestured him in. "Hi, Jim. Have a seat."

"I'm good." She flicked a dismissive glance at Jim, then gave Alex a conspiratorial nod, raising her hand in a peace sign. "Remember, I go by V now. Veronica sounds so stuffy. Even my patients call me Dr. V."

"V," he nodded, even as he turned to Jim.

Working with Jim Barrow was one of the few times when his faculty job didn't feel very satisfying.

Barrow sat facing him, laptop balanced on his bony knees and scrolling through his patient's chart as if searching for something he'd lost. Although Alex hated to admit it, he disliked Jim's nickname and pretended to forget it. Jimbo. What was it with these nicknames? V and Jimbo—seriously? Jim struggled as it was, so why saddle himself with that? It felt juvenile, demeaning. Residency seemed like a good time to drop those adolescent hangovers. A nice enough man, Jim harbored a gentle soul, but his brain circuits flowed like cold syrup. Alex wished he knew how to guide him better.

"Now then," Alex said brightly, setting an efficient tone. "Tell me why you think this man's diabetes is making his left foot feel numb."

Jim's gaze dragged across the laptop, then his mud-brown eyes wandered up to Alex. "It must be, right? I mean, he's diabetic, and diabetics get nerve damage. It makes sense."

"That's all correct, of course. But there are two problems with your theory. Any ideas what?" Don't just tell him. Give him a chance to figure it out. That was the art: instead of throwing him solutions, show how to think the problem through. Simply supplying the answer was quick but mindless, while coaching analytical skills took patience. And though Alex considered himself a patient man, even his endurance had limits.

Jim stared at the screen again, as if the answer might materialize there.

Alex prompted a little more. "It's just on one side of his body, just his left foot…"

"Ah." Jim pursed his lips, still lost.

"And you've got his sugars pretty well controlled…"

Jim nodded slowly, waiting for help.

Enough torture, thought Alex. "When high blood sugars cause nerve damage, it's widespread—so both feet would be numb. Since it's just one foot, we have to think about something local, like a pinched nerve in his left leg. Besides, his sugars are decent, so it's probably not his diabetes."

Now Jim nodded rapidly, avoiding Alex's eyes. "Of course. Of course."

"Let's go see him together and check it out." Alex didn't trust Jim to find the heart of this alone. And it grew late. His nurse would want to go home as soon as he finished.

A considerable time later, they exited the patient's room with a diagnosis of left sciatica…an inflamed nerve running down the leg, a common diagnosis. Jim thanked Alex profusely, apologetic about missing the obvious. The nurse Connie gathered up discharge instructions for the patient and threw a concerned look at Alex.

Jim Barrow was a problem, functioning almost like a medical student instead of a resident. Alex carefully documented the clumsy encounter, feeling bad for Jim, then sent a copy to Stewart Burns, the residency director. The last time Alex talked with him, Burns muttered about an intervention for Barrow if things deteriorated. A formal evaluation. Alex felt puzzled, because last year Jim seemed like a normal intern. Had something changed? Residents commonly suffered from depression and sleep deprivation, might develop problems with alcohol or drugs. Alex had gently probed Jim's mental state, pointed out that a quarter of doctors in training grew downhearted. Jim turned wary and vehemently denied it.

"I'm just tired." He sounded defensive, his dull hair unkempt. "Nothing else."

Maybe.

Well, it would be a slow process. One step at a time, with painstaking documentation of his lackluster performance. Jim would need a psychiatric evaluation, a thorough physical exam and labs, a learning specialist, drug testing. All daunting, but increasingly inevitable. When physicians began running off the rails, you did everything you could to figure out why and get them back on track.

Alex moved to his office and found a pink note stuck on his keyboard "Sorry I couldn't wait. Maybe tomorrow? :) —V"

What a relief. Alex sent her an email, arranging a meeting the next day at noon, just before the daily lecture.

But he looked forward to tomorrow. Maya Summer would be there, seeing her patients in the morning and teaching alongside him in the attending office all afternoon. While trained in family medicine like him, she followed a different path, working at Arizona Public Health. He appreciated her high energy, her public health stories, and he enjoyed teasing her about mosquitoes, like whether she kept any pet mosquitoes at home, to learn their perspective and see how they felt about being vectors for deadly diseases. He liked how she playfully poked back at him, about his reserve. *You know what they say about people like you*, she laughed, *all quiet on the outside…* Then she never finished the phrase, left it unspoken. Those unusual gray eyes—truly gray, not an altered shade of blue. Something else there, too, something shadowed, but he hadn't yet figured it out.

Alex changed clothes and strapped on his bike helmet, adjusted the clasp. Best idea he'd ever had, riding his bike to work. The growing heat made it tough, but there was a shower in the residents' study lounge that he used every morning. His weight and fitness felt good. Something new for him, shedding that pudge.

Still a little weak from the stomach bug, he took his time and didn't push himself. Avoiding the main road traffic, he slipped through neighborhoods, dodged a few kids playing baseball in the street, smiled at a little girl romping with her dog in a dirt yard.

Halfway home, Alex enjoyed the light ginger sky above and the soft breeze drying the sweat on his face, then recalled Veronica's note with its smiley face. Such a witless, vapid image. That wasn't really her—he didn't buy it for a second.

4

Maya draped herself over the pipe rail of the large corral. Still very warm, evening settled around the dusky hills as the orange sky dimmed, a soft glow. She loved living here in her parents' old house, nestled against the low mountains of Piestewa Park, right in the middle of Phoenix. The house seriously needed work, but she would think about that later. It was on the list.

"Hey Luna," she called.

Thank goodness for her neighbor Rosa and her ten-year-old son Rafael, who always came over and fed Luna if Maya wasn't home. It would be his job this summer, feeding the horse twice a day, checking her water, cleaning her hooves. Maya gladly paid him for the chores, although he would have done it for nothing. Rafael loved Luna and hung out with her, groomed her, and brought her carrots. When he talked to her, Luna flicked her ears, listening closely.

The old mare raised her head, munching hay. She shuffled over and thrust her sorrel face against Maya's cheek, a whiskery rub. Maya huffed out a breath and Luna put her nostril to Maya's mouth, inhaling her scent, gently blowing it back. Maya touched the delicate nasal arc, then stroked the white crescent on her forehead.

"Luna," she murmured, "you funny old mare."

The mare smelled fragrant, of warm dust and crushed hay.

Maya wondered what horses thought. Was Luna completely in the moment—here's my food and here's the human, warm sunlight in January and blessed shade in July? Or maybe she worried every morning if the sun would rise, if someone would appear with breakfast or care enough to rub that spot on her neck. Maybe she dreamt of past days, when Maya climbed on and they cantered through the desert, skirting prickly cholla and laughing at roadrunners, startling those stinky javelina that scuttled up out of a draw, grunting and squealing. Maybe Luna longed for that again. Or maybe she felt relieved it was over.

And what do you long for, you silly human, Maya asked herself, sliding off the fence as Luna moved back to her hay. Maya checked on the tortoise lounging under the mesquite tree in the yard, his beady eyes following her.

"Hey, Twinkie." Maya rubbed his leathery head with two fingers. He raised his neck, pushed back. "Did you move much today?"

Twinkie blinked slowly. Contemplating something, Maya thought. Or nothing.

Damn Mel and his prying questions, catching her off guard. Her inane response about Whit: smart and handsome. Could she possibly sound more shallow? She should have told Mel how thoughtful Whit could be, always aware of her schedule. How hard he worked, taking every patient's success or failure personally. He brought her little things, a nice pen or a book of poetry, a music album. *I thought of you when I saw this*, he'd say. Sometimes it was sentimental rhymes or smoky jazz, neither her taste, but he certainly tried. Why didn't she tell Mel about that? Whit supported her career. He worried about her hip and wanted her to take better care of herself. She felt safe with him, and this month they started discussing a future together.

Her hip ached now. She shouldn't have walked so far last night, but the moon was too inviting and she strolled on and on under that overflowing light. The desert luminous, cactus spines glowing. She became a night creature, slipping past brittlebush and spicy creosote plants, nudging at stones. Coyotes yipped, then went quiet. Once, she paused in the long shadow of a saguaro and felt herself disappear.

Well, everything had its price. Her hip would settle down.

And now here Whit came, his sports car crunching slowly down the gravel drive so no rocks flew up, no dings. The car shone dull in the dusk. When he first bought it, Maya teased him that it looked like a scarab beetle, iridescent green.

"Like what?" he asked, uncertain whether to be amused.

"A scarab beetle. *Cotinis mutabilis*. They're beautiful."

He laughed then. "Why do you even know the Latin name?"

"Massive amounts of nerdy trivia." Maya tapped her head. Since childhood, she'd been fascinated by scientific labels. In college she even took a semester of Latin.

Now she hurried toward him until she noticed his lips moving, a squint of concentration as he parked, talking on his phone. She felt struck anew by his face, that long sharp jaw. Instead of waiting, she waved and swerved into the house to prepare a quick supper.

"Nothing fancy," she announced when he entered the kitchen, hanging his suit coat on a chair. He pecked her forehead as she fussed at the stove; he smelled strongly of antiseptic soap and faintly of aftershave, something musky. She'd meant to stop at the Mexican market on her way home, get fresh handmade tortillas and veggies for fajitas. But instead she went out with Sheila. "Just grilled cheese sandwiches and fruit. I can add some ham or bacon to your grilled cheese if you want more protein."

His fine eyebrows lowered slightly as she scooped butter into the skillet, arranged thick slices of cheddar and ripe tomato on brown bread while the butter sizzled.

"That's a lot of fat," he commented. "Our poor little coronary arteries."

"Clock out, Dr. Cholesterol. Have some fun." Maya elbowed him in the ribs. Then she realized she sounded like Mel and laughed. She pulled a bowl of chopped melon from the refrigerator, glistening green and orange cubes.

Whit sighed, gripped her shoulder.

"What's wrong?" Maya asked, now alert. His smooth cheek looked hollow, a crumple in his lips.

He drew the phone from his pocket and glanced for messages, then slid it back. "My last patient didn't do so great. Blood pressure problems, ventricular arrhythmias. If his heart doesn't settle down, I might need to go back in."

"I'm so sorry." Maya hugged him, then turned back to her skillet, flipped the bread. "Let's have supper right away just in case."

"Yes, I should eat something."

Whit conducted himself thoughtfully, made certain he was hydrated and fed so nothing impaired his function. He worked out and watched his cholesterol. A little obsessively, Maya thought, but that felt like an occupational hazard, seeing so many hearts clogged and floundering.

He said he just wanted to relax, so they ate in front of the television, not really watching. Maya ran through channels between bites, finding nothing interesting and eventually settling on an old movie, the sound low and nearly inaudible. But she was pleased to see him polish off the grilled cheese.

Whit leaned back and closed his eyes. Even tired, he looked dashing, a spray of dark hair across his forehead. Maya leaned against him, reached up and loosened his tie. Eyes still closed, he smiled and took her hand, kissed it, then slid his fingers up her arm, wandered across her shoulder and climbed her neck, traced her lips. Maya murmured, aroused. He leaned over to kiss her cheek and halted.

"Um. You kind of smell like a horse. I think."

"Yup. That would be horse. You might find a few horsehairs there, too." He pulled back. "Really?"

His day had been difficult so she let it go, made light of it. "Relax. I'll go wash my face. I forgot I was kissing my horse. Don't be jealous."

She heard his phone ring while in the bathroom, and by the time she returned he was deep in conversation. Brisk words about arrhythmias and drips, anticoagulants—it must be a nurse or a resident doctor. He hung up, finally, and sat thinking, his fingers skating back and forth on his thigh.

"Problems?" Maya asked.

"Yeah. I have to go back. I'll give those meds a chance to work first."

"I'm sorry." She snuggled up to him.

They sat in silence, his expression distant and preoccupied, when he suddenly turned to her.

"I should have just stayed there. But I wanted to talk tonight." He touched her hand.

"About…?"

He played with her fingers, his eyes on the screen as the movie reeled, the muted mumble of a soundtrack. Then he shifted to look into her eyes, a trace of smile. "Really caring about someone is different, isn't it?"

"Different than what?" she asked, a little lighthearted, not certain where he wanted to go.

"Than the usual. You know, different than just dating and going out."

"What are you saying?" He surprised her, starting such a conversation with a critical patient in the wings and about to return to work.

He touched her cheek, stroked her hair. "It's different. Deeper. Like I want to take care of you."

Maya gripped his hand. He talked on but she could barely track him. Unusual for him, to be so scattered. Dry and clinical, he analyzed his feelings this way and that until they seemed like laboratory rats, bumping back and forth, as if through a maze. Maybe it was her, the mosquito interview still lingering in her head. She just let him go on; he clearly felt stressed. She could never do his work, life and death at her fingertips. Coaxing hearts to throb slower, run faster, pump stronger. Her mind wandered and became aware of her own thumping pulse. She pictured her heart, that strange hollow fist of muscle that never quit contracting, that never got to rest.

His phone rang again, summoning him in.

"Thanks for supper." An apology, another quick kiss. He suddenly seized her tightly, arms wrapped, then left abruptly.

He'd behaved awkwardly before—this was not the first time. You'll get used to him, Maya told herself. He's a decent man. He had difficulty expressing emotions sometimes, especially intense ones, and she knew he needed room to find his way. But she also felt a little relieved that he'd gone. She wanted to shed his odd soliloquy, wished she could shake herself down to the bones like a wet dog, that tooth-rattling tail-shuddering sort of quake.

What bothered her most was how she never thought too deeply about Whit until today, when Mel asked. She and Whit came together a year ago; they got along and it seemed simple, automatic. They supported each other. She accepted his traits as part of the personality needed for scrupulous work, and certainly he put up with her flaws. Both physical and mental. Yes, he could be fussy and precise, a little stuffy, but a good steady partner. Never late, rarely aggravated, never rude.

Never anything.

Maybe a little tedious at times, the way he intellectualized. Like tonight.

Still, people acted impressed when they discovered Whitaker Thicket was her boyfriend. They nodded respectfully and a few women pretended to swoon a little, fanned their faces with their hands. Lucky you, they said.

Maya grimaced. Even his lovemaking could be analytic. He first touched her exactly like this, then like that. And he knew her, as if he had calculated how she worked. Almost as if checking her pulse, her breathing, as she heated up. When she thought about it now, it seemed rather rote. Not exactly mechanical, but so…scientific. His protocol checklist, another successful procedure.

"You're nuts," she told herself aloud. As if anyone was perfect. Look at yourself in the mirror.

She should consider herself fortunate.

Maya scrubbed the dishes clean and stepped out back to admire the night. Still warm, not a breath of breeze. She sensed the immense heat gathering force as the seasons shifted and summer approached, inevitable, about to strike. Luna dozed in the corral and a soft silver burn shone behind the hills, the moon on its way. One ridge bristled with saguaro, spiking into the sky. The moon took its time, so she gave up waiting and went inside.

With Whitaker gone, she now had time to gather data on melanomas and skin cancers. The annual sun safety campaign would not organize itself. And earlier that night, as she drove home from work, the radio reported another child drowning in a backyard pool. Such wretched sorrows, never ending, year after year. She wanted to analyze those numbers, too—find better ways to increase awareness, diminish the tragedy. Maybe she should launch a new study, look again for risk factors, find a new key.

Definitely a trait she shared with Whit, both doggedly determined to solve the challenges before them. They weren't so different after all.

Her phone pinged, an email from Sheila about the drowning. Sheila knew Maya would want to be aware. That was the problem with this work. Maya knew she took it too personally, but often it felt up to her to find the way.

JOURNAL

I hoped this place would be an improvement. I always have hope when I move, when I start over and meet new people. A fresh beginning. Maybe this time, I think, I'll be happy. I invent my past, again and again, into a normal childhood. One with both parents, both kind. Some days I even start to believe it myself.

Wishful thinking is a terrible trap and I should avoid it, but sometimes I slip up.

And it turns out, they're no better here than anywhere. People always disappoint me.

Maybe there's one, that Dr. Reddish. He doesn't look at me like most people do. But I don't trust him, either—there's something different about him. Hard to tell if it's good or bad.

Today I spent the entire afternoon just thinking. I could have been more productive but sometimes I need to make plans, figure things out.

I thought a lot about cancer and how those twisted cells take over. When a person first gets cancer, they don't know it at all, not for a while. Sometimes not for months, for years. But it's there, working, reproducing, like a hidden monster that's busy in the cellar. All it takes is a tiny glitch, a tortured piece of DNA, and it begins. It's like a horror show. If the body can't stop it, can't keep it from multiplying…game over.

You have to admire that.

5

Alex Reddish was having a good morning. Lots of chubby babies, gurgling and squirming, sticky drool on their chests. Except this mom was distraught. She licked her chapped lips and hugged her infant. "I'm still scared of these vaccines," she repeated. She looked weary, her clothes rumpled, the toll of infant care. "I can't help it. There's so many side effects."

Alex took his time. "Not that many side effects, actually. I've been doing this for years and have never seen a serious reaction. Neither has any doctor I know. Maybe a little swelling, occasionally some fever and irritability. Younger babies actually seem to tolerate it better."

"But the internet..." Distress crowded her face.

Alex touched the baby's dimpled hand, smiled when she giggled. "I would never do anything to harm this beautiful child. I just want to protect her. I'm sure you've heard about the outbreaks in other states. That's bound to happen here, sooner or later—it's just a matter of time. You'll want her covered."

Alex patiently reviewed measles and mumps complications: pneumonia and encephalitis. Brain damage, lung damage, and seizures. Death. He pointed out that he was vaccinated as a child, and the mom probably was too. But he had to move on. He left her with handouts, asked her to read them before leaving and then let the nurse know what she decided. The baby, snugly wrapped like a little burrito, slept against her shoulder.

Later the nurse Connie patted him on the back. "Nice work, Dr. Reddish. She got the shots."

Alex smiled, relieved. He certainly did not always succeed, but he was fairly adept at reading people and often knew when to push a little more. Spending all those years across a chessboard watching the other players, their cautions and resolves, helped hone those skills.

Childhood viruses were really such dunces, he thought, so easily vanquished. Almost never resistant to vaccines. Not shifty like the influenza virus, so nimble and clever, altering itself each year so the previous vaccine fell flat. Not brilliant like HIV, too agile to pin down at all. Those elusive superstar infections learned to conceal themselves, almost like a castling move, the virus running and hiding behind the king but still dangerous.

Stop it, he told himself. A virus didn't think or strategize—it just mutated.

His last morning patient shuffled in. Arthur Mason, a most frustrating case. Eighty years old, Arthur complained that he sweated too much in winter and shivered too much in summer. His joints creaked and he couldn't touch his toes, so his toenails grew unchecked, thick as roof tiles. His feet cramped and his heart jolted, and sometimes his lungs didn't seem to breathe.

Arthur went to the emergency room last night about that breathing. They X-rayed his chest, checked his oxygen level, and ran an electrocardiogram. They tested his blood and monitored him for an hour. Finally, the emergency doctor said it was probably his "nerves." Arthur took that diagnosis literally and asked Alex to refer him to a neurologist.

Alex nodded sympathetically. "When doctors say that, they mean you have a type of anxiety, something making you nervous, not something wrong with your actual nerves."

Arthur peered skeptically. Rheum puddled in his crusty eyes and thin gray hair wandered across his mottled head, his small nose pink and drippy, making Alex think of elderly rabbits. His clothes hung on a narrow frame of bones, a pouch of belly protruding, but his shirt was clean and he smelled of Old Spice.

"You've lost a pound." Alex tried refocusing Arthur's fears. It was no small task, convincing a chronic worrier to stew about something constructive. "I'm concerned about what you eat. Or what you don't eat."

"I must be careful," Arthur lamented. "Most food doesn't agree with me."

"Did you ever see that dietician? Order Meals on Wheels? You need good nutrition and protein or you'll lose your muscle. You don't want that."

"I eat boiled eggs and canned tuna. Plenty of protein there. My dogs love it, too."

"How many dogs do you have now?" Alex ventured.

A smile cracked Arthur's stern face. "About eight. Sweet little boys and girls. They keep me going, the little darlings."

"Mr. Mason. Can our social worker come visit you? She's so helpful, and she knows what services you might be able to get. Some housekeeping, some meals." Then it dawned on Alex. "Are you spending all your money on dog food?"

The old man insisted he only wanted a referral to that neurologist. Alex explained again, then taught Arthur breathing exercises for when his lungs felt wrong. He recommended a visit with the office psychologist, to explore his anxiety. Arthur made a rabbity twitch with his moist mouth and left muttering.

Alex suspected Arthur's home was a disaster: maybe a hoarding fiasco, maybe filthy from the dogs. Or perhaps the opposite, spare as a cell, just a narrow bed and bags of dog food. And dust, piles of dust and dog hair. No wonder the man felt he couldn't breathe.

Veronica Sampson waited in his office—Alex had forgotten their meeting and came in late. Not that he could have escaped Arthur any sooner.

"So sorry, Veronica. Let me get your file." Alex opened the confidential website and quickly entered his passwords.

Veronica looked stern and raised her hand, making that V. Delicate gold bracelets clicked on her wrist, the same kind of bangles his mother used to wear. Distracting little clinks. Once in high school, he asked his mom to please not wear those jangling bracelets when he played chess; she slid them off quickly and he never saw them again.

Veronica smelled faintly of fruit. Maybe strawberry, maybe apple.

"Sorry. *V*," he corrected himself, and she rewarded him with a wide smile, generating a dimple in one cheek. He focused on the computer. "Well, you only have one evaluation here, I'm afraid. That means two are overdue."

Besides seeing clinic patients two or three days a week, residents spent each month with a specialist, learning as much as possible about that field: dermatology, pulmonology, orthopedics, and so on. Afterward, those specialists sent a report to the resident's advisor about their performance. But busy specialists sometimes put off the reports or forgot, and often the evaluations trickled in weeks or months later, sometimes never.

Veronica's lip pouted. She scooted her chair close and leaned against

Alex to see the screen better. "All right. I see which ones are missing." She pulled back, annoyed. "I'll talk to them—I'll make it happen."

"That would be helpful," Alex admitted. He shifted to make more room. "But look here. Your review from cardiology is fine. Dr. Thicket said you were good to work with. They're a picky bunch, so that's a strong compliment."

Veronica stood, resting her hand on his shoulder, now in a hurry. Definitely strawberry. "Thanks, Dr. Reddish. I'd better get going."

"Any time. And next month is your annual review. Let's do some self-reflection. I'd like you to create a list of what you think are your strengths and your challenges for this last year. Okay?"

She studied him openly, her eyes roving his features as if memorizing the angles. It was a prolonged odd moment, and he resisted touching his face.

"Sure, Dr. Reddish."

Alex hurried to finish his morning charts. By the time he moved to the attending office, ready to supervise the afternoon residents, Maya Summer already sat there. She shook her head at him, her dark brown hair swinging back and forth across her shoulders, a glint of copper. She had a short straight nose and deep gray eyes rimmed in black. He found her subtly attractive.

"I was starting to worry," she said, pulling folders from a shoulder bag. She always carried work with her, articles about mosquitoes or helmets or who knew what, and always seemed to accomplish work between staffing resident cases, taking notes and jotting stats. Now she pretended to look anxious. "I was afraid you'd left me here alone with the wolves."

Alex grinned. "The residents are mostly friendly wolves. They just want to drain your brain of knowledge and feed on your compassion, and then they'll scurry off."

Maya laughed, her eyes now merry. "Scurry? Men never say words like scurry."

"Hey," he said, remembering. "I saw you on TV last night. That interview about Zika."

She groaned. "That was awful. I felt like he was trying to trap me."

"No," he protested. "You were really good. Especially the way you turned the conversation to West Nile, asked him to pay more attention to that. I was impressed."

"Well, thanks. But it felt terrible. I didn't even watch it."

"How are your pet mosquitoes doing, anyway?"

Two residents appeared and Alex and Maya became quickly immersed. The clinic teemed with acute and chronic issues, children eating too little and adults too much. A man with a swollen prostate and a sullen teen who might be using drugs. Diabetes and shin splints and gonorrhea. Welcome to family medicine, Alex thought, never a dull moment.

Third-year resident Jackie Canter staffed a woman with a seeping uterus, irregular bleeding. Another one of Alex's advisees and, unlike Veronica, Jackie was a total joy, with a short dark cap of hair, quick to grin, and intense devotion to her patients. Alex nodded approval, pleased with her thorough evaluation. Having grown up in northern Arizona, she planned a career with the Indian Health Service and hoped to work on the Navajo Nation.

"Nice job," he said. "You'll do great next year. Your patients will love you."

Jackie beamed.

Maya talked with Jim Barrow now. Alex heard her ask Jim what medications he liked to use for hypertension, then about his antibiotic choices for cellulitis. Heard her gently correct him. Then she went with Jim to examine the patient.

Alex felt a little badly, that he was glad it was her this time and not him.

6

Based on Jim Barrow's disorganized description, Maya could not tell if his patient's rash seemed serious or not. He could only specify that the woman had "funny red bumps."

"Let me see it," Maya suggested.

Jim led her to the patient but failed to introduce her, so Maya presented herself to Mrs. Hicks, a middle-aged woman quite pleased to be the center of attention. Masses of auburn curls sprang from her head and framed her freckled face.

"Oh my, Dr. Barrow," she said happily, "I didn't know you were bringing an expert!"

Three pea-sized red nodules humped up on the back of her hand, and three similar lumps marched up her forearm. Two of the little domes had broken open, raw and weeping.

"Fascinating," Maya murmured. "Mrs. Hicks. By any chance do you spend much time gardening?"

"Goodness, yes," the woman exclaimed. "I've got a huge flower garden—it's my pride and joy. Getting it through the summer is such a challenge! How did you guess that?"

Maya smiled. "Just a hunch. Lots of roses?"

Mrs. Hicks's mouth dropped open. "How on earth could you know that?"

Maya felt acutely aware of Jim hovering behind her. She knew how awful it could be, to have no clue about a diagnosis and then someone else waltzes in and nails it immediately. Sooner or later, they all experienced it. She tried to soften the moment.

"Actually, this is uncommon. I've only seen it once, years ago." Maya glanced at Jim, giving him another chance. "Now that you know it might come from rose thorns, do you have any idea, Dr. Barrow?"

Jim shook his head, looking miserable.

"Don't worry," Maya assured him. "Like I said, it's pretty rare. I'm just lucky I've seen it before. It's called sporotrichosis, and it's caused by a fungus that lives on rose thorns. *Sporothrix schenckii.*"

"See, Dr. Barrow?" Mrs. Hicks said brightly, her curls bouncing. "No one expects you to know it. You can't know everything, now, can you?"

Maya found herself admiring this sweet, upbeat patient, trying to make her young physician feel better. Clearly Mrs. Hicks liked her Dr. Barrow, acted almost protective of him. Maya promised the patient that he would be right back, and pulled Jim into the nursing station.

"Okay," Maya instructed. "Describe those skin lesions in medical terms."

"Well…" Jim's eyes slid back and forth. He looked weary. "Like I said, red bumps."

"That's a start. But you should describe the size, the shape, the color. Are they solid, like a nodule, or are they fluid-filled, like a blister? Are the edges sharply demarcated, or vague? And how would you describe the ones that are open and weeping?"

"Um. Can't I just say that?"

"Yes. But a more correct term would be that they're ulcerated. Right? So, can you describe them medically now?"

He slowly put it together, drawn out but correct. "Okaaay. Soooo. There are these four-millimeter solid…nodules. Dark red, the edges sharp. In a line. I guess you'd say a linear pattern?" He paused to look at her and Maya nodded. He actually smiled. "And the two nodules most… distal…," another look and another nod, "show central ulcerations."

"Perfect." Maya said. "We should do a biopsy to prove the diagnosis, but in the meantime, let's start treatment. Any idea what to use?"

His bright moment faded and he stared at her, almost listless. Maya took pity and discussed antifungal medications, then showed him where to look up the dosage.

She didn't expect him to recognize sporotrichosis—many seasoned physicians wouldn't know that—or which antifungal drug to use.

But something was off with him.

7

Alex looked up when Maya returned, her face thoughtful. He leaned her way and quietly asked that she document the encounter carefully and send a copy to Stewart Burns, the residency director, and to Scott Sherman, Jim's advisor.

"What's going on with him?" Maya whispered.

"We're not sure. Some days he's normal. Then other days he barely functions."

But they could hardly discuss it there, and he changed the subject.

Veronica stopped by with a question about hyperthyroidism, and even though Maya sat available at the moment, Veronica waited for Alex. Alex sensed Maya watching them…not that Maya wasted a moment. If Veronica wanted to talk with Alex, Maya had things to do. She pulled a file from her stack and scribbled hurriedly, running her finger down a column of text, marking with a yellow highlighter.

"What are you studying?" he asked after Veronica left. The afternoon was winding down. "You look like you're attacking that article."

Maya raised her head, wielding her marker. "Sometimes this helmet data makes me crazy and I do attack it. At least, with my pen." She tilted her head. "Does she always flirt with you like that?"

Alex caught himself pausing.

"No," he said, uncomfortable, because it wasn't true. Veronica almost always flirted. But he understood she had no real interest in him. More like a game of hers—so like his mother. It annoyed the hell out of him that Veronica made him think of his mother, more than he'd done in years. The gold jewelry, the gratuitous touching. Alex shook it off and focused on Maya. "Did you say you're preparing a report? For a proposed new helmet law?"

"Yes." She warmed to her subject. "I'm looking at the bicycle data, too. And horseback riders. All things helmet."

"Please don't tell me not to ride my bike to work," he begged, playful.

Maya didn't smile. "Please tell me that you always wear a helmet. Or so help me, I will hide your bike and never give it back." She frowned when he laughed. "It's not funny, Alex. You're smart, you know the data.

Seventy percent fewer head injuries on bicycles. Forty percent fewer deaths on motorcycles."

"Of course."

"I mean it." Her eyes stormy.

He raised his hand in a pledge. "I will *always* ride my bike with a helmet."

Maya squinted at him as she gathered her papers.

She finally softened and smiled. "All right, then."

The patients had gone and residents sat busy at their stations, charting and making phone calls. Alex and Maya chatted about difficult diagnoses and treatment strategies. When she told him about the sporotrichosis, her acumen impressed him.

"Next time, please come get me if you find something interesting like that," he said. "I'm not sure I would have remembered sporotrichosis. I wish I'd seen it."

"For sure," she nodded. "I should have thought of that."

He suddenly wondered if she had supper plans, wondered if it would be strange if he asked her to grab a bite with him. They could talk about her work and her research, so interesting. Not a date, of course, just talking. Like a colleague. Everyone knew she had a boyfriend, or he was pretty certain she still did. He imagined himself saying it, *grab a bite.* Her possible replies: She might say, *Sure, why not?* Or maybe she would say, *No, I'm seeing my boyfriend.* She might act flattered, or perhaps annoyed. The potentials branched out, more and more pathways.

He blinked and saw her watching him, waiting. Crap. How long had he sat there, inside his own head? Had she asked a question? Say something.

"Are you still with Thicket?" he blurted, instantly regretting it. He'd met Thicket a few times in the hospital. A smart man, no doubt about it. Polished and urbane, a stylish suit. Cardiology was a lucrative specialty, while family medicine languished at the bottom of physician income. You didn't go into family medicine for the money.

"Yes, thanks for asking." She ignored his muddle. "This was fun. I love getting away from my office for a day. Seeing patients and teaching, so down to earth. So immediate."

"Hey, we really appreciate it. We can always use the help." Alex mumbled more words about seeing her next week. She rose and he saw her step oddly, a sideways hitch, a small grimace. Then she walked on and seemed fine.

His partner Scott Sherman sauntered down the hall. Scott glanced appreciatively at Maya as he moved past her, then zeroed in on Alex. The newest and youngest faculty member, recently divorced with two small kids, Scott had a keen medical mind and a roving eye. Deeply tan, he slicked back his pale blond hair and looked like a surfer.

Why did someone like Scott get the eidetic memory? It hardly seemed fair. Scott could pull complicated data quickly from inside his brain, pluck it up easily like weeds, while Alex scrambled with textbooks and online resources.

"Hey." Scott whispered confidentially, put his mouth close to Alex's ear, checking up and down the hall to be sure no one else could hear. "You want to trade advisees? I'll take V off your hands any day. If you know what I mean."

Alex shook his head. "Inappropriate, Scotty."

Scott elbowed him and chuckled. "Just say the word, buddy. Just say the word."

I get lonely. Doesn't everyone? But when I try to fit in, it never works. I take part in their futile charities, though I always wish I'd stayed home. There we are, putting canned peaches and beans in boxes for homeless families. Pathetic. You can't help people, and I hate wasting so much time. Isn't that what the government is for, to give them assistance? Isn't that what churches are supposed to do? I'm sure there are programs they could sign up for if they bothered. They're probably too lazy.

But if you don't volunteer, you get that look. Like something's wrong with you, like you're too selfish. So every now and then I go along. I try to impress them. I can smile and chat. I can pretend.

Sometimes I wonder what they think about me, deep down inside. We all have private thoughts, the ones we never share. I know Dr. Reddish has secrets—I can tell he's got a past.

Maybe they think I'm good and kind, simply quiet. Maybe they think I'm hard to know, distant. Sometimes I enjoy being mysterious. A mysterious person can be whatever they want, a hero or a villain.

No one knows me, of course. Not in their wildest dreams.

8

Maya dawdled on Sunday morning. Two glasses of wine the night before left her a little sluggish. She and Whit enjoyed a lavish dinner out, celebrating both his birthday and the Friday news article about her proposed helmet law. Although the reporter presented all angles of the issue, briefly mentioning regulation of personal decisions, he applauded the wisdom of Maya's measures.

Maya felt cautiously positive, despite increased blowback from bikers. Reactive comments appeared online, swift and brutal, about individual freedom and government interference. About her personally, calling her a milk-white do-gooder, someone with a neurotic need to mother. Someone who should get out and live a little. Offers to help her do that. A media monitor at the health department said he saw more graphic remarks, ones he immediately deleted. He declined to be specific.

Last night Whit chose his favorite elegant steakhouse and for once Maya didn't care. Formal restaurants made her edgy, but it was his birthday after all and they had fun. His week had gone well, and she sensed them moving forward together in a confident way.

Because Whit started his on-call shift this morning and would rise early for rounds, she came home from his place late last night. Now Maya moved leisurely around the corral, forking manure into the wheelbarrow as sweat crept under her straw hat and trickled along her nose. Luna followed, nudging Maya's arm now and then to scratch her neck. Maya glanced up once, the burning sun a bright cyclops eye in a washed-out blue dome, not a cloud to be found. The forecast predicted over a hundred degrees today. She loved the desert, but the difficult months were just beginning.

Get going, she urged herself. The mucking done, Maya stretched her back, wiped the sweat away with her sleeve. She waved at Rafael next door, who emerged from his house and ran over with an old apple.

"Can Luna have this?" He showed Maya the wrinkled fruit, well past ripeness.

"Sure. Horses don't care."

He carefully extended his hand, fingers flat to avoid Luna's teeth. A small, intense boy, Rafael sprouted a mop of black hair, and his somber eyes rarely missed anything. Maya felt for him, fatherless now for three years, since the day his dad went off to work and never came home. With that same dense flop of hair, robust and cheerful and known for his mechanical wizardry, Rafael's father worked two jobs yet was always quick to help anyone in the neighborhood with a broken window or leaky pipe. When he disappeared, Rosa tearfully confided to Maya that he was undocumented. Maybe he had been apprehended and sent back to Guatemala, maybe he'd had an accident. They never found out, and he never returned. Rosa feared contacting authorities, terrified they might focus on herself and Rafael, who crossed the border with them when six months old.

Luna mouthed the apple from his palm and crunched contentedly, eyes half closed, juice and saliva dripping. Rafael beamed, kissed the white moon on the mare's forehead, and ran back home.

Maya quit procrastinating and cleaned up. She chopped up greens and fruit for Twinkie, who slowly explored along the low backyard wall in that lumbering tortoise crawl, as if looking to escape. He trundled over and bumped his beak against her foot, then settled down to his feast. Maya promised him fresh water that evening and slid into her car, finally headed for The Best Years.

The Best Years retirement community covered twenty acres of desert near the outlying town of Cave Creek, a long drive for Maya every Sunday afternoon. A few years ago, her aging parents fled their large property, too much to manage, and turned the place over to her. Maya happily sold her downtown condo and took over the rambling home, complete with her childhood horse and tortoise. Weathered and dull, the house seriously needed paint inside and out, and the outdated kitchen cried for remodeling. She could tackle the painting herself—it was just elbow grease and good exercise—and she had budgeted for the remodel. She just needed inspiration to make it happen. Maybe she would start painting this week. The place looked shabby, and she already bought the paint.

Maya did some of her best thinking during this drive. And some of her best worrying.

First, she reminded herself, she should get a little appreciation gift for Sheila. That wonderful woman made her work not just bearable, but downright enjoyable.

Then there was Mel. Most of the time he seemed fine, caustic and clever, but sometimes sadness swept over him and he stepped off a cliff, dropped into a dark place. She never knew how much to be concerned and often tried to elicit his mood.

"Do you miss seeing patients?" Maya asked him recently.

"Hell, no, I don't miss patients," Mel replied gloomily. "I wasn't doing them any good, anyway. Held them together with baling twine and glue. I'd say to them *what the hell do you mean, you're not taking your meds?* And they'd say they couldn't afford them. Said they needed new tires instead. We'd go around in circles. What a pathetic health care system, if you can call it a system."

"I don't believe it. I bet you helped them tons and I bet they loved you."

"You're lucky I'm not a betting man." Mel scowled and slumped away. "I'd be a lot richer and you'd be a lot poorer over that wager."

So Maya never knew how much to fret about Mel.

She did not plan a career in public health until she discovered her knack for research, discovered herself drawn into intricate healthcare policies, the impact on both society and individuals. Still, she felt unwilling to lose her clinical skills and was not ready to stop seeing patients. So Maya arranged for her day at the clinic each week. While her job didn't require it, treating patients and teaching family medicine kept her connected to reality and patients' tricky lives beyond her office full of paperwork and strategies.

Not to mention that, if she spent every day with patients, on her feet those long hours, her bad hip ached and her limp deteriorated. She doubted she could physically endure it.

And what about that resident, Jim Barrow? He had a likeable sideways smile and his patients seemed truly fond of him, despite his untidy appearance and his cognition that waxed and waned. He performed competently when he took a skin biopsy on the sporotrichosis patient, showing some skills. Alex Reddish disclosed that they were about to require a formal evaluation of him, probably warranted.

Alex. What an odd, intriguing man. Offbeat, but congenial. He wore frameless eyeglasses, bookish in a cute studious way, and a pile of light brown hair fell into his hazel eyes. His wit kept catching her off guard, and he often displayed a peculiar mannerism, a hesitation before he spoke. Thank goodness the schedule put them together on Thursday afternoons—what if she'd been paired with that self-centered Scott Sherman? Once, when both Maya and Alex were swamped with questions in the attending office, Maya suggested that someone go staff with Dr. Sherman, who was listed as backup. The resident rolled her eyes, muttered something about Sherman playing video games, and waited for Maya.

Maya parked at The Best Years Retirement Village and hurried through the stifling air, past an empty tennis court and a glinting aqua pool where a woman in a pink bathing cap paddled slowly along the edge. Lantana blooms flourished nearby the walk, a red and yellow riot, and a large vegetable garden sagged in the heat, doomed to wither and die in a week or two. No matter how much you watered such a garden in summer, no matter how well you shaded the plot, the heat sucked the moisture from the leaves and roasted the plants into oblivion. Only vegetation well adapted to aridity survived.

Her parents occupied a large apartment with a glimpse of dry desert hills. They ate their suppers in the main dining room and contentedly dabbled in the daily activities. Her father seemed relieved with this simpler life.

"Hi, sweetheart," he crowed, taking a bag of groceries from Maya and setting it on the table, pushing aside dirty dishes, a clatter of plates. A pile of magazines splashed to the floor. "Oh, hell."

"No problem, Dad." Maya scooped them up and dumped them in a recycle box. "Were you done with these?"

"I don't know…"

Maya cleaned up the kitchen and fixed lunch. Too hot now for her favorite spot, sitting at the picnic table under a pungent eucalyptus, so they stayed inside. Maya turned off the television, laughing at her father's stories about the "inmates." People who glared if you accidentally took "their" chair in the dining room or—heaven forbid—left a newspaper on the couch in the library instead of replacing it on the rack.

"Bossy old biddies," he chortled. "Sometimes I do it just to rile them up."

Her mom shuttled about, putting food away, asking Maya about work and her boyfriend and if there would ever be a wedding. Her long gray hair hung messy, unbrushed.

"We'll see." Maya watched her put a box of cereal in the refrigerator. She caught her dad's eye.

"*Que será*," he said quietly. What will be.

"How's Luna?" her mom asked. "I miss that old mare."

"She's good. Maybe next week you could drive down and visit her, get out a little bit."

"I don't know, hon," her dad said. Tentative. "It's getting pretty hot."

Maya realized with a funny pang that he might rather not drive so far now. "You're right, Dad. Maybe next fall."

Eventually they made their farewells. Maya drove home strangely empty and sad, the cold stale air blasting against her. It's not like you haven't seen this coming, she told herself. And they did seem content. But still. They were always so lively, so engaged, spent large chunks of their lives in places like Haiti and the Dominican Republic, teaching math and English to rural children.

Don't go down that rabbit hole, Maya warned herself, but she did anyway. When Maya graduated from medical school, they hoped she would join them, would help staff a medical clinic in those needy and faraway places. Or at least do it part of the time, maybe volunteer for a month or two every year. But Maya found she could not, too uneasy about an imagined illness or accident in such remote locations. *You'll get over it*, her mother said kindly, *you just need a little more time to recover*. But she did not get over it. They hid their disappointment.

Get off that, she chided herself.

She arrived home, the sun inching down and burning a trail toward the horizon. Maya left her car in the lacy shade of a palo verde tree and retreated inside to read. Soon she must put aside all other tasks and prepare for the nuclear disaster drill. Sheila already started the paperwork.

She still felt hollow, thinking about her parents. Maybe this week she would start painting, tape off the baseboards, beginning with the bedroom. Something mindless, soothing. Whit said he would help, but he was too busy and she would never ask him. He actually thought she should just hire someone. You've got better things to do, he remarked. But something inside her resisted.

Later that night, ready for bed, she heard a disturbance out on the street, a snarl of engines. Again, louder. Shouting and raucous laughter.

She lived in a quiet neighborhood where disruptions were rare. Maya moved through her dark rooms and peeked between the front blinds. The asphalt sheened in the moonlight where a swarm of motorcycles milling before her house, gunning their engines, a shattering racket. One broke away and roared down the street, skidded in a circle and came tearing back.

"Hey, babe," a hoarse voice shouted, "come on out here and ride with us."

"Yeah, sugar. Let's get something hot and heavy between your legs."

"Wait, man. You got a helmet for her?"

Hoots and catcalls.

Maya backed away, heart pounding. How had they found her? She kept a low profile, stayed off social media, avoided everything except official venues. Nevertheless, she had a unique name, and it probably would not take a determined person long to locate her through public records.

She heard more, something behind the house, and her pulse slammed in her throat. Maya moved to the kitchen, picked up her cell, and tapped 911 into the phone. But she didn't press *send* because she saw it was Luna, snorting and trotting back and forth, her head flung high. Her trot uneven and jerky, arthritic, the gait of a frightened old mare. Sweat dark on her flanks. The clamor from the street gnashed on, rising and falling.

Then silence. A red light pulsed through the night, and Maya saw a police car in the road, an officer talking with the bikers. A neighbor must have called, although the men would of course suspect her. Gradually, one by one, the motorcycles peeled away until a lone man remained speaking with the cop, a large tattooed figure in a torn sleeveless shirt and heavy boots, straddling his bike. His muscled arms shone dimly and tangled hair trailed down his back. Then he nodded and drove quietly off. The patrol car followed shortly.

Maya went out to where Luna stood anxiously, ears pricked. She nervously swung her head to Maya and snorted. Maya crooned to her, stroking her, and looked back over her shoulder at the empty road. Her heart began to slow.

The moon glowed, a lopsided bulb, hanging aslant in the hot still air.

"They're gone, Luna. It's okay. I think."

9

Alex used to hate parties. Awkward with women, cautious with men, he said too much or too little, always strangely aware of his hands. They stuffed themselves in his pockets, until he realized how graceless he looked and pulled them free. Then his loose hands gestured with a will of their own, odd disconnected motions, as if they had invented a sign language known only to them.

Finally, after abandoning chess partway through college, Alex willed himself to become more normal. He made a point of conversing with both men and women, learned to inquire about their work, their dreams and disappointments. Pretending at first, he found himself absorbed in their stories before long. He played observation games, watched people, and predicted who would be next to speak or laugh, which man would touch what woman and where—her arm, her back. Who would engage with him and who would light up at a compliment. He copied the behaviors he admired and tailored them to fit; he discarded the rest. He began looking forward to parties and gatherings, and his hands settled down.

He developed real friendships, enjoyed real relationships.

The residency's formal graduation dinner had yet to occur, still a few weeks away, an official ceremony at a swanky resort. But this easygoing annual party, a celebration for third-year residents about to launch their medical careers, always bubbled with excitement and relief. A wealthy attending physician hosted the event, a man who left his clinical practice long ago. He instead made his fortune writing unlikely medical detective novels, which became even more unlikely but wildly popular movies. His books stood prominently along one wall, a display of lurid, sinister covers. Alex read one a few years ago and, while he didn't consider himself squeamish, he found the violence disturbing and cruel. He never read another.

As a former graduate of the residency himself, the author loved sponsoring this party early each June. His home perched high in the Paradise Valley hills, with floor-to-ceiling glass windows overlooking Phoenix. Sunset flamed crimson and gold, and city lights began sparking across the valley. Alex tried to imagine the house's summer cooling bills with so many south-facing windows.

Because the host loved games and intrigue, tables placed about the rooms were set with Scrabble, Clue, checkers, and chess. People gathered around, laughing and goading. More games stood stacked on a sideboard, ready for takers. A lap pool flickered outside and a hot tub frothed on the deck, but only a few confident people donned swimsuits. Alex watched as a woman he didn't recognize climbed from the pool, hair dripping down her back. Scott Sherman sat in a patio chair talking with her, a martini in his hand. Although Scott told Alex he had joint custody, his ex-wife seemed to always have the kids.

"Alex! I was hoping you would be here." Maya Summer appeared before him in a long grass-green sundress with narrow sparkling straps, her arms bare. Her skin carried a toasty tan and her shiny dark hair skimmed her shoulders, curving against her neck. He looked up quickly into her gray eyes, hoping he had not been staring at her chest, the gentle swell of her gentle curves in that soft green dress.

"Maya. Great to see you. Did you bring any of your mosquitoes to meet me?"

She made a face at him and gazed about. "Quite a place, isn't this? And anyway, the mosquitoes have to wait. I'm working on the Palo Verde disaster drill."

"What? Should I worry?"

Maya explained about the Palo Verde Generating Station, the largest nuclear power plant in the country, located west of Phoenix on a lonely stretch of desert. Debate about the wisdom of nuclear power so near a major city was a moot point, since it had been operating for decades. Every other year, federal nuclear investigators appeared to evaluate the health department's readiness for leaks and accidents, so Maya must drop everything else until that drill concluded. It would take her another week to prepare. She just finished updating warning systems for the ten-mile zone around the plant, which affected over ten thousand people, and for the fifty-mile radius…which crossed through Phoenix and potentially threatened several million.

"Sheesh," exclaimed Alex. "That's sort of incredible, isn't it? And sort of scary, to be so close."

Maya sighed. "And yet, here we are. Who knew that a desert city, with almost no water supply but eight months of great weather every year, would keep growing?"

Alex kept glancing around for Thicket while Maya admired the smoldering sunset, the sky broiling down to red embers. He finally asked, "Is Whitaker here with you?"

She shook her head. "No, sadly. He would have loved this. But he's in San Diego for a cardiology conference."

"Oh. Well, that's too bad. Can I get you a drink?" Alex tried not to sound pleased.

Maya stood on her toes to survey the options. A full bar occupied one corner, complete with a bartender, a busy bow-tied man amid a forest of deep glassy liquor bottles and people waiting.

"Just that fruit punch, maybe, over on the buffet," she said. "I think I'll skip alcohol tonight—I haven't been sleeping very well, and I need to drive a way to get home."

Alex retrieved two cups of punch and informed her that the mosquitoes were not waiting for her, nuclear drills or not. Their doctors just diagnosed a new case of West Nile virus, an old woman hospitalized with fever and headache, too sick to eat or drink. They worried she might not survive.

"Make sure it gets reported," Maya said, eyes alight. She pulled her phone from a small purple purse and tapped in a note. "There were just two cases in Apache Junction, too. And one in Surprise last week. This isn't good—we need to ramp up our mosquito work, now. Stupid nuclear power plant." She looked grim, then glanced down and inspected her fizzing pink punch. "Does this taste funny to you? It's like someone spiked it or something."

Alex hadn't noticed. "Why would anyone spike the punch when there's an open bar?"

Maya laughed. "Sometimes it takes a while for doctors to grow up. You know? They've been students forever. They can't let go of old pranks."

She put her cup down, still half full. Alex took a few more swigs to finish his, but now he could taste it, too—a tang between acid and sweet. Maybe something raw like whiskey, but not that, either. Maybe tequila.

Stewart Burns, the program director, nudged his way through the crowd, nodding at Alex and smiling at Maya. Alex admired him, for Stewart expected excellence from his crew and he got it. The faculty all worked hard, all honed their different areas of expertise, and the physicians in training were an intelligent, eager bunch. Doctors like Jim Barrow, struggling and under-performing, were rare at this place. Alex reminded himself that last year Barrow also seemed eager and intelligent, but something had changed.

"Hi there, Maya. I saw your report about helmets. Strong work." A small man with a strong presence, Stewart had a dark full beard and keen eyes. He shook her hand enthusiastically, then turned to Alex. They spoke a few minutes and he moved on, making his rounds.

Alex grimaced, watching Stewart. Just yesterday, he asked Alex about his research plans.

"I've got to get a project going," he said to Maya. "My last idea fell through."

Her eyebrows raised. "I've got all kinds of studies that need to be done, if you're interested. Mostly qualitative research, people's impressions. And their prejudices."

"Like…?" What a treat that would be, he thought, working with her.

"Well. Helmets, of course. Have you ever seen a family out biking, the kids wearing helmets and the parents not? So naturally the kids will quit using helmets as soon as they can, because it seems grown up. Or a study about mosquitoes. Most people don't use enough protection, and they don't drain their standing water. People are terrified of Zika but we may never see it, while West Nile is here and they don't pay attention. Everyone worries about the wrong things. Should I go on?"

Alex agreed to write up some ideas and get back with her. She dipped into her little purse again and, after extracting a tiny pen and scribbling her email address on the back, she handed him a card with her personal phone number, too. Then someone across the room called to her and she drifted off.

Alex leaned against the wall to survey the crowd, suddenly tired. Veronica stood by the window with several classmates, elegantly posed with a drink, wearing a short shimmery dress and backlit by the hectic sky. She glowed golden amid the others, the low sunlight catching the glass in her hand, molten yellow. When she laughed, Alex predicted she would touch the man nearest her on the elbow, and she did. Alex wondered why he let her disturb him, why she lodged uncomfortably against his brain. She wasn't his mother. He ought to be able to ignore her and focus on what mattered.

Jim Barrow hunched slowly past and joined a group hovered around a table, a checkers game underway. Although no one cared, Jim wore cargo shorts and a Nogales T-shirt, thick huaraches on his feet, noticeably underdressed. Alex predicted he would plunge his hands in his pockets just before he did. Barrow was not the kind of man who would presume to touch anyone, and Alex thought vaguely of his own former life.

Alex filled a plate from the buffet to perk himself up. He wondered if Maya was hungry. The food tasted excellent and he pondered taking her a few appetizers. Then he discarded that notion—what was he thinking?

"Dr. Reddish! Help us," someone called from another table.

Two third-year residents, among those about to graduate, waved him over to join them. Stewart Burns sat across their small table, arms folded, grinning at the chessboard where he'd just made a move. Scott Sherman stood alongside him, nodding.

"You just got *burned*," Scott teased. "Get it?"

"It's not fair…," one of the residents complained good-naturedly, "faculty against residents. You have to help us, Dr. Reddish. We need some faculty power over here on our side, just to even things out."

"Not you, Reddish," Burns groaned. "Aren't you some sort of chess expert?"

"Not anymore." Alex shook his head, studying the board. The pieces were positioned poorly, no real foresight. He glanced at Stewart, who seemed overly confident and not seeing the risk. Alex never talked about his chess past, but somehow someone always knew.

"Come on, Dr. Reddish," the resident pleaded. "Give us one move. Just one."

Alex examined the board again. He became aware of a green dress as Maya came up and stood nearby.

"Just one." Alex reached over and hovered above a knight, assessing the board a final time. Then he took the piece and moved it. He leaned over, spoke quietly to the residents. "That move is called a fork. He can't save both the pieces that you've threatened now, so he'll have to choose which one to save and let you take the other. And they're both valuable." He leaned even closer, whispering, suggesting a few moves. Then he walked away.

He stood at the buffet when, five minutes later, the resident cheered and jumped up, fists raised in victory. Alex heard Stewart call out something like *You're in trouble, Reddish. Whose side are you on?*

"That was inspiring," said Maya, joining him.

Alex changed the subject. "Do you want something to eat?"

She shook her head. "I'm suddenly really tired. I'd like to stay longer, but I don't think I'm up for it."

She did look drained. He walked her to the door, feeling disappointed. There were two stairs down to the entry, and he noticed she stepped funny, a hitch as she came down. He remembered a similar catch in the attending office.

"What's wrong with your leg?" he asked.

"Just an old injury." Dismissive.

He started to ask her more, but he felt exhausted himself. As if he should sit down, curl up in one of the soft armchairs, and fall asleep. What was wrong with him, to be so tired? Within ten minutes after Maya left, he said his farewells and took off too.

His sleep that night was strangely deep and pierced with desperate dreams.

10

Not only did the Palo Verde Generating Station produce more power than any other nuclear plant in the country, it also held a distinction as a rare dry-land nuclear structure. Most were built near lakes and rivers, a ready water supply for cooling the reactors, but Palo Verde gleaned wastewater from nearby communities instead. Whether that would be enough in a disaster situation would hopefully never be tested.

Then came the wind, another problem. Prevailing winds swept Phoenix from west to east. Since the nuclear plant stood west of the city, any radiation that escaped could be blown into town. Millions of people lived in that path, and the city continued to spread.

Maya massaged her forehead. Updating all the data had triggered a dull headache, and she was not normally a headachy person. The morning started badly enough, ninety-eight degrees at seven o'clock, the sun blasting like a blowtorch. By the time she checked on Luna and freshened Twinkie's water—not that he needed it, for he was a desert tortoise and these were his glory days—she'd turned salty and had to wipe herself down before enduring the roasting rush-hour streets into downtown Phoenix. Sunlight through the window stung like a laser on her arm.

Maya opened a new email from the federal nuclear inspectors. Crammed with acronyms, she could barely decipher the message "Dr. Summer, your spot on the Org Chart has changed. We will place you in the TOC instead of the HEOC like last time. All LPIOs will be at the JIC to coordinate with both the AZDEMA and the MCDEM, and of course the MCDPH. Look for your SME vest in the IC section. Please confirm."

Sheila stuck her head in Maya's office. "Crazy much?"

Maya showed her the email and they both laughed. Fortunately, by the end of the week it would be over and wrapped up for another two years. Unless their department performed poorly and had to remediate.

"Hey." Mel Black appeared and walked around Sheila, nodding at her fondly, then dropped into a chair. He pointed at the materials spread across the desk, thick protocol binders and detoxification manuals. "You need any help with this crap?"

45

"No…" Maya wished he could help. "If we threw a new person into the mix, they'd probably have a meltdown. If you'll pardon the expression. Just be glad you're stuck with narcotics and not nuclear power plants."

"Oh please." Mel scowled. "Do you want to tell a bunch of surgeons that they can only prescribe five days of pain meds after a procedure? Even though the patient barely needs one day of narcs? If any. The rest of the world uses ibuprofen. I'm stuffing cotton in my ears before that meeting, so I can't hear all the cursing and shouting. I'll take nuclear fallout any day. Hell, I'll go bathe in it."

"Will that make a difference? I mean, limiting the amount of post-op pain meds?"

"For sure. There are so many opioids floating around. Pills that were over-prescribed and never taken. Pills given away or sold or recirculated. I'm surprised you can't just scoop it up off the ground. Come to think of it, there's probably places where you can." He sighed, dismal.

"You think you'll get lots of resistance to your new guidelines? I mean, from physicians?"

"God, yes. How dare we tell them how to practice more safely? But they don't throw a fit if a dangerous drug is taken off the market. What's the difference? Heaven forbid they might have to spend thirty seconds and check the pharmacy database, look to see if their patient is getting narcotics from other docs. Hell, their staff could check it. Some of the old guys—and I'm talking about docs way younger than me—don't even use computers. Freaking dinosaurs."

"Well, your new program sounds good to me," Maya assured him.

"There's a big meeting in two weeks. We'll see how good it sounds after their outraged feedback. Outrage over nothing. I think I'll wear an armored vest to that little shindig." Mel glowered and his fingers roamed his chest, as if checking for bullet holes.

After Mel and Sheila left, Maya pulled up her data on potassium iodide. In a nuclear emergency, exposure to radioactive iodine was especially dangerous within the ten-mile zone; it could cause thyroid cancer. If a radiation leak occurred, the health department would try to give everyone a dose of ordinary potassium iodide right away, to block the radioactive kind. Because timing was critical, the health department kept thousands of doses on hand, prepared to dispense it widely on very short notice.

Maya's phone chirped, an unexpected text from Alex Reddish.

Were you sick after that party? I need to talk with you. Call when you have a minute.

It didn't sound like something that would take a minute.

11

Alex wondered what Maya must think of him. The way she quietly regarded him during that chess game, as if making a diagnosis. The way he acted so lethargic when she announced she was leaving. He should have gone outside with her, walked her to her car instead of just to the door.

Grow up, he scolded himself. She has a boyfriend and is practically engaged. Get a life.

But he really did need to talk with her. A dozen people suffered peculiar symptoms after the party, a strange fatigue that lasted for hours. Some experienced dizziness, and one complained of vertigo. And much worse... an older nurse fell asleep or passed out at the wheel while driving home. She plowed across a median, causing a head-on collision. Fortunately the other driver had not been injured, but she was hospitalized with a concussion, prompting both a head scan and drug testing. Her medical record should have been confidential, but rumors flew quickly and soon traveled to Alex that her benzodiazepine level was positive. Benzodiazepines included drugs like Valium, or one of Valium's many cousin drugs.

The nurse denied using any benzos, that night or ever—not that her muddled memory could be considered reliable. But everyone felt troubled and let down because she was an upbeat, sweet woman near retirement, especially popular with residents. She listened closely when they felt discouraged and often performed small kindnesses, reheating a cup of coffee or triaging a patient's call, printing a handout ahead of time to save them the effort. It now looked like she might not return, and resident morale slipped a little.

Alex himself had trouble staying alert when he left that party. Once home, he dragged himself to bed and collapsed, still dressed. When he awoke to urinate, he stumbled and nearly fell down.

He vividly recalled Maya peering into her punch, saying *Does this taste funny to you?* And then setting it aside. He wanted to know if she had symptoms. Already he had discreetly checked around, asking the people who became ill if they had consumed the punch. The nurse in the crash, whose recall remained hazy, thought she had. So far in his unofficial poll, those who indulged with alcohol from the bar did not develop the stupor—just those drinking the punch.

Maya finally called him back after eight that evening.

"Hi, Alex," she said warmly. "Is it too late to call? We're having those federal nuclear exercises this week and things are insane."

"No problem. I won't keep you long." Alex took a formal tone. "But quite a few people went home sick after that party, and I wanted to make sure you were okay. We're looking for the cause."

"I felt weird," she admitted. "But I thought I was just tired. I haven't been sleeping very well. There were these bikers last week—" She halted. "Anyway, you think it might have been something from the party? Some sort of food poisoning? I never ate anything."

Alex explained his thoughts about the punch and told her about the nurse.

"Very interesting. Nice work." Maya sounded instantly engaged. He could practically see her lean forward, her eyes sparking. "What are you thinking? Can fruit punch go bad, or suddenly ferment? I don't know much about brewing alcohol."

"I think you might have to add yeast," Alex said. "Or maybe bacteria."

"Well, you hear stories of animals getting drunk on fruit that's fallen on the ground. Maybe fruit can ferment naturally. Perhaps that happened with the punch? It did taste off."

Alex went on to describe his other concern, unlikely, but…could someone have put benzodiazepine in the drink? He recalled the way he felt that night. Not really drunk, more like drugged.

Maya laughed. "Alex. You must be watching too many crime shows. Why would anyone do that?"

"I'm sure you're right." The idea did sound outlandish and he felt a little embarrassed. He tried to remember the punch flavor, some kind of citrus. Grapefruit? That acid tang could have been fermentation. "The nurse probably does take benzos but didn't want to admit it."

"The combination of alcohol and benzos is very sedating. Especially in an older person. You said she was older, right?"

Alex started to affirm but Maya wavered. "Wait a second."

He heard her speak away from the phone, muffled words.

"Stop that," she said, muted. "I'll be done in a minute."

"Is someone there?" Alex felt suddenly awkward.

"It's just Whit. He thinks he's being funny."

"I'm sorry. I had no idea you were busy, Maya." Alex imagined an intimacy between them. He pictured Whit touching her, maybe kissing her, while she talked on the phone. Whit trying to distract her, disconcert her, a kind of a joke. Which made him feel like the brunt of it.

"No, really," she said. "I'm going to look into fruit juice fermentation. See if there have been other cases."

She sounded earnest, but he couldn't get that vision out of his head, of Whit playing with her while they talked.

"That's okay," Alex said abruptly. "I'll see you on Thursday."

Grow up, he thought. You know better.

12

Maya stood in the clinic hallway and watched eighty-nine-year-old Gloria Gonzalez thump toward her, the woman's good hand tightly gripping her wooden cane. The beauty in that cane inhabited the carved handle, an elegant dragon with a fierce face.

The cane's rubber foot banged down on the thin gray carpet, which looked rather dingy. The hallway seemed worn, tired, the walls scuffed here and there. Maybe she should say something to Alex about getting the carpet cleaned, but she knew she was used to a new municipal building where everything shone with polish and glass. She'd heard talk of replacing this old carpet with linoleum, but residency budgets were stretched thin—a downtown practice like this always needed cosmetic updates, every niche clamoring for dollars that simply weren't there.

"Ms. Gonzalez." Maya joined her in the room, helped her onto the exam table. "So nice to see you. Are you feeling better?"

Gloria hooked the dragonhead on the edge of the table, then arranged her withered left hand in her lap; she seamlessly managed the residual damage from her old stroke. A tight bun of iron-gray hair crouched on her neck, her bronze cheeks spattered with pigment.

"Better than last week, when I felt like death." Gloria pretended to be surly. "That kidney infection almost did me in."

"I wanted to put you in the hospital," Maya reminded her.

"Pah. I hate hospitals. Noisy, drafty old places. Cramped little rooms. Bossy old nurses." She smiled now, a gleam of gold tooth, triumphant. "And I'm fine, aren't I? I didn't need your old hospital after all, did I?"

"Maybe not. Or maybe you were lucky." Maya allowed her a smile, then tapped her fist on the woman's low back, one side then the other. "Do your kidneys hurt now when I do this?"

"Yes, that hurts. Because you're hitting me, you meanie."

"Not very hard."

Gloria laughed and slipped her good arm around Maya in a hug. "Thanks for calling and checking on me the first few days, *mi querida*." Then she pulled back and scowled. "My *doctorita* looks tired. She needs more sleep."

"Who's the patient here?" Maya protested. She had Gloria lie down and carefully palpated her abdomen. She reviewed the urine test, now normal. "You lost some weight with that infection. Be sure to drink enough fluids to keep your kidneys running. I want to see you again in three or four weeks. Sooner if you have any problems. You're still taking your aspirin, right?"

"*Sí, sí*. So I don't get another stroke. I know." She rolled her eyes.

Maya helped her down. Gloria tucked her useless hand into her blouse and picked up her dragonhead cane. She started for the door, then suddenly turned back.

"Wait, I almost forgot. I brought you something." Gloria clamped the cane under her elbow and fished into a large cloth bag hanging across her chest. She handed Maya a paperback book, a playful expression. "You study too much and don't get enough sleep. Read this instead. Much more fun."

"Ms. Gonzalez. Really." Maya pretended to be shocked at the torrid romance novel, not the first one the woman brought her. On the cover, a blond female physician wore an alarmingly low neckline under her white coat, stethoscope askew, her scarlet lips open in surprise. The title: *This Doctor Is in All the Way.*

Gloria chuckled. "You can give it back to me after you're done."

That would be never, Maya thought. But she hugged her and watched her clump crookedly down the hall, her weak leg trailing along.

Maya still felt tired from last week, that intense nuclear review. Her next tasks swam before her: make more infographics for the helmet law, analyze the well water contaminated with arsenic and uranium, and of course, mosquitoes. The patient Alex told her about, the older woman with West Nile encephalitis, had died.

And every two or three nights near midnight a motorcycle blasted through her neighborhood, back and forth in front of her house, ripping the air with noise. It never lasted very long, never enough for anyone to call the police. Worse, she started noticing that items in her yard were moved. The birdbath by the front door shifted to the back. A heavy stone bench under the old mesquite tree now stood by the corral; no one person could have lifted that, not even a strong man. Days went by and she thought it was done; then a bale of hay moved from one side of the corral to the other.

She made the mistake of telling Mel, who insisted she call police and file a harassment report. Maya dragged her feet, uncertain of the point, but a few days later Mel rapped sharply on her door and ushered in an officer. Mel's thundercloud face boded no arguments, and he wouldn't leave until Maya gave her story; he stood there the whole time as if guarding her door. The officer promised to patrol her neighborhood frequently and urged her to call if something changed in her yard again. Maybe they could get fingerprints.

You can't take fingerprints off a bale of hay, Maya felt like saying.

When the policeman left, Mel stood staring at her, arms crossed for a good long moment before stamping away, cowboy boots ringing on the floor. Maya felt both grateful and aggravated.

Now Maya shook that off and focused on her work. In the attending office that afternoon, she told Alex that she had uncovered very little about fruit fermentation.

"I think I should let it go," Alex admitted, self-conscious. "It's going nowhere."

"Don't rule it out completely. I'll keep looking."

But Alex seemed subdued, as if holding back. As if keeping distant. When she asked him about his chess background, he deflected and talked about the West Nile case instead.

Late in the day he handed her a small sheaf of papers, well-constructed proposals for several studies. He'd written a questionnaire for parents about bicycle helmets and suggested a program for free helmets at a nearby middle school, with a "Helmet-Head Club" for students. His last idea involved an exercise and nutrition program for senior patients who earned perks from local merchants by collecting points for healthy behaviors.

"Alex, these are great ideas." Maya paged through his proposals. "I mean, there's real community impact here, and both residents and medical students could get involved."

Alex looked pleased, a small smile. He could use a trim, she thought, his light brown hair in his eyes. Bachelors. Maya felt an unexpected impulse to reach out and brush back his hair. She straightened, startled by such a whim.

"Thanks," he said, stacking the papers, finally more animated. "I'll see who wants a new project. We can write these up, start a literature search, get going on the IRB."

All research plans must be cleared through the hospital IRB, the Institutional Review Board. They scrutinized every study for ethics problems, for any violations of human rights, or any potential harm to participants. No project could proceed without that approval.

"Great," Maya said with enthusiasm. "I'm really excited about this."

"Cool."

She still felt something missing…and it was him. No teasing, not one mention of mosquitoes.

"Is everything okay?" she asked.

"Sure," his eyes deep behind his glasses, unreadable. "What do you mean?"

Maya shrugged, unsure. "Nothing really. You just seem quiet today."

"I'm a quiet kind of guy," he quipped. For the first time, Alex grinned.

"Maybe on the outside," she fired back, feeling more natural, exchanging tiny barbs.

His eyebrows rose, disappeared under his hair. "How are your pet mosquitoes?"

"Well. Whiny and Tiny are doing well, but we lost Pinchy and Itchy. I mean, let's face it, their lifespan is pretty short. But it's still sad. They had big dreams, that they might get to spread some important diseases." Maya looked sad.

"Pinchy and Itchy?"

"Hey, I try not to judge. If they said that's their names, that's what I called them. They're kind of simpleminded, after all."

"Let me know when the funeral is." Alex turned to go, then inclined his head toward Maya's bag, where the romance novel lay.

"Love your taste in literature," he said formally. "Can I read that after you're done?"

She flipped the book over. "One of my old patients thinks I need more entertainment."

Alex laughed. She felt better to have their banter restored.

Driving home, her car thermometer registered one hundred fourteen degrees. Sweat crept under her hair and her armpits quickly turned swampy as the AC ramped up, trying to cool the car and not quite succeeding. Heatwaves shimmered over her hood and the sky looked almost white, a boiled-out blue. Trees drooped along the road, stunned and still, as if holding their breath. The forecast predicted five more days of severe heat.

She hurried into the house and shed her work clothes, pulling on shorts and a T-shirt. The sun began its slow slant toward the west, shadows lengthening. The heat might drop below one hundred by ten or eleven o'clock. Maybe. Maya looked around her yard, relieved to see nothing out of place. She checked that Rafael had been there, saw a flake of hay on the ground. Luna stood motionless beside it, her head low. Usually she came to greet Maya.

"What's up?" Maya called, climbing through the rails and walking over. The mare stood at a strange angle, her left front leg held slightly off the ground, the toe of her hoof barely touching the dirt. Her head rose, just a bit, and her leaden eyes looked into Maya, clouded with misery and pain.

Maya rushed back to the house to call her vet.

13

"I can take an X-ray," offered Dan without much enthusiasm. Ripe with perspiration, his face rimmed with salt, he kept rubbing at one irritated eye. Salt or dirt or both, Maya thought.

Luna's veterinarian for at least twenty years, Dan Karmichael had the strong, callused hands of most horse vets, the muscular build that it took to wrestle with thousand-pound animals genetically wired for fright and flight. For the last two hours, he told Maya, he labored over a beloved Arab gelding with severe colic, touch and go. Since the owners could not afford surgery, he pulled out every trick he knew. Right now, that horse seemed marginally better. Once done with Luna, Dan planned to return there and reevaluate.

"There's not much point in an X-ray, is there?" Maya asked dully. She gazed at the sky, a dull copper backdrop to the jagged black hills. As if there might be solutions there. The heat, rising from the baked ground and clogging her lungs, made it hard to breathe.

But she knew the answer, and Dan knew the answer. When he examined Luna's leg, carefully palpating from the hoof and up, he reached a boggy spot on the bone and the mare's entire body flinched desperately. A hollow groan escaped her, a wrenching sound Maya never knew a horse could make.

"Some people just like to see the X-ray," Dan said neutrally. "So they know."

Maya said nothing because the outcome was inescapable. She debated not asking, but it would eat her inside out if she did not. "This couldn't be from trauma, could it? I mean, like someone striking her, hitting her? Or something like that?"

Dan looked at her oddly. "I don't think so. Because the skin isn't damaged. There would most likely be a wound of some kind, an abrasion, a laceration. At least some swelling. I guess it's possible, but I doubt it. Why would you ask that?"

Her lips pressed together. "There have been some problems around here lately."

Maya heard scuffling steps and Rafael appeared beside her. He timidly touched Luna's nose.

"What's wrong with her?" Wary, his eyes darted from Maya to Dan.

"Rafael." Maya gestured at Dan. "This is Dr. Karmichael. He's Luna's doctor, and he thinks she has a broken leg. Dr. Karmichael, this is Rafael. Rafael helps me take care of her, and he does a very good job."

Dan leaned over and solemnly shook the boy's hand.

"She's really sick, Rafael." Dan glanced at Maya.

"But why?" Rafael's voice quivered. "Why would her leg break?"

"Because she's so old," Maya explained, gripping his small hot hand. She felt his pulse hammer in his thin wrist, like the heart of a delicate bird. "She's over thirty, which is really old for a horse. Sometimes their bones get weak and they crack, for no good reason."

Dan nodded confirmation.

"Go get your mother," Maya said. "Bring her back with you. And bring some sugar cubes, if you have any."

"But—" His wide eyes fixed on Luna. Tremors ran through the mare's muscles. "Why is she shivering? It's so hot."

"Hurry." Maya gave him a slight push. He backed up a few reluctant steps, then whirled and ran. She turned back to Dan. She felt entirely empty now, like a vacant container. No organs, no brain, no blood. "I guess we know what we need to do."

He squeezed her shoulder. "I'll get my stuff ready."

"You won't have to hurt much longer," Maya murmured to Luna, rubbing her neck, her face. The mare breathed heavily now, as if she'd been running, her flanks working in and out, her hide wet. Maya's fingers turned sticky and dark.

Rosa came walking across with Rafael, holding his hand. Her dark eyes met Maya's. Rafael opened his other fist to show a clutch of sugar cubes, crumbled from his grip.

"She loves that," Maya said. "See if she'll eat them."

He extended his palm. Luna flicked her ears, smelling the sugar, and lipped up the cubes. She stood with the offering in her mouth, not chewing.

"She's not eating it," Rafael wailed.

Maya rubbed his back. "She's just sucking on it, honey. Like candy."

Dan came up, a clean steel bucket in hand, vials and syringes.

"Give her a kiss goodnight," Rosa said, her voice choked. "It's getting late. You have to go to bed."

Rafael took Luna's long bony head in his hands and touched his lips to the moon on her forehead.

"Goodnight, Luna," he whispered, his cheeks wet. Then he turned and seized Rosa. They clutched each other and made their way clumsily through the yard, his arms wrapped around her.

"Ready?" asked Dan. Maya nodded, and he handed her a halter. "Put this on her. That way I can help control her when she falls."

Maya slipped the halter on while Dan drew up the drugs. He tapped for a vein, quick and efficient. Maya looked away. Luna suddenly shuddered and loosened, and Dan grabbed the halter as her legs buckled and eased her head down the best he could. It still was a violent thing, a thousand pounds of animal collapsing to the ground with a thud. He glanced at Maya, checking on her, then switched syringes and finished the last injection. Luna's sides heaved once more, then stopped.

Dan bent over and listened with his stethoscope. Then he moved beside Maya and put his arm around her shoulders. "You okay?"

She nodded, unable to speak because there was still nothing inside her. Certainly not words.

Dan wiped his equipment, put it all back in the bucket. "You want me to call Last Trail?"

"Yes, please," she said, finding her voice. She couldn't just stand here, staring.

"Do you have something to cover her? An old blanket, a tarp?"

"Yes." Maya shook herself. "I'll go get it from the garage."

She heard him talking on the phone as she pulled a dusty canvas from a shelf. He helped her spread it over Luna and they both searched the ground, picking up stones heavy enough to weigh down the edges. Maya cast her eyes away and performed the task with peripheral vision. Luna's mouth, frozen in a grimace, teeth showing, a small froth of sugar on her lip.

"Brenda has a job way out in Casa Grande," Dan told her. "She has to get some sleep after that, but she said she could be here around five tomorrow morning. You okay with that?"

"Sure."

There wasn't much choice. Disposing a horse carcass in the city presented a challenge. Maya could call the county livestock service, which might take a day or two. Brenda Tilling, who ran Last Trail, was a lively middle-aged woman with a truck and flatbed trailer, a winch, and heaps of compassion for her clients. Brenda tried her best to come pick up within an hour because no one wanted a dead horse in their yard, but some days were busier than others.

"Here." Dan handed her a foot-long golden strand he had clipped from Luna's tail and braided together. Maya thought how that tail once flew out like a pale flame, catching sunlight, a magical plume. She almost declined the offer, couldn't imagine what she would do with it, then realized Rafael might want it. Dan hugged her again and climbed into his truck, headed back to the horse with colic. Maya thought of the night stretching before him and wondered if he would be doing this twice tonight.

She wandered into the house, moved slowly through the dim rooms. She thought she would cry, but for some reason she did not. Thirty years was a long life for a horse; many didn't make it very far into their twenties.

No foot, no horse.

Was that Shakespeare? No, Shakespeare said *He's mad that trusts in the tameness of a wolf, or a horse's health.* Maybe from King Lear. Early in college she played at being a literature major, wanted to be a professor— all those lit classes she took. Then something shifted. Maybe it was the student in her dorm who succumbed to leukemia after a long semester of losing weight and vomiting in the bathroom every night. Maya still regretted not talking with her more, not trying harder to help. She'd been clumsy, clueless how to behave. Late in her sophomore year, Maya bent toward medicine and scrambled to take all the science courses. She discovered she was good at it, better than her skills with literature, and more passionate about her future. She never looked back.

But sometimes those writers and poets and philosophers returned to her, reappeared with their wisdom or observations. It no longer surprised her.

Her fingers trailed across the old pecan-colored piano. She hadn't played in weeks, but now she sat and opened the keyboard, plinked out scattered notes. Both hands next, a few chords. She closed the keyboard and stared blankly, then took up her phone and called Whit. She'd spoken with him briefly while she waited for Dan.

"What happened?" he asked quickly. "Is the horse okay?"

"No." Maya's voice cracked and she swallowed hard. "We had to put her down."

"Oh." A pause. "I'm sorry, Maya. Is there anything I can do?"

Part of her wanted him to come over, and part of her did not. She was afraid they might end up making love, which felt wrong. And she knew he was scheduled in the cath lab very early the next morning.

"No. I think I'm okay."

"Well. All right. At least the horse was really old, wasn't it?"

Irritation flashed through her. But she knew Whit never grew up with animals, never had a dog. Not even a fish in a tank. He had no idea, didn't understand the bond, and she lacked the energy to be upset.

"She, Whit," Maya said. "Yes, she was past thirty. That's extremely old."

They hung up and Maya tried to eat, but had no appetite. Only thirst, so she mixed a pitcher of lemonade and made herself drink.

The isolated cries began, that eerie lament. Coyotes, *Canis latrans*. First a thin wavering call, drawn out in a mournful thread, then a cluster of bright yips. Another answered, then another, a different pitch. The wails escalated into canine chaos, a wild chorus of barks and howls, a frenzy of screams and snarls. Maya stood outside, staring into the desert and seeing nothing, as the noise dwindled away. The coyotes might be only a few hundred yards away, or half a mile. Impossible to tell. A few more yaps, then silence.

She looked at the mound of Luna. Would the coyotes approach, looking for meat? The stones on the tarp would not deter a cunning coyote. Maya retrieved a pillow from the house and dragged the lounge closer, prepared to spend the night. If coyotes rustled the tarp, that would surely awaken her, although she doubted she would sleep. Maya made herself relax into the pillow and closed her eyes. A tiny touch on her hand startled her, but when she looked she saw nothing, wondering if she imagined it. Then a miniature whirr at her ear. A mosquito.

She found the repellent, stepped out in the moonlight, and generously sprayed herself, holding her breath against that chemical reek. Spritzing her fingers, she rubbed a little on her face, then returned to her vigil. A crackle along the low wall drew her attention, but it was just Twinkie, moving through dead leaves. He stopped and raised his head, aware of her. Twinkie was twenty-five years old and could potentially live nearly a century, although he spent half of each year asleep, hibernating. It hardly seemed fair and made no sense.

She must have drifted off because a sound broke through and Maya opened her eyes. Rafael stood over Luna, his black hair shining in the moonlight. Slowly, dreamlike, he lifted an edge of the tarp and looked for a long time. Then he squatted and touched her, held his hand on her nose.

Maya wondered what she should do. Go to him, comfort him. Or pretend to be asleep and give him this time alone. She felt strangely incapable. Though young at ten years, he was not a baby to be placated with sweet nothings; his life had already been tough and full of loss. Maya wished she knew how his mother processed this with him. She didn't want to contradict her. Horse angels, heaven, green pastures, eternal sleep? Their house swarmed with friendly dogs and Rosa raised chickens, so Maya doubted death was a complete stranger. In fact, she remembered him gravely telling her last winter about a hen's funeral.

Rafael dropped to his knees by Luna's head and Maya stirred, but he started talking and she stayed put. His soft words rose and fell, like he was telling a story. He finished and stood, tucked the tarp back in place, and walked home.

Maya tried again to sleep but her skin stung, tacky with sweat and repellent. Around the neighborhood she heard air conditioners kick on and off, groaning with robotic effort. Maya pictured all the people inside, peacefully asleep beneath their vents. Pictured the millions of humans all over the city, huddled in the vapor of their mechanically cooled air.

A half-moon hung pasted to the gray dome. The sky here never turned truly dark, always flushed with city glow—she could almost taste that charcoal air, burnt by heat and smothered by exhaust. A few stars trembled and sizzled in the hot iron skillet of sky, and every now and then one shifted and blinked and moved across, not a star at all. A plane, a helicopter, some machine churning its way. She grew sick of the artificial sky and the brine and stink of herself and wondered why there was a city here at all, why anyone lived here.

Little water, long seasons of unbearable heat. They must all be insane to stay.

A diesel engine rumbled into her driveway as Brenda from Last Trail pulled up, and Maya went to meet her.

14

One thing Alex could say about Veronica Sampson was that, despite her flirting, she never dressed provocatively. She wore professional, business-like attire. Until today. Because she had enrolled in a research project for the month, which meant spending her June days working at the library and from home, she saw her patients in the clinic only twice a week. She scheduled her annual review with Alex on a non-patient day, coming in from home just for that meeting, so she dressed casually.

Admittedly it was a scorching day; the humidity barely registered at six percent. Streets bubbled and wood cracked, and a wet towel dripped dry in minutes. Paint blistered and pavements crumbled, lawns withered and turned to dust. Cold tap water no longer ran cold.

Arizona stood apart in time, refusing to adopt daylight savings because no one wanted the sun aloft any later. Only the Navajo Nation, a vast northeastern expanse of the state, embraced the time change. The Hopi, a separate tribe with lands encircled by the Navajo, did not. Confused travelers driving through tried to adjust as the hours hopped back and forth, while Arizonans just shrugged. July would bring relief of sorts when summer monsoons began, thrilling thunderstorms that marginally cooled the air and raised humidity to miserable levels.

Veronica breezed in wearing skimpy cutoff denim shorts and a blue cotton top tied in front, a glimpse of midriff. Her golden hair waved unrestrained and a new fragrance wafted from her skin, something spicy like cloves.

"Are you ready for me?" She paused in his doorway.

"Of course," Alex replied, carefully looking only at her face. "Come on in."

She shut the door and slid into the chair by his desk, curled onto the seat, catlike. They chatted about her trajectory, one more year to go. Since Veronica had no special ambitions for her first job and her plans remained vague, he encouraged her to investigate opportunities and gave her resources. Then Alex reviewed her latest evaluations from specialist preceptors, uniformly enthusiastic. They used words like smart, analytic, and efficient. Easy to work with. Only one attending, an older rheumatologist known for her crusty comments, mentioned that Veronica should study more about lupus.

"I hardly staffed with her," Veronica protested, her face clouded. "Maybe one afternoon. I mostly worked with her partners. Those." She pointed at other remarks.

"Do you remember discussing lupus with her?"

"No," she said shortly. "I'm sure we never did. She must be thinking of someone else."

Alex let it go. The observation wasn't even a criticism, just a suggestion. He didn't completely believe Veronica's claim but decided not to pursue it.

"Did you make your list?" he asked.

A puzzled line between her light eyebrows. "List?"

"Remember? We wanted to discuss your strengths and challenges, what you do best and what to work on this year."

A tolerant expression. "I think I'm doing pretty well. I think I'm especially good at creating a differential diagnosis. Getting a history. Ordering the best tests and studies—I sort of take pride in not ordering too much. Or too little. Getting it just right."

Her eyes grabbed him, almost insolent. Maybe he imagined it.

"I agree, I've seen that. But of course no one is perfect. Self-reflection is a tool that we should use, all our lives. We should never quit learning… about medicine, and about ourselves." That sounded a little preachy, so he softened it to keep her on board. "You're a curious person, V, so I imagine you can do that fairly easily."

"Hm." She did it again, searching the angles of his face, roaming. His chin, his nose. His forehead, then his jaw. It made him feel flawed, wanting to touch his face, but he resisted. She crossed her legs and her denim shorts rode up into her groin. "What do you struggle with, Dr. Reddish?"

"That's easy," he said lightly, though her question felt defiant, switching the focus from herself. But he could act as a role model, demonstrate vulnerability. "I should be more efficient—my notes could be shorter. And I sometimes get impatient with anti-vaxxers. They don't see my impatience—I try not to let it show—but I'm working on understanding their views better. Their fears. It helps me be collaborative instead of confrontational." He nodded. "That's just for starters. I've got lots of issues. We all do."

"I see." She fingered the gold chain dangling on her chest, a small sunburst pendant. "Now that I'm in my last year of training, should I call you Alex?"

His annoyance rose. He recalled that time his mother talked with Gary Anderson, his chess instructor, her hand on his arm, while Alex sat ready at the board with the pieces waiting in place. As if the pieces themselves felt impatient. *Mr. Anderson—Can I call you Gary?* she asked. Alex was only nine years old, his father away on business as usual. His mother should have dropped him off and left, but she often came in. Then it took her a while to exchange pleasantries with Anderson, and even longer when she picked Alex up, lingering to talk. *I'm so impressed with Alex's progress, Gary. You must be brilliant. I must confess, I've always been fascinated by gifted men.*

Alex waited long enough now to make Veronica wonder.

"You can call me whatever you like. Whatever you're comfortable with." He allowed her a small smile. "Usually I have the opposite problem, getting residents to quit calling me Dr. Reddish, even years after graduation."

"Some doctors are very stuffy," she laughed. "So formal." She looked at the door then, as if deciding whether they were done.

"So." Alex picked up the topic again. "Can you think of what you might want to work on this year?"

Veronica sighed. "All right. I'm not sure this is actually a problem, but maybe I could do a little better. When I talk with depressed patients. If it's a busy day, sometimes I have trouble slowing down, paying close attention. I like to stay on schedule and those patients take longer."

Alex controlled his surprise, that she would admit such a shortcoming. While she realized she must say something to placate him, it seemed a startling choice.

"Excellent," he said, his mind scrambling to get it right. Flattery went a long way with her. "I mean, an excellent insight. Everyone struggles with this—depression is a complicated task to accomplish in a short time. For one thing, body language is critical."

"I see." She shifted in her chair, tugged at her shorts as if they might be uncomfortable. "Maybe you could show me more about that."

Alex forged on gamely, his eyes on her face. "I've got a good article I'll send you. And did you know there's a depression inventory in the electronic chart?"

"No." She looked bored.

"It's under the 'documents' tab. I can show you the next time we're in the attending office. And V—when you have your next patient with depression, you might make a recording of that encounter. Then we could go over it."

She nodded absently and stood. "Thanks, Dr. Reddish. Alex. I'll see you later."

When she pushed out the door, Jim Barrow waited across the hallway, lounging against the wall. Veronica flicked a glance at him, then turned her back and walked away.

"Hi, Jim. I didn't know you were waiting," Alex said. "Did you need something?"

Jim wanted to review an abnormal lab test. Alex knew that Stewart Burns planned to meet with Jim later in the week, start an evaluation and likely an intervention. Stewart wanted Alex there, too, in the role of witness and support. It should be Scott Sherman, Jim's advisor, but Scott had left town on vacation. Alex thought highly of Stewart and knew he would be firm but fair.

Even as Jim talked, Alex chided himself for allowing Veronica under his skin. Overall, she was a good physician, and he could have much worse problems to deal with. He only had to endure her for one more year…he simply must ignore her manipulations, her ego. It wasn't that difficult.

He shook it off and focused on Jim. That's where his energy belonged. Hopefully this would be one of Jim's better days.

JOURNAL

I stopped in Papago Park to think. It was hotter than hell, but I like the heat. I like sitting in the sun until I feel weak and dizzy, until I see those little spots dance around like gnats in my eyes. Until my skin hurts. The sunlight here feels like liquid fire pouring over you.

Sometimes I sit there just to see how much heat I can take. I never drink water then, because that would be too easy. I feel like I'm proving something.

I'm keeping my eye on Dr. Summer. She isn't around as much, so it's hard to tell if she's like the others. She's hiding something.

I sat on those strange bare rocks and burned. I watched a vulture circle, searching the ground

…it never once flapped its wings, but it flew so low I saw its ugly bare head.

They only eat dead meat, something rotten and rancid.

What a stupid way to evolve.

It's like they have no pride.

15

Time flies over us, but leaves its shadow behind.

That quote nagged at Maya for days after Luna died, until she finally looked it up to see who said it. Nathaniel Hawthorne, a man so haunted by his ancestor's role in the Salem witch trials that he changed his name.

Names. She never asked her parents if they named her Maya because they liked the cadence of the word, or if they actually knew the meaning. During her teens she discovered that in Sanskrit, Maya meant *illusion*. She concluded they must not have realized, because who would call their child an illusion? Maybe there were other interpretations.

Would it have been so terrible for her to work in the Caribbean with her parents, staff a medical clinic for a month or two every year? They dreamed of that. Maya tried it once, just for a week. She deteriorated, too nervous, afraid to travel on a bus or ride a bike, imagining jagged wounds and broken limbs, crushed beneath a truck without brakes. No adequate hospital for hundreds of miles. Perpetually overcome by a dread of remote places, she never returned.

Now when she told them about Luna, her mother wept and her father wished aloud that he had driven to see the mare when Maya suggested it. Maya consoled him, reminding him that the weather was indeed much too hot, as he had said.

But Hawthorne had it right. Regardless of shadows, time flew on, and Maya had much to do.

Maya felt she was managing; she was no stranger to stress. She enjoyed her patients today. First, a shy teenager with severe acne whose treatment finally showed improvement…Maya spent extra time with him, discussing how to handle bullying. She saw a woman who missed too much work because of excruciating menstrual cramps, whose unsympathetic supervisor claimed it was all in her head and threatened to fire her. Maya drew pictures of her uterus and explained endometriosis, what tests they needed to order, then wrote a strong note to the supervisor. Dealing with the physical body was one challenge, but trying to manage troublesome peripheral humans could sometimes be worse.

Gloria Gonzalez appeared with a badly scraped knee. She had tripped over a loose brick on her patio and went down hard, peeling off a wide strip of skin. Maya had little to do but apply ointment and advise keeping it clean, to watch out for infection. Gloria seemed confused about her last tetanus vaccine, so Maya administered that too. People still died from tetanus bacteria, *Clostridium tetani*, wily little organisms that lived in soil and prospered in wounds. While only a few people succumbed to tetanus each year in the United States, they were often elderly and had let their vaccinations lapse.

"And be very careful about falls," Maya cautioned. "I know your knee hurts a lot, but at least it's only skin. Skin grows back. I worry most about broken bones. Can someone fix your patio?"

Gloria nodded and asked Maya if she enjoyed the romance novel. Anticipating this question, Maya had forced herself to read the first chapter so she could be truthful.

"I've started it," Maya said. Satisfied, the woman gave her a sly wink.

The last two patients distressed her more, a married couple in their sixties. Carrie and Carl McAllister. Longtime patients of Scott Sherman, they needed med refills for their diabetes, arthritis pains, cholesterol, and blood pressure—a remarkably identical list of problems. With Scott out of town, the McAllisters couldn't wait because they were down to their very last pills. So Maya saw them instead.

Carrie drove down the hall in a handicapped scooter and Carl wrestled with a walker, grumbling and cursing.

"It's my turn for the damn scooter." He angrily shoved the walker along. "My knee is killing me."

"My pain's worse than yours is, and you know it," Carrie retorted, parking the scooter outside the exam room and clambering off. The doorway was too narrow for the deluxe scooter, with wide padded armrests and running boards, hung with bags of tissues and water bottles. "You nasty old crab. I've got a *disc* in my back."

Maya glanced at the nurse who helped them in. She sent Maya a consoling expression and left the room quickly.

When Maya remarked that Carl's blood pressure looked too high, Carrie accused him of skipping his meds.

"Yes, sometimes I do," he griped, "because they make me feel tired."

"You're tired because you stay up all night watching porno." Carrie's eyes met Maya's, a look that implied a shared disdain for males.

When Maya mentioned they both had gained weight, Carl accused Carrie of buying chips and cookies.

"Yeah," snapped Carrie, "except you eat them faster than I do. I have to practically swallow them whole to get my share before they're gone." She folded her arms.

"At least I don't take your pain meds," he reproached.

"I told you, my pain's worse than yours."

"No, it's not. I just have a higher pain tolerance. That doesn't mean you should take my meds."

It was a long thirty minutes. Despite asking twice, Maya couldn't tell whether either felt better or worse than usual. Unsatisfied, she refilled their meds and silently vowed to see them separately if they ever appeared on her schedule again. She recommended they follow up with Dr. Sherman next month.

Is this what marriage turns into, this sniping resentment? Maya wondered. Surely Carrie and Carl once cared for each other. There must have been tenderness, something they called love.

Maya gathered her work and moved to the attending office. She had vowed not to let her personal problems interfere with work. So much had happened since she'd been there, the persistent bikers and Luna's death. She made certain to tease Alex at least a few times. But he kept studying her in a new way and, when she looked up from her computer, more than once she found his attentive hazel eyes on her.

"What?" she finally asked during a lull.

He paused and she suddenly got it, an inkling of why he did that. She remembered the party, his fingers over the knight. Making certain. Like now—just a slight beat, before speaking.

"Is something bothering you?" he asked. Not a gibe this time.

"No, I just—" To her dismay, her breath caught and tears stung her eyes. What the hell, she thought. It had been a week, and suddenly she felt like crying for Luna for the first time, here in front of Reddish.

A resident appeared, looking for help. Maya abruptly turned away, pretending to search for something. Alex took over and calmly answered the questions. Then another resident entered, asking Maya to look at a vaginal smear. Back on keel, Maya jumped up and followed him to the lab. They peered through the microscope at the puddled secretions, where Maya pointed out the big flat epithelial cells, the scattered white cells, a few discs of red blood cells. And there, tiny wiggling creatures, spinning and twisting. *Trichomonas vaginalis.* Trich.

Maya took every chance to leave the attending room and see patients with residents, to escape Alex's surveillance. At last, everyone done, Maya hurriedly put her files together. Alex stopped her, his hand on her elbow.

"Let's go talk," he said quietly. "Come on to my office."

"I'm in kind of a rush. I probably need to get going." She pulled away, expecting him to let go. Instead his grip tightened.

"Come on. Just for a second."

"Okay, sure," she said lightly, as if it was nothing. "For a sec."

Alex waited until she sat, then shut his door.

"If you don't want to tell me anything, then say so." He raised his hands defensively, though his eyes were soft. "But you seem really upset and I thought maybe you should talk about it." He smiled briefly. "I know, it's not my business. Feel free to tell me to go to hell."

Maya exhaled, regarding his benign face, and decided to go ahead. Maybe he was right, maybe she should vent. Slowly at first, Maya told him everything. She heard her words escalate like they had been caged, escaping and running downhill, faster and faster. Luna's death. Her parents. Rafael and Rosa. Rafael's missing father—why on earth was she telling him that? And now the bikers, blasting by at night, coming into her yard when she was gone and rearranging her things.

Alex listened intently with hardly a word, grimacing now and then, until she was empty.

"Jesus, Maya," he said. "Every single thing you told me is very upsetting."

"I know. Right?" She was relieved she had not cried, and it did feel better to let it out. Much better.

"Are you staying with Thicket now, while this is going on? Or is he staying with you?"

Maya stared at him. "Well. I haven't told him yet. I mean, about the bikers."

Alex stared back, incredulous. Not just a pause, but genuinely speechless. Maya could practically see his mind turning, sifting this information, mixing it in with the string of disasters.

"I probably should tell him," she added lamely.

"Maya." Alex picked his words carefully. "Won't he be upset? That you've kept this from him?"

She shrugged. "His work is so stressful. Sometimes I feel like I should shield him from my problems."

He started to reply, then his nose wrinkled. "Listen, do you want to talk some more? We could go get coffee. Or maybe a drink. Grab a bite."

Maya shook her head. She wanted to, for this was the best she'd felt in days, talking with him. But it seemed wrong.

"I probably shouldn't." She cast about for excuses. "I need to go check on Twinkie."

"What's that? Another horse?"

Maya laughed. "It's my desert tortoise."

"Twinkie?"

"You know, hard on the outside, soft on the inside."

"But—a Twinkie isn't hard on the outside." He gave her a look.

"Close enough. Don't be so picky. I was a little kid when we named him."

Alex chuckled, teasing her now. "I think Ding Dong would have worked better." Then he sobered. "Hey. I'm really sorry about your horse. That's tough—I can't imagine. It sounds like you had a real connection with her."

"Thanks." A small burn started again behind her eyes. "I've really got to go."

They stood and Alex hugged her. Not a friendly sideways hug but a real embrace, arms around her. Pulled up against him, the scent of his skin, the cotton fabric of his shirt. She nearly broke down.

Maya straightened and fled.

16

Maya drove home through the sweltering streets, barely aware of her path. She avoided the Piestewa freeway, knowing the traffic would only creep right now and unable to face that broiling crawl. Nothing cooled her off, even though she adjusted the AC repeatedly. She felt flushed with discomfort, bright with embarrassment, because Alex Reddish just told her how she should behave with Whitaker. And the worst part was that he was right. She should have told Whit about the bikers, immediately. What was wrong with her? She kept seeing that incredulity on Reddish's face.

Maya vowed she would call Whit tonight, explain everything. She couldn't imagine how he would react.

You really are messed up, she told herself. Twice now, she'd spent the night with Whit since Luna's death and she hadn't come close to crying. Then today with Alex, in the midst of work, she fought tears more than once. What the hell.

And that pathetic excuse, checking her tortoise. She might as well have said she needed to wash her hair—he must have been offended. Native to the Sonoran Desert, *Gopherus morafkai* needed very little care. Twinkie only required shade from the seething sun, a little forage, and occasional water. In the warm months he enjoyed roaming the yard and digging his burrow, but he passed much of his life at rest, watching Maya come and go, settling his chin on the bony shelf of his lower shell. He could endure many days without sustenance. The rest of the year he hibernated.

Maya knew she panicked. Unsettled by raw emotion and Alex's consoling embrace, she bolted. She barely knew him, after all. An odd chess champion, full of strange mannerisms and behaviors. Sure, he was funny and considerate, and she enjoyed him in the attending office—a work friend. If she were single, she might be interested. But she was not, so why go there?

Almost home, Maya halted at a red light and lowered her window to empty half a bottle of tea that sat in her cup holder, sweating and dribbling, making a mess. Maya reached out the window and dumped the old drink, nearly burning her arm on the metal strip as heat poured into her car.

A large clattering motorcycle braked alongside, far too close. Aggressively close, just inches from her car. If she tried, she could stretch her arm and touch the man's wrist. Her heart thumped—it had to be one of them.

Don't look, don't move, Maya told herself, staring straight ahead. Her sweaty palms gripped the wheel, slipped a little. Unnerving, the clamor and heat battered in through her open window. Then his hand moved on the throttle and the engine gunned, making her jump.

She sensed him staring, watching her startle. He gunned it loudly again and she jerked again, unable to help herself. In her peripheral vision she saw a scorpion tattoo on his sunburned forearm, saw tendons play in his hand. She wanted desperately to raise her window but sat immobilized, as if any movement might attract more attention. His skin burnt dark red, chapped and charred by sun. Incongruously, ridiculously, she thought of sunscreen.

Don't you dare look, she kept insisting, but something inexorable pulled her. Against her will, her head turned a fraction and her eyes rose and she saw his face, saw her own distorted features reflected in his sunglasses. Dark ropes of hair snaked around his head and tattooed lizards climbed up his arm. He leaned toward her and his mouth broke into a smile, yellow teeth.

The light changed to green and Maya tramped on the accelerator, lurching forward and flying across the intersection. When she looked in her mirror he still sat there on his bike, staring and grinning, getting smaller and smaller as she raced away.

17

Alex knew what he must do. He needed to start dating again.

Six months had passed since his previous girlfriend, an attorney who worked for the county prosecutor. Carla Canterbury took a while to recover from, that long rusty hair against her milk-white skin, those ferocious blue eyes. Maybe not exactly ferocious, but close. She seemed animal-like in her core, impatient and alert. Alex liked Carla's wicked intellect; she pounced on information like a tiger, as if knowledge was food to be devoured. Then she licked her lips, hungry for more. Their discussions, complicated and rich, could go on for hours. Sex with her felt animalistic as well; sometimes he felt like her prey in exciting, unpredictable ways.

He found Carla attractive, mentally stimulating, and intimately rousing.

But he never felt relaxed with her, and he sorely missed humor. Carla laughed less than anyone and never made jokes, never made fun of him or herself, never kidded around. His best puns elicited a deadpan stare. He could recall only a few times she came close to amusement, the ghostly smile of a deep cynic. Eventually they drifted apart.

Maya made him laugh, and she triggered him to poke back. He grinned to himself, just thinking of Whiny, Tiny, Pinchy, and Itchy. Mosquitoes and their dreams. She encouraged his research, shared patient stories. She had creative, original ideas. She threw herself into her work and she worried about Jim Barrow. He couldn't quite figure her out—there was some piece missing—but he felt good around her.

And here he went, thinking of Maya again. He had to stop—only a jerk would pursue an engaged woman. Or nearly engaged. He couldn't ask. Except he remembered that moment when confusion flashed across her face, when she admitted not sharing the biker problems with Thicket. Was she reckless, or simply naïve? Neither felt accurate. But it made him wonder about that relationship.

It also made him feel oddly protective. Made him want to park outside Maya's house overnight, a kind of sentry.

Are you becoming a stalker? Back away.

So now Saturday night loomed, and Alex faced his first date since Carla. For months, Scott Sherman prodded Alex to ask out Scott's neighbor, Wendy Jones. For months, Alex ignored him. Finally, last week, feeling too drawn to Maya, he decided he must act. He got the phone number, disregarding Scott's winks and nudges, and invited Wendy to dinner.

"You won't regret it," Scott promised.

Alex did not ask why. Better not to know.

Wendy Jones, a fourth-grade teacher, looked just like the photo Scott showed him: short, curvy, bubbly. She laughed easily, small straight teeth, and touched him often. She hugged him when they met and clung to his arm as they walked into the restaurant. He'd never been with a woman so merry and upbeat. It felt unreal, but pleasant enough. Within twenty minutes, Alex imagined she would share his bed that night if he asked.

"Parents can be so bad!" she exclaimed, sipping her margarita. Her small pink tongue lapped at salt on the rim as she watched him. Suggestive. "If their kid gets in a fight, they always say it was the other boy's fault. Even when there are witnesses."

"How do you handle that?" Alex was curious.

"It's really hard, and often there aren't any witnesses. One time we had a meeting with these parents and their son, and the mom and dad insisted it couldn't be him being a bully. Because of course he was an angel. Always so good at home—as if. These parents were sooo obnoxious. And their kid finally just stood up and shouted *Shut up, Dad. I did it. Exactly like they said!*"

"That's fascinating. So sometimes the kids are more honest than the adults."

"Yeah. Maybe they should be more in charge." She giggled. "Just kidding. What a zoo that would be, right?"

"Like *Lord of the Flies*." Alex tried to add to the conversation, tried to be more present. He kept losing track of her stories and forced himself to focus, finding it difficult to get in a word. "Those children created their own society. Of course, that went terribly wrong."

"Right? Because it's never good when you end up in Mordor."

Alex smiled. "I think that's from *Lord of the Rings*."

She gave him a curious look, then grinned. "Has anyone ever said how cute you are when you smile? I love a man in glasses. It makes you look so smart." She covered her mouth to laugh. "But of course you're smart! You're a doctor!"

Alex soldiered on. He wanted to like her. She was sweet and comical, sexy and flirtatious. He wanted humor, after all. Big deal, so she confused *Lord of the Flies* with *Lord of the Rings*. Don't be such a snob.

It's not her fault, he told himself. It's me. I'm trying, but I just cannot do this. Not with this woman—it would never be right. Damn you, Scott Sherman.

He tried to give her a pleasant evening, told some amusing medical stories at her urging. She ordered another drink, and he almost questioned that because she had turned silly, a little sloppy. But why did he care? He was driving, and he didn't mind if she had fun. Maybe it would soften the outcome. Chatting happily, she ate slowly and lingered over her flan. Once she squeezed his knee and once she rested her hand on his thigh. Alex endured, losing the conversation a few more times, but she didn't seem to notice. He thought of Maya only twice and considered that an accomplishment.

Finally he drove her home, past Sherman's dark house, and parked outside her duplex. He unbuckled his seatbelt to walk her up, but before he could open his door Wendy scooted against him, squirmed half into his lap. Her warm mouth all over his, her tongue delving deep.

"You should come in," she murmured, panting softly.

Alex resisted, pulled back. "No, I don't think so."

Wendy straightened his glasses on his nose, looked amused. Her breasts against his arm. "You're very cautious, aren't you?"

"No, I—"

"Don't worry. That's sort of a turn-on, that you want to go slow. I'll let you off the hook tonight. But not next time." She slid back across the seat and out, shutting the door and leaning in through the open window. Her breasts spilled over the edge, barely covered.

"No, Wendy. Listen, I just don't think—"

"I'll walk myself to the door," she laughed. "I'm a big girl. In lots of ways—you'll see."

She turned and flounced up the sidewalk.

Alex laid his head back on the headrest, waiting to see that she was safely inside before driving off. Damn you, Scott Sherman.

But it wasn't Scott. It was him.

18

News tickers ran beneath Bluff Barrington's smooth determined face on KTAN, as his warnings grew more and more alarming.

The hidden killer with wings that lives in your yard!
Wear long sleeves or die!
Drain your standing water—you could be murdering your neighbors!

Bluff gleefully launched a personal campaign against mosquitoes and West Nile virus. With a blaze of fervor on his carefully powdered face, his brow dramatically furrowed, he hammered the public with offbeat mosquito stories while offering practical solutions. At Maya's insistence, he referred his audience to the health department's website to learn about proper clothing and repellents, especially DEET and picaridin. He emailed or called Maya often and frequently quoted snippets from her in his reports.

"I just think you should be careful," Maya cautioned over the phone. "Don't make it out worse than it is."

"Dr. Summer." He sounded impatient. "People are *dying*."

She remembered the SARS epidemic of 2003—Severe Acute Respiratory Syndrome. Travel to China cut back dramatically, and even to Toronto because of an outbreak there. Alarmed Canadians and Asians wore masks in public or stayed home, and media coverage became intense, almost histrionic. Despite the hype, not one American contracted SARS on home soil and no Americans died of it.

Some felt the media frenzy helped slow the spread.

On the other hand, every year West Nile virus infected thousands of Americans and killed over one hundred. Climate change gave mosquitoes longer, balmier seasons for growth and helped them spread to warming parts of the country.

Logic did not always dictate what the public feared most, Maya told Bluff, and thanked him for his help even as she counseled restraint. She wondered if she dared approach him about motorcycle helmets—he could be a great asset or it could backfire horribly. What if he took the other side, the individual freedom argument?

Sheila appeared abruptly, interrupting Maya's phone call with Bluff, her face contracted in worry, her hair awry. Maya welcomed the excuse to disconnect.

"Maya. Come check on Mel. I can't talk any sense into him." She looked anxiously back over her shoulder. "These old men are the worst."

"What's up?" asked Maya. Sheila's comment amused her because Mel and Sheila were nearly the same age. "Did another surgeon complain about the opioid rules? Is Mel threatening to resign again?"

Sheila pulled Maya from her chair. "He's scaring me. He's really sick. And he says he—never mind, just come."

Mel looked terrible. He stood weakly, propped against his desk, one knobby hand pressed against his ribs. His corduroy blazer had fallen to the floor, his armpits wet. He looked up dully when Maya and Sheila hurried in, his face gray, although he still managed to lower his eyebrows and scowl.

"Mel," Maya said urgently, taking his arm, moving her fingers to his wrist. His pulse sped and his skin felt too warm, fevered. "What are you feeling?"

"It's just a virus," he grunted, shrugging his arm away, talking in little gulps. "You women. Always meddling. I'm fine." A cough broke deep in his chest and his hand clutched at his side. "Goddammit."

It took them a while to find a stethoscope because they never examined patients there. The irony escaped no one. Once she listened to his chest, Maya heard what she feared, congested crackles in his lung. She quickly diagnosed pneumonia and insisted Mel go to the hospital. He needed his oxygen level checked, and he needed an X-ray. Antibiotics. Depending on the tests, he might have to stay a few days. Maya predicted to herself that he would, for pneumonia like this at his age could be serious. Occasionally life-threatening.

"Can't do it," he said slowly, breathing carefully. "I've got to go back to the ranch. No choice."

Haltingly, Mel tried to explain why. Sheila shushed him and took over, already knowing the story.

Maya knew about Mel's sprawling ranch, run by his brother now, a handful of cows and a nice bunch of horses. Mel spoke fondly of the wide rolling spaces, and his office walls bore photos of a lonesome landscape, yellow grass sweeping over hills, vermilion rocks and azure skies.

Sheila caught Maya up. With his brother traveling this week, Mel kept watch on the place, and that morning he put a dozen horses in a corral with a treatment chute for the vet, who came by midday to administer equine vaccinations. Mel must return and move the horses back to their fenced range for feed and water. The trough at the corral would be empty by now.

Sheila took a breath. "So that's the story. Right, Mel?"

"They were behind in their shots. Can't have the horses getting West Nile," Mel growled, hunching into his chair. He rubbed his mouth, his hand trembling. "It makes no goddam sense why horses get a vaccine for West Nile and humans don't." He coughed again, a scraping sound. "So, I've got to go back."

"That's ridiculous," Maya exclaimed. "You'll do no such thing. You can't drive in your condition. Isn't there someone you can call to manage the horses?"

Mel frowned, thinking. Then he straightened and winced, pressing his hand against his ribs. "Nope. I'll be okay—I've had worse."

His face turned brick red, a sudden choke, and he grabbed a tissue, spat into it. He examined it briefly and wadded it up, tossed it in the trash.

"Well, that's not good," he muttered.

Sheila glared at Maya. *Do something*, she mouthed.

"This is ridiculous," Maya repeated. She thought of the horses waiting, watching the road where the humans always appeared. Nickering, restless. She thought of Luna. "I'll just go do it myself."

"Really?" Mel's brows rose hopefully, then fell. "No. I can't ask you to do that, Maya. I can't—"

"Just be quiet before I change my mind. I'll deal with the horses, and Sheila can take you to the hospital. It all makes sense."

Sheila wagged her head, made a face. "Remember your calendar, Maya. You've got that thing tonight."

"Thing?" Her mind blank.

"You know, with Dr. Thicket. Dinner with his new partner and his wife. You said it was important."

Maya gazed at her watch, already past four o'clock, figuring the times in her head and realizing the numbers were not good. Mel's ranch was an hour away, and she would need to stop by home to change her clothes and shoes. These were ranch horses, not docile backyard mares, and wearing sandals might risk a few toes.

"This is obviously an emergency—I'll have to beg off," she said. "Or maybe I can make it back in time for dessert. I'll call Whit in a minute." Mel looked relieved, his face pale, eyes closed. He spoke without opening them, stopping twice for a swig of air.

"You'd better take my truck. That road's kind of rough. And you'd better tell your boyfriend to eat really slow if he expects you to see dessert."

19

Alex dreaded the meeting with Stewart Burns and Jim Barrow. He couldn't imagine how it could go well. Jim showed no signs of improvement…he seemed stuck in a lethargic, unmotivated cycle, barely getting by. Occasionally he had better days, but not often. And twice in the last two months he'd called in sick for a day.

What annoyed Alex most, though, was that he himself had become so involved. Jim's advisor Scott Sherman should have been there; only Scott suddenly had plans in California and took the week off. His absence felt deliberate, but someone had to be there because Stewart needed a witness and an advocate for Jim. Scott once admitted to Alex that he hated confrontation.

Stewart wasted no time at the meeting. His tone was humane, expressing concern, but he laid out Jim's issues and a remediation plan in no uncertain terms. Alex reflected that you didn't get to Stewart's level by soft-pedaling problems or beating around the bush, and wondered if he himself would ever assume such a leadership position. Probably not.

"Wait. Wait." Jim blinked several times in disbelief, his eyes sliding back and forth between Stewart and Alex. He set down his insulated coffee cup, his constant companion. More than once, Alex winced at the Superman logo on that mug. "You're saying you think I'm *incompetent*?"

Alex stepped in. He saw that Jim did not quite grasp what Stewart presented, and Alex figured he should contribute something. He didn't exactly play good-cop bad-cop, but close.

"Not actually incompetent." Alex ignored how Stewart squinted at him. "It's that you don't seem to be functioning at the level you should. Does that make sense?"

"No. Not really." Jim looked at the floor, then up at Stewart. "I haven't hurt anyone. You can't name any bad outcomes, can you? And my patients like me. Mostly."

Stewart leaned forward. "Jim. You're not listening. We're not talking about overt neglect, overt bungling. We're talking about knowledge level, basic skills, creating a differential diagnosis. It's like you've hardly progressed this year." Stewart lifted a stack of papers, thumped it on the desk, and pushed it at Jim. "There's about thirty of your patient encounters here. I know Dr. Sherman reviewed these cases with you. Every single one of them reveals significant clinical flaws. Weakly done histories, important symptoms not asked about or explored. Poorly described physical findings, major differentials missing, incomplete plans and follow-up. No one else in your class gets anywhere near this much critique."

It was much to absorb. Alex saw devastation creep over Jim: his face sagged and his eyes turned moist, and for a moment Alex thought he might cry. Then Jim twisted his neck and raised his chin. Stubble grew under his jaw on one side, as if he'd missed it when shaving.

"I'm trying really hard."

"We know that," Alex interjected. "That's why we want to understand why you're not advancing. Some days you seem fine, and then other days you seem so tired—I've seen you fall asleep sitting at your desk. And I mean on days when you haven't been on call, when there's no reason. We want you to get checked out."

Jim turned on him. "*Want* me to? Don't you mean you demand it? It doesn't sound like I have any choice." His face fell. "I drink coffee all the time, all day long. I read every night. I'm working as hard as I can."

"I know," Alex agreed. "And some days you're better. Some days you seem pretty good, then other days you're so exhausted, almost dull. Do you have any idea what makes the difference?"

Jim stared at him. "No."

Alex nodded sympathetically and waited. Stewart waited. Jim finally sighed.

"All right," he said listlessly. "Tell me what I have to do."

Stewart reviewed the remedial contract, went through the items one by one. A physical with his personal physician. A psychiatric evaluation for depression. Drug testing for substance abuse. An assessment by a learning specialist. He must staff all his patient cases with an attending like a new intern, not just the difficult ones. He could not miss any work without a doctor's excuse. Jim listened bleakly, a forlorn nod as Stewart read each requirement. When Stewart finished, Jim picked up a pen and painfully signed the agreement, as if each letter in his name was torture.

The whole process felt disheartening, and Alex wished he wasn't there.

"Come to me any time," Alex said as they stood. "You know, if you have questions. Or if you want to talk. I mean it."

Jim shuffled down the hall and said nothing.

Well, that sucked, Alex thought as he drove home. Despite the heat, he wished he'd ridden his bike. He wanted the exercise to pump away this bad mood, the stinging salt to scrub away that vision of Jim's pain.

July had arrived, the monsoon season edging closer. Humidity rose a fraction and clusters of cumulus bordered the valley, as if the clouds contemplated their futures, bulging and climbing. Far to the north, he saw a yellow-tinged thunderhead swelling up, its smooth white crown rising over the hills. Alex thought of his empty house and then thought of Wendy Jones, who had already texted him. *Don't be shy.*

Then a smiley face with a semicolon. A wink.

Alex had grown to hate those things.

20

Her fury frightened her. She could not bring it down.

If it were not getting so late, Maya would have pulled off the highway and closed her eyes, would have slowed her heart and head until she figured it out. Or least until she found some control. But the canted hills and mesas transformed, gone slate blue, sliding long shadows away from the tarnished sun—darkness was too close for stopping.

Damn it. Damn this stupid old truck of Mel's, and even damn Mel himself for insisting she take it. Damn the sun for moving so fast. Damn Phoenix for its stagnant rush hour traffic, making a quick getaway impossible. And damn you lousy son-of-a-bitch bastard Whitaker Thicket. She wanted to rip the silk tie from his neck, throw it in the dust and grind it under her feet. The red haze in the lowering sky and the scorched air roaring through the stuck passenger window mixed up with the heat in her head and the rage behind her eyes until the whole world was nothing but furnace and noise.

How dare he say those things about her.

Flighty. Immature.

Disloyal.

She pressed her toes against the accelerator and the truck lunged up a long grade, the powerful engine galloping under the hood. Stupid old truck. She slapped her hand on the seat in frustration, sending up a puff of dust. The bench would not slide quite all the way up, making her strain to reach the pedals, and the passenger window stuck at two-thirds up. The air conditioner hardly functioned, emitting a thin spill of barely chilled air. Her hair kept escaping the ponytail and flew into her eyes and mouth, making her swipe it constantly, her neck wet with sweat. Another reason to pull over, collect herself, secure her hair. But it would be nearly dark by the time she reached the horses. She stretched her toes and pushed harder.

The air turned a trace cooler at the top of the grade. Not really cooler, she corrected herself, just less hot. Maya drew a long breath and slowly let it out. Let it go. He's not worth it. But thinking of him released another surge that burst from her heart and spread like a tsunami to her temples and hands, until each fingertip throbbed with a hard angry pulse. She chewed at her lip, afraid she would taste blood any minute. She forced another deep breath, held it, and released it gradually.

It didn't work. Every thought, every cell and nerve in her body still focused on her phone conversation with Whit and she could not shake it off.

"Come on," Maya had pleaded, feeling a bit silly but charged by Mel's gratitude. "Come with me. Reschedule the dinner and let's have an adventure. Let's go save the horses."

"Reschedule?" Even over the phone, she saw the arch in his brows. Her enthusiasm slipped a notch. "We've planned this for days. You said you would come. You told me."

That was peevish, even for Whit. He took pride in his cool logic when stressed. Maya knew she should pull back and start again from a different direction, a less threatening angle. She wondered if he'd had an especially bad day and started to ask, but he plowed on.

"Obviously, you would rather spend the evening with this old man's smelly livestock instead of having dinner with me and my new partner. And his wife. They're expecting us." He paused, as if difficult to say it. "I need you."

Maya understood her role, to welcome the woman, to paint a nice picture of Phoenix life. Maya had gathered a small amount of background, a few stories and photos online; the woman seemed like a social climber, an arts patron and clotheshorse. No discernable occupation. Probably there was more to her. Maya would be polite, and they would likely never speak again. But that was hardly the point.

Be rational, she had reminded herself. Appeal to his sensible side.

"Please. Whit. It's not my preference. It's priority. These horses could be in danger. I offered to do it because Mel is my partner and he's really sick. I'm terribly worried about him—if you could have seen him, how bad he looked. Maybe it wasn't the best decision, and I'm sorry. But at the time it made sense, and now I'm committed to it. You can understand that." A plea to responsibility.

"Great. Just great. Really great, Maya."

He must have had a horrible day. "Whit, are you—"

"Tell me," he interrupted, cross and rude. "Just tell me about this guy. This Mel Black. Is he enamored with you? I mean, do you like him? Is this some kind of winter-spring attraction or something?"

Maya felt shocked to her core. That Whit would be jealous of Mel, that he would express it so bluntly. She hardly recognized him. The words from his mouth sounded alien, clumsy and stiff—who used the word *enamored*? — but his accusation took her air.

"What is wrong with you?" She barely knew how to be angry like this, hardly knew how to quarrel. Maya could deliberate and debate nearly anything, could listen calmly when others heated up. Maybe that explained why she aligned with Whit…they shared that composure. She grew up in a home where indignant arguments rarely happened. If her parents disagreed, they smoked a little weed and laughed and then made up. They waited until the next day to discuss it, when clearer thoughts prevailed. Sometimes they wrote letters to each other, explaining themselves. They celebrated passion, denounced wrath. *Anger is wasteful*, her father once said. *Destructive. Deny it.*

"Nothing's wrong with me!" he shouted. "What's wrong with you?"

Shouting. Whitaker shouting, the most controlled man in the universe—it had to be a first. No man had ever yelled at Maya in her life.

"You sound like a child," she said quietly. She turned suddenly intolerant, in a chilling way.

Whit sputtered. "Me? Listen to yourself. I've never seen you so—so—flighty. So immature. I'm counting on you and you don't even care. Don't I deserve some loyalty?"

It sounded ridiculous, so misplaced, that Maya could not even respond. But he built up steam.

"And what the hell, Maya. You can't just take off into the desert at night by yourself. Think for a minute. You're a woman. And what about your hip—what if you hurt yourself?"

The silence stretched. She never should have told him about her injury. No one really wanted to know, no one knew how to react. Which was an absurd thought since they were lovers, and he would see the scars anyway.

"Quit acting like I'm defective," she finally said, quieter. "I'm going to go. I thought it might be a nice thing to do with you, but obviously I was very mistaken."

She heard him swallow, imagined him closing his eyes, trying to be charitable. She'd seen that look a thousand times, only it never bothered her before. She'd actually admired it.

"Maya, please. Let's start over. Be reasonable. This has been a hell of a day. I'll go there with you tomorrow. Can't you bend a little?"

"Apparently you have no grasp of the situation. Have you listened at all? I have to go tonight."

In a minute he would fall into that patronizing voice, the one he used when convincing a patient they needed a cardiac catheterization. Trust me, it will hardly hurt at all. We'll just thread these little tubes up your veins and through your heart, nothing to it. Every once in a while there might be a problem, like someone has a heart attack or dies while we're doing it. But not very often.

"Maya. Don't leave it like this. Let's talk it over. Can I meet you? Are you still at your office?"

There it was, that tone. Like he needed to calm her down, talk her off the edge. Maya suddenly hated him and hated herself too. Because maybe she was wrong, maybe she had gone too far, assumed too much. She couldn't tell anymore. Then she remembered his accusation and her face flushed.

"No. There's no time to sit down and be civilized." She heard her voice rise, fought it back down. "Damn it, Whit. I don't mind that you don't want to go, or that you don't want me to go. I understand if you're angry. I get that. Maybe I didn't handle this well, and I apologize—again. But what you just said about my motives, about Mel. How can you think of me like that?"

"I'm just upset. Anyone would be. You said some mean things to me, too, in case you didn't notice. I just—"

"I'm sorry. It's getting late. I have to go."

"All right, all right. Just call me when you're on your way back so I—"

"Whit. Goodbye."

She hung up.

21

So that was that. Whit didn't call back. She would not have answered.

Maya braked hard, the tires squealing softly. She'd almost flown past the turnoff. The sign marked *Esperanza Pass*, Spanish for *hope*. The truck bounced over a cattle guard with a loud thrum and rattled onto a graded dirt road, throwing up a wall of dust behind her. Covering my tracks, she thought. She suddenly realized that no one but Mel knew exactly where she was, and Mel was not in great shape.

Off the highway, she grew more relaxed. Four miles, Mel said. He hadn't mentioned the twists and dips and narrow sandy washes, making any speed over fifteen miles an hour hazardous. The sun lay low, a painful searing orange, the sky around it poached pallid as the heavens deepened. The hills dark mustard. Maya managed to slow her mind somewhat and leaned into the road, maneuvered the lumbering vehicle through the turns. She wrestled it over deep furrows and washboard ruts and now felt grateful for the truck.

Whit surfaced in her thoughts, over and over, and she violently shoved him out, made herself focus on the road.

Finally. A skeletal windmill, blades motionless in the hot purple air above a brimming tank, a liquid mirror of sky. Barbed wire ran glistening in two directions, traveling out of sight. Beside her, an aluminum gate opened to the fenced range, and several hundred feet away stood weathered wooden chutes and a timbered corral. A small barn by the corral had collapsed into a heap of splintered slats. Dust rose in spurts, and she heard the anxious whinnies of horses.

Let's get this over with, she thought irritably. Maya cranked open the door and slid from the seat, her sneakers plopping in the dust. It last rained in early April, three months ago, and rain would not drop again until the monsoons said so. Hopefully soon. *Esperanza.*

A row of equine faces peered over the top pole, ears perked, eyeing her intently. Hooves scuffled and air whooshed in and out their nostrils, trying to smell her. Knowing she was not their usual human.

"All right, all right. I'm coming." A simple task. Mel said halters would be hanging on the fence. She planned to tie up all the horses, then lead them singly or in pairs to the pasture. Or what passed for pasture in this part of the world—acres of sparse pale grass and old rock.

"Oh, wonderful." Maya stopped short. Only two halters. Two halters and fourteen horses. She counted them—no, fifteen.

"You'd better behave," she muttered. They crowded against the gate, jostling and nipping. The sun retired and darkness gathered along the ground, although the sky stood light at the edges, fading to black above. A single golden thunderhead towered and shone over the hills behind her, splendid and luminous.

She grabbed the halters and two faces shoved immediately into her hands; they knew the process. Maya rubbed their foreheads, breathed the strong scent of sweat and manure. These were no well-groomed city ponies. They had no friend like Rafael to curry their coats and comb out their tails, and their dirty hides felt like the stiff fuzz of old stuffed animals. She buckled the halters and reached for the latch, where it got tricky. She had to open the gate and lead these two through without letting others crowd past. A loose horse would probably run straight to the water, but if it took off in another direction it could disappear quickly into the open desert. No water there at all.

Thank goodness—the gate opened inward. Maya maneuvered her horses in place and pushed the gate just wide enough for one to surge through, the other on its heels, and then she slammed the gate shut. Panting in the heat, she led them across to the pasture and released them. Happy, they snorted and bucked, galloping to the tank and plunging their faces in deep.

Maya repeated the routine over and over. If a horse seemed touchy, she took it alone. Back and forth, she began to feel a simple pleasure, seeing thankful horses at the tank, water dripping from their muzzles. The thunderhead faded to an ashen heap, but the soft evening light remained enough. She had gone many minutes without thinking of Whit: quite a feat.

She also sensed an old shadow, that dark aura mounting inside her head. Not welcome. Too much angst and aggravation today, too much self-doubt.

Maybe it would go away.

Only two more, a small bay mare and a large pinto gelding. These did not wait eagerly at the gate, but stood warily across the corral. A white rim flashed around the pinto's eye as Maya approached carefully, talking gently.

"Come on, you idiots," she crooned. "Come on, you dingbats. Don't you want to come get a nice drink of water? Cool yummy water?"

The mare's ears swung forward and Maya extended her hand, creeping closer until she felt the warm breath on her fingers. She slid her hand up the jaw, stroking, talking, and was gently passing the rope around the mare's neck when the pinto whirled and bolted for the gate. The mare leaped, knocking Maya down, and for an awful moment she couldn't remember latching the gate. But the pinto merely crashed against it, slamming it shut. On his heels, the mare collided, sending him off in a frenzy, bucking and kicking.

Maya wiped the dust from her mouth and clambered up, but her hip caught painfully, making her stagger and nearly fall. She wanted to turn and leave, and had to remind herself that the horses could not grasp the magnitude of her efforts. She stood and waited, letting the spasm pass, then cautiously tried a step. Still painful, but better.

The aura expanded inside her, a slow grim flood. It was inevitable now.

Twice more she approached the mare, on the verge of capture, and twice more the pinto exploded at the last moment, sending the mare flying. Livid, Maya picked up a small stone and hurled it at him. She aimed poorly and the rock landed harmlessly at his feet, but he understood the intent, for he spun and scooted to the far side.

"Ah ha," Maya crowed. She searched the ground and loaded her pockets with stones, then again went after the mare. When the pinto stirred, she threw a rock in his direction and he stayed back. Tired of the chase, the mare stood still for Maya and followed willingly to the pasture.

"Now for you."

The sky dark now, with just a pewter stripe in the west. The towering cloud had either dissolved or stood invisible in the enormous night. Maya felt very alone. The hills undulated around her and the sky curved hugely, sprinkled with tiny stars too distant to look familiar. She was grimy and exhausted and her hip throbbed. And she felt oddly empty, knowing that when she finally got home there would be no one to call, no sustenance.

The pinto scrutinized her, his four hooves—two black, two pink— slightly spread for action. Every muscle tense, his eyes glittering.

"Come on, crazy horse," she coaxed. Horses were social animals; he might want to join his friends now. "Come on and have a nice drink of water." One step closer. "That's a nice stupid horse. Pretty spotty horsey. Stupid, pretty, lame-brained horsey. Come to Maya so she can go home and be all alone." Two more steps. His neck shortened, drawing back. "Easy, big man. Come on." Almost there. If only she had a carrot or a pail of oats. Horses were easy, really. You just had to know what to do. Just like a man, she thought. Offer the right favors and play their games and they were happy.

One more step and the horse erupted, leaping straight up in the air, spinning and lashing out. His hind leg whizzed past her ear so close she saw a nail gleam in the shoe before she ducked and fell. The pinto cavorted around the pen, enveloping them in a dense dusty haze.

"You could have killed me," Maya screamed, bracing against the pain, climbing back up. He slid to a stop in a ghostly plume of dust, bugled a snort of hot air. A jagged patch of white hair started at one ear and zigzagged down his neck like wild lightning, and his eyes glowed red in the dim light.

"Monster," Maya breathed. Her eyes watered, her lips thick with dust. Her hair loose, heavy with dirt and sweat. She brushed off her hands and the horse went into a crouch, muscles rigid, waiting for her next move.

"I hate you," she shouted, throwing up her hands. He whirled and galloped around the corral several times before slowing.

"Oh, no." Maya reached into her pocket for the stones. "You just keep going. You just run all that energy right into the ground."

She hurled a rock and he took off again. Around and around. Every time he slowed, she spurred him on. The dust hung opaque and his hide shone with perspiration, and Maya thought she would suffocate from the heat and haze and the hate welling up in her. She hated the horse and hated Whit. She hated Mel for getting sick and hated Luna for dying. She hated summer and the desert and the sky and she hated herself because she could not understand what she wanted and had no idea how to cope.

Her pockets were empty. The horse stood gasping through wide nostrils, frothed, gleaming. He was so still and the night so quiet that between his rasping breaths she could hear sweat drip from his belly and plop in the dirt. His dark parts dim in the night, the white parts disjointed segments.

Go on, she told herself. Do it the way you should. Her father, who spent his teenage years on a ranch, taught her long ago that if a horse came to you, the bond began. Resist the temptation to rush in and conquer.

She turned her back and sat down in the dirt.

His breathing changed. A long pause, followed by a curious sniff. Maya crossed her left hip, the good one, and bent forward until the tips of her hair dragged in the powdery dust. Whit would be appalled. She heard a stir behind her, the drag of one hoof. Her hair made faint tracings in the dust, like grasses blown over. More slow steps, and then his breath huffed her hair. He nosed her shoulder and she cupped her palm, rubbed his dirty nostrils, one black, one pink, worked up to his sweaty ears. Very slowly she stood and slipped the halter over his face. He trailed her then, docile. She released him in the pasture and he ambled off to the water, too tired to hurry, a shuffling of hooves as the others made room.

Defeated by his own pride. By a small weak human with a pocketful of sharp stones and a mind full of sharp thoughts. A human who could not choose a decent companion or even keep a mediocre one.

Maya leaned against the bug-spattered bumper of the truck, swept with a crushing sorrow and loneliness. She let go and sobbed, tears sliding through the dust on her face, adding more salt to her sweat. The stars spun and swam, hot and crazy in the vast black sky.

Eventually drained, she gulped and quieted. She tried to clean her face with the backs of her hands, but every inch of her was filthy and she gave up. The aura kept coming, stronger and stronger. It had been months since she relived her accident; she was overdue. At the beginning it came every day, many times a day. Then as the days passed, the months and then the years, it appeared less often, and now she only had to play it in her head a few times a year.

She sat back against the truck, closed her eyes, and gave into it.

22

Near the end of her junior year in college, Maya needed to get back to Tucson, back to the university for final exams. The weekend trip to Phoenix probably hadn't been wise, visiting her parents for a few days, but they'd been gone nine months and she missed them tremendously. Just returned from the Caribbean, they brimmed with tender stories and delightedly embraced her. They were so excited about her pre-med plans.

Now her senior year barreled toward her like a freight train, but first she must wrestle four final exams and the looming MCAT.

The MCAT, the Medical College Admissions Test. That score, along with a high grade-point average, provided the basic platform for acceptance to medical school. If either element came up lacking, regardless of other accomplishments, her prospects dropped. For months, she studied all day and half of every night. She studied while she ate and while she jogged on the treadmill, between classes and while she fell asleep and when she awoke. It felt like she studied as she slept. When she closed her eyes, she saw rafts of multiple-choice questions floating before her.

A hot day in May. The I-10 from Phoenix to Tucson crowded with thundering semi-trucks and lumbering RVs, the tourist season in its fading throes. The sky a warm blue ceramic bowl, cupping them in the oven of early summer. Settled in the right lane, creosote and cholla whizzing by, Maya kept studying, mentally reviewing the coagulation cascade. The intrinsic and extrinsic pathways, all those steps in the body's exquisitely complicated system of making a blood clot.

A motorcycle crept past her, a rugged young man, brown hair wild in the wind. He wore a bulky backpack with a University of Arizona logo, books strapped down by a bungee. He gave her a two-finger wave, grinned at the U of A sticker on her car. Maya smiled and nodded as he moved by, something flapping from his pack. A little later she saw him pulled off, fixing it, tucking it away.

Coagulation began with platelets, those sticky little cells in the blood, cells covered with tiny spikes. They formed a mesh, a framework for the clot. So many convoluted steps to get there. The illogically named factors.

Factor XII, then Factor XI. Factor IX then Factor X. What's next? You know this, she thought to herself. Come on.

A lifted pickup rushed by, places to go. The bright chrome bumper flashed in the sun, a loaded rifle rack, Arizona flag. Now she remembered—factor X needed Factor VII. Then along came prothrombin and thrombin, and now the clot was ready to form.

Maya never saw the coyote that ran in front of the truck. They told her about that after.

Too late, too late, her foot crammed the brakes as the shiny bumper flew at her. Too close, too close as something jolted her from behind and then everything spun, screeching metal, blinding bursts of wheeling light and tumbling dark and horrible mind-splitting pain. Showers of dirt and sand. Silence. Then cries and shouts, the desert sideways, a mangle of cactus in her windshield. Spears of sun and a man's face beside her, his eyes wide and his mouth moving, but she heard no words because all she knew was pain, that shredding tearing pain, knew that her right hip, her right leg must have been severed, ripped away.

She opened her eyes, being carried, lost in agony. The sunlight skewered her face and she turned her head and saw. Tousled brown hair matted red, his face masked in red, red running down his neck down the pavement down the dirt, blood everywhere sticky in the sun, blood sparkling like glitter, endless blood streams trailing into the sand, starting to dry. Small black ants already scuttling, industrious, busy with bounty.

Failed, failed, failed. Failed platelets, failed factors, failed coagulation, everything abysmally failed.

They crowded over her, snatches of medical talk…

hurry with that IV damn it she's getting shocky
must be internal bleeding somewhere
can anyone get a blood pressure
damn would you look at that leg what a mess
Billy if you can't get that IV going, find someone who can
fuck it man you try it if you're so smart
can we have some oxygen
does anyone know her name hang in there honey
nope she's out again not sure she's gonna make it
hey nice job with that IV you get a gold star…

94

The replay stopped there. In retrospect, she knew she couldn't possibly have seen those ants. Yet they were always there. Memory had its own interpretation.

Maya recalled nothing more until after the surgeries, an exploratory laparotomy that opened her up, that located and stopped the pelvic bleeding, then pins and plates in her hip and femur. Repairing her crushed calf. Five units of transfused blood. If it had taken twenty or thirty more minutes, the surgeon told her, we would have lost you. She missed a year of school.

Even with a helmet, they said later, he probably would have died. It wasn't your fault, they told her, the truck swerved right in front of you. The motorcycle was following you too closely. Maybe they were right. Maybe not. If she had been more alert, not mentally trapped in the coagulation cascade, perhaps she could have braked a fraction sooner, changed lanes. Given him a nanosecond more time to react. She would never know.

Wrung out now, Maya breathed heavily and pushed herself off the truck. She looked at her dirt-caked hands, then remembered the water tank. She walked over and reached through the wire, dipped her hands and rinsed her face. The water felt wonderful, still tepid from the sun, so soothing that she carefully slipped through the wire strands and dunked her head. Holding her breath, she let her hair float and spread, soaking her neck and shoulders. Then she stood and squeezed the water from her hair, her T-shirt drenched.

"The hell with it," she said aloud. She glanced around—as if anyone was there—and tugged off the shirt and her salted chafing bra, rinsed them out and hung them on the fence. The warm evening air bathed her clean bare skin, her breasts pale in the starlight. The horses stood back in a group, watching her.

"Whatsa matter? Never saw a half-naked woman before?" All their heads rose an inch at her voice, all eyes blinked, making Maya laugh. Except the pinto, who had withdrawn.

The water soaking her hair evaporated rapidly, and she shivered despite the hot night. Welcome to the desert, Maya thought, land of weirdness. The invisible thunderhead suddenly twitched with lightning and glowed hugely, lit up for an astounding moment. Maya grinned and applauded.

She looked at her phone. No cell service here, of course.

The stars stood closer now, more friendly. Maybe she should call Whit when she got home, try to make peace. Well, probably not tonight. Or maybe she should let him call her. She wasn't certain who should take the next step, or if there should be another step. She felt impossibly guilty and innocent, wrongful and wronged, all at the same time.

Maya pulled on her clothes, already nearly dry, and climbed back into the truck.

Once out of the hills, Phoenix shone before her, radiant in the night. Her phone cheeped awake as it came into range, two texts flipping up on the screen. Maya knew better than to look while driving, but she did anyway, expecting something from Whit.

One text from Sheila, saying Mel was stable but needed oxygen. And a text from Alex, asking if she'd like an update on Jim Barrow. To call him when she wasn't busy.

Nothing from Whit.

23

"Good morning, Dr. Reddish," crooned Allie June, the front desk clerk at the nursing home. A wide round woman, Allie June had bright yellow hair that had been permed into frizzy oblivion, a sunny mist around her head. Her tiny flaming fingernails always matched her tiny flaming lips, those lips always curved up in an impish smile.

"Good morning yourself," Alex answered, trying to recall if he had ever seen her away from her chair. "Have you got any work for me today, or should I just go home and watch the soaps?"

"Don't you tease me," Allie June cried with delight. "If there wasn't any work for you, I'd find some, just to make you stay."

"Probably wise," Alex agreed, "to keep me off the streets."

"You're such a menace," she chuckled. She craned to see the front door as if expecting someone, squinted at the blinding square of sunlight. "Where's your resident?"

Alex shook his head. "I've been abandoned. On my own."

He was supposed to meet Jim Barrow here to make nursing home rounds. Jim once expressed an interest in geriatrics and palliative care, and Alex looked forward to this interaction, to see if it seemed a good fit. Then twenty minutes ago Jim paged him to say he couldn't make it because he had his psychiatrist appointment. Surely Jim must have known before this morning—you didn't call a psychiatrist and get an appointment that quickly. Unless maybe you were suicidal, which Alex doubted. Suddenly uneasy, Alex wondered if he had misjudged. But Jim's poorly timed message seemed passive-aggressive.

Unless Stewart Burns made it happen. A determined phone call, doc to doc, can you see this guy now? Things with Jim had fallen apart. That drug test. Jim's reaction.

Alex fought his unease, for Jim would now be in better hands with the psychiatrist. And he fought his irritation, for he could have found someone else to meet him here if he'd known sooner. He tried not to be angry at Jim, who faced a personal hell right now, but second-year resident Jennie Burger would have come in a heartbeat—she paired a long somber face with a cheeky sense of humor, and older patients loved her. They clasped her hand, laughing, wanting more. Or Alex could have brought a medical student. Caring for these long-term patients took different skills, art more than science, empathy more than art. Alex felt drawn to them, these souls lost in a shadowy limbo between life and death.

Well, doing it by himself was easier anyway. He should consider it a break.

Allie June handed him a paper with just one name today: Beulah Harms. Okay, not a break. Difficult and depressing. Alex sighed and headed for H Wing. "H" for hopeless, the staff said. H Wing was situated farthest from the front entrance by no accident, away from most visitors' eyes and ears. And noses, Alex thought, sniffing the taint of incontinent urine, of leaky bowels. No one visited H Wing unless they must.

H Wing aide Frances seemed the polar opposite of Allie June, a thin, jaded woman with a deeply entrenched glare. Flat drab hair, pasty skin, bleak eyes. A large pink nametag perched precariously near the tip of one breast, the plastic square crowded with smiling yellow stickers. Her smile surrogates, he thought. She placed a thick chart in Alex's hands, and he wondered again when this place would go electronic. They promised it every year and every year came and went, still paper charts.

"I'll get the nurse for you," Frances said gruffly. "To help with Beulah."

"Thanks, Frances. But I can see her by myself if everyone's busy."

"No, no." She apparently took pleasure in saying that word, for a faint disagreeable smile stretched her lips. "The nurse said to get her. Beulah's bedsore is worse."

Frances's fingers banged on the intercom key, her voice blurting down the hall.

"Well," she said indignantly after three attempts with no response.

"Well," agreed Alex mildly. "I'll just start by myself, then the nurse can join me when she's able."

As he turned away, Alex heard her slam the intercom with new fury.

"Hello, Beulah," Alex said cheerfully to the waxen form. Her knees poked up like tent poles, making sharp white peaks in the sheet. "How are you today?"

Beulah stared unblinking at the ceiling, her stiff, contracted body the product of a well-meaning family who took her home after her stroke and bypassed the recommended physical therapy. They tucked her in a soft clean bed and never moved her limbs for her, and soon her limbs no longer could move. Her dry mouth hung open, smelling like seaweed. Now the family surrounded her bed every Sunday afternoon, according to staff, warily holding her hand and afraid to touch her anywhere else.

Beulah did not like to be touched.

"I'm going to listen to your heart." Alex placed his stethoscope gently on her bony chest. The instant he contacted her skin, Beulah's eyes sprang alive and darted wildly, shrieks flying from her lips. "Your heart sounds good," Alex told her, lifting the stethoscope for his ears to recover. "And now your lungs." He grimaced, eliciting another long screech. Truthfully, he could hear nothing in her lungs except the squealing, which seriously threatened to damage his hearing, but the exam was a formality anyway. Designated a "no code," Beulah would not be treated or resuscitated, no matter what.

Stacy Flagg appeared at his side, a kind RN with long gray hair in a ponytail and a purple mass of scar tissue crowding her left face and neck. Some horrible burn. Every time Alex saw her, he thought he might ask what happened, and every time he did not. He realized now that he never would.

"Poor Beulah," Stacy said, moving to the other side of the bed. They plowed through the exam as quickly as possible, positioning Beulah's frozen limbs so Alex could palpate her abdomen and check her legs, wincing at every shrill protest. He worked around the feeding tube in her belly and the flabby bag that drained her urine. Then they rolled her on her side, still cringing against the screams, to see the decubitus, the open bedsore on her sacrum.

"Ouch," Alex remarked unhappily, peering closely at the deep maroon wound, wet and swampy. The rank odor constricted his nose.

"I know," Stacy agreed, carefully removing the putrid packing. Beulah began wearing down, less vocal now, more like groaning. "I should never go on vacation. Temporary help—you know."

They devised a plan: more air to the wound, more time on her side, special dressings. If it didn't improve soon, they would call a wound specialist.

Alex's phone rang. Maya Summer. Finally something nice in this day.

"We good?" he asked Stacy before answering.

She nodded, stacking pillows around Beulah to prop her in place.

Alex sought privacy, taking the heavy chart under his arm and moving outside to a small empty courtyard, strewn with leaves and broken twigs. "Hi, Maya. How's Tiny and Whiny?" Alex swiped off a bench under a drooping mesquite. He saw the mazy cobweb of a black widow and broke it up with his shoe, hoping the spider would stay away. Clearly, it had been a while since anyone sat out here.

"So sad, Alex—Tiny and Whiny finally died of old age," Maya said, feigning grief. "They were already ancient, two or three months old. So many great-grandkids."

"Will you adopt some of their children?" He found himself grinning.

"I'll just foster," she said. "The paperwork for adoption is too complicated. You know, one species trying to adopt another...there's a lot of intolerance."

Alex laughed. He could see her smile, that shine in her gray eyes. He wished he could ask her to lunch, just friends, to talk about Jim Barrow, for she might actually have some insight. Working with her this year, he had come to value her observations, her opinions. But the last time he asked her to grab a bite, on that afternoon when she was so upset about her horse and the bikers and everything else, she fled like he was poison. That flimsy excuse, checking on her tortoise. Part of him wanted to say *tortoise, my ass*, but he knew that she was being loyal to Thicket. Which he respected.

"So," Maya was saying. Pay attention, he thought as she paused. "Something new with Jim?"

"I'm afraid so. I know you've been working with him, so I thought you should know. And there might not be a chance to talk at the clinic. At least, not very confidentially." Alex almost hated to tell her. Though inescapable, it didn't feel right. "His drug test was positive. For benzos."

"Oh no, Alex. What happens next?" Dismay in her voice.

"Normally? Counseling and rehab. Monitoring. But Jim's incensed. He says he doesn't take any drugs, doesn't drink alcohol, nothing. He's insisting on another test, at another lab. It's gotten hostile."

Alex didn't tell her everything, how Jim acted almost paranoid. Saying they were out to get him. Suggesting they falsified the test so they could fire him.

But benzodiazepines were a problem. Alex knew the data; he recently gave a lecture on it. Prescribed to treat anxiety, benzos were ruthlessly addictive drugs, among the most abused medications in the country and second only to narcotics. Benzos included diazepam, lorazepam, and alprazolam, better known by their brand names of Valium, Ativan, and Xanax. And the problem kept escalating. In the first decade of the century, annual benzo prescriptions leapt from eight million to thirteen million. The daily doses rose, too.

For a person like Jim Barrow, struggling to cope with the demands of residency, taking a benzo could be tempting. It could also cloud his mind and cause sedation.

"It might explain a lot," Alex admitted. "His lethargy, his trouble learning and remembering."

Alex knew that over a third of medical residents suffered depression or anxiety, or both. They faced long hours, felt insecure about their knowledge. They feared making a mistake, hurting someone. But there were far better and safer treatments than benzos. Hopefully Jim could get real help now with the psychiatrist.

Alex's personal problem with this, though, centered on Jim's insistence that he never took any pharmaceuticals. Alex read people fairly well, and it seemed like Jim told the truth.

"I feel so bad for him," Maya said quietly. "He's a nice man. What should I do?"

"Nothing really, not right now. He's being evaluated by a psychiatrist today, then we'll have a better idea. We may recommend he take a leave of absence to work on this."

The little courtyard baked in the heat and Alex began to perspire. He saw a stripe of dust on his slacks. What a stupid idea to sit out here, just because he wanted to feel alone with Maya.

"Thanks for letting me know. I always worry about him, and now I'll worry more."

Alex felt a deep pang. Maybe it was the heat, this sad dirty courtyard. Maybe it was Beulah with her hollow, truncated existence, maybe it was Stacy with her burn scars and Frances with her sourness. Whatever the cause, Maya's genuine compassion swept through him and he felt suddenly adrift.

"You're very kind," Alex said, subdued. Then he remembered his other agenda and vowed to be generous. "Not to change the subject, but I meant to tell you. There's a picnic for the new incoming interns this Wednesday. You should come—you should meet them. Bring Whitaker, too. It would be nice to see him."

Silence.

"Maya? Are you there?"

"I'll have to check my calendar." She sounded cold.

"Okay." Alex pushed on. "Maybe I'll see you there."

He could not imagine what he'd done now.

24

Maya discovered how isolated she had become.

Before Whit, she went out with friends, made dinners with Rosa and Rafael. She and Sheila often shared happy hour on Friday. Everything changed when Maya started keeping evenings open for Whit, in case he could get loose from his work. But that's what being a couple meant, wasn't it? She and Whit had fun, went to concerts and lectures. They enjoyed the Desert Botanical Gardens and driving out to the Boyce Thompson Arboretum, strolling among exotic arid plants, laughing at boojum trees and admiring endless varieties of succulents. Succulents that looked like rocks or brains, some sprouting hair-like tangles of spines, others smoothly bald.

She quit socializing with other faculty, too. Like Agatha Mercer, the most colorful and senior faculty member, one of Maya's best mentors. Agatha came to work armed with biting sarcasm, the latest medical evidence, and thick homemade pecan cookies. She told entertaining stories about the old days, when haughty, patronizing men utterly controlled medical training. As some still did. When Maya saw more of Whit, though, she saw less of Agatha, and it had been months since they shared a meal.

Maya felt wakened from a daze.

It made her reluctant to call Whit now, although the analytical part of her brain thought she should. That night with the horses had been her predicament, her fault—not his. It made sense that she should reach out to make peace. Couples quarreled, after all. You didn't just throw away a yearlong relationship because of one disagreement, even a hot one.

Then she remembered what he said and made no calls. She felt caught between petulance and self-righteousness and could not imagine what to say.

"Earth to Maya." Sheila waved a hand in front of Maya's face.

"What?" Maya straightened and tried to focus.

"Something's bothering you."

"Nothing I can't manage," Maya insisted. "What's going on?"

"Hm." Sheila looked at her, rubbing her green curl, as if trying to see inside Maya's head. "There's been another bobcat attack, this time in Sun City. On a golf course. Really aggressive behavior, probably rabies again. We need to respond."

"Of course. Was someone bitten? Was the animal captured?" Tasks formed quickly in Maya's mind as she began planning: news announcements, flyers, educational programs. Alert the schools and law enforcement. Emails to physicians and other providers. She needed to organize a robust campaign for both the public and for physicians, make certain doctors knew the proper triage and treatment protocols. This was not just a problem for rural physicians. Bobcats roamed into city parks and stalked the many golf courses, searching for water, preying on birds and rodents. Occasionally finding cats or small dogs from nearby homes. Even handling a dead infected bobcat could transmit rabies.

Sheila relayed the story. The bobcat bit the woman, and authorities killed the bobcat. Rabies testing would be performed on it right away, and the patient already started treatment. Humans exposed to the virus, *Rabies lyssavirus*, must quickly receive rabies immune globulin, then a series of three vaccinations over the next two weeks. Delay could be fatal, for once the virus infiltrated a person's nervous system and brain, once they developed symptoms, survival was rare.

The word *Lyssavirus* fascinated Maya. *Lyssa*, Latin for *rage* or *fury*, aptly described a mammal's belligerent behavior, its brain inflamed and tortured by the infection until it died. While bats carried most of the rabies, small wild mammals like skunks, raccoons, foxes, and bobcats succumbed as well.

Maya and Sheila spent the rest of the day on rabies. By late afternoon, Maya still worked at her computer, typing and making calls. Deeply absorbed, she heard someone enter and turned to see Mel Black settle himself by her desk.

"Mel. Aren't you supposed to be home, recuperating?" Maya's worried eyes ran over him, but she couldn't stop her smile. He looked pale but his eyes glinted.

"Home is boring," he complained. He coughed once, lightly, then thumped his chest. "Got most of those gremlins out of me now."

"You're not actually working today, are you?"

"Of course I am. We just got our newest data." His mouth pulled down.

"Nearly three thousand deaths from opioid overdoses in the last few years. Three thousand, just in Arizona. Of course, the actual numbers are worse—those are just the ones we're certain about."

Maya grimaced. "Is that more or fewer than other states?"

"We're somewhere in the middle. And that's not counting the twenty thousand accidental overdoses that might have killed people but didn't."

"Twenty thousand?"

Sheila entered with an armload of papers and stopped short when she saw Mel. She dropped the stack on Maya's desk and turned to him, hands on her hips.

"Melvin Black. You've got no business being here, and you know it. Why aren't you taking care of yourself? Shame on you."

Mel regarded her sourly. "Aw, pipe down. If I thought I needed another wife to yell at me, I would have gotten one by now."

"Well, obviously you need one, since you've got all the common sense of a baby cricket."

"Damn, I've missed you, Sheila," Mel said, slapping his thigh.

Sheila glared, then stomped from the room. Maya covered her mouth to suppress a laugh.

Mel sighed loudly. "I suppose I do owe her something, for taking me to the hospital that day. And I owe you, too, for helping with those horses." He studied Maya and she felt his eyes pierce her armor. "Everything work out that night? I mean, you had important plans, didn't you?"

"It turned out fine," she said shortly. She grew tired of being asked about Whit—why was everyone suddenly curious? First Alex, now Mel.

"Sure it was." Mel seemed dubious, then looked at her work. "Rabies now?"

"One crisis after the next—you know how it goes. I'll start ramping up the helmet stuff later, as the election gets closer. And mosquitoes never go out of style."

"You still getting trouble from those bikers?"

Maya shook her head. "Not much lately."

"Good." Mel scanned the papers. "You need help? I could double check some of the statistics for you."

"Mel. Please go home."

"Okay, okay, I get it. Send the old man packing." He pushed himself up. "Oh hey. You want another horse for your backyard? There's a gelding

105

that's not getting along with the herd. The others are beating him up and he needs a break. Can you take him for a little while? No obligation, of course. But I thought you might like having another pony out back."

Maya realized it would be nice. She still missed Luna sharply, missed her nickers at feeding time and those communal moments, face to face, breath to breath. She often caught herself checking the empty corral, just out of habit. Maybe Rafael would like that, too.

"That sounds good," she admitted.

Mel walked to the door. "Great. I'll see about bringing him down next week. Now I'd better go make nice with Sheila. You don't want to be on her bad side."

After Mel left and Maya returned to her work, she grasped that the horse was probably that damn pinto.

She drifted out to Sheila's workstation. Her phone buzzed in her pocket, briefly, then stopped. Maya took it out and saw Whit's number, stared at it. No message. No second attempt. Maybe it was accidental. Maybe he started to call and changed his mind, or maybe he was interrupted. Maybe he was testing her. Impossible to know, but it sent her sideways.

"Sheila. You have any supper plans? Want to join me?"

Sheila's mouth popped open. "You're free?"

"Seems so." Maya felt suddenly determined. Tomorrow she would call Agatha Mercer and set up lunch.

Sheila grinned and grabbed her purse.

25

Alex went out of his way to be available to Jim Barrow, but Jim didn't want much to do with him. Or anyone. When Alex asked Jim to stop by his office one day and inquired how Jim was handling things, he responded cautiously, short and guarded.

"Do you care?" His eyes rose but didn't quite connect. He looked over Alex's shoulder instead at a framed painting of the Grand Canyon at dusk, deep shadows and ruddy rock. Jim's eyes trailed the landscape, as if longing to escape there. Heat beat on the tinted window, making the office warm and stuffy.

"Jim. I know this is painful. I'm very sorry," Alex said.

"Not too sorry to quit watching me like a hawk. I can't relax for a second." Jim stared at the floor now.

"Have you thought about taking a leave of absence?"

Alex knew Stewart Burns offered that. The second drug test came back positive for benzos, again. So far the psychiatrist offered little insight, only stating she wanted more time, more sessions with him.

"Out of sight, out of mind, right?" Jim replied. "Maybe I'll decide not to come back—you can hope, right? And just so you know, I'm not taking any drugs, no matter what those tests say."

"Jim." Alex spread his hands, palms up, as if to say *what can I do?* Alex hated that he had become an enemy, all because Scott ran off. "I worry about you. It's incredibly stressful, what you're going through. It's difficult to take care of yourself."

Jim's eyes flared up. "Yeah, right. I'll try hard to take care of myself. I'll take my vitamins, and you can imagine how well I'm sleeping. And exercise? When I can't sleep, I get up and go walking. I walk for hours some nights. Sometimes I walk when I get home from work, sometimes before I come to work. How's that for taking care of myself?"

"I'm so sorry," Alex said quietly. He took small comfort that Jim seemed engaged with the psychiatrist. But Jim's denial made everything difficult.

And what could a person like Jim do if he recognized medicine might not be the right fit? He carried huge loans, and he would disappoint his family. Heartbreaking scenarios. Medicine looked inspiring and noble from the outside, but could appear very different once you climbed inside it. The endless learning, more than anyone could really know. The fear of errors, the fatigue. So many needy patients, the unhappy patients. Occasionally angry patients. Of course the rewards were great, but some days the positives did not balance the negatives.

Jim did not attend the welcome picnic for the interns.

But Maya Summer came, arriving late in a rush, full of stories and information about the recent problems with rabies. Residents gathered to her, clarifying the vaccination protocols, how to triage a suspicious animal bite. The interns hovered, impressed to meet someone with an impact in public health. Once again, no sign of Whit.

Alex considered her curiously. She looked animated, eager to meet the new interns, inquiring about each person's background. Not that Maya wasn't always friendly and lively, but he sensed a different energy. Stewart Burns stepped over to her, and Alex predicted that Maya would turn to him, say something that would make Burns grin, but she surprised Alex by suddenly looking his way. Her eyes found Alex, her hand half raised in greeting. Nice. He nodded back.

Something had changed.

Veronica held court under a tree. She sat on top of the picnic table, a small group of newbies perched on the benches and soaking up her words as she gestured and told a story. Wearing a white top and white shorts, her hair catching the low light—she shone in the early dusk.

Because Maya came late, people soon started leaving. Ridiculous weather for a picnic anyway, everyone red and sweaty, fanning themselves. The food limp, unappetizing, the drinks watery from melted ice. Storms stacked up behind the mesas as the sun incinerated the sky on its way down. One of these days those clouds would start moving, push into the city and let loose.

Someone began collecting trash in large plastic bags, so Alex grabbed another bag and helped. If Maya wanted to talk to him, she would find him.

He barely finished that thought when she appeared, picked up the other side of his bag to give him a hand. She wore a long striped skirt with a camisole top, having shed her shirt and tied it by the sleeves around her waist. She always dressed in slacks or long skirts, never shorts or a short skirt. Had he ever seen her legs? Her face pink from the heat. She blotted perspiration from her forehead and laughed.

"Whose idea was it to have a picnic in July?" she asked.

"I think it's a tradition. Which is a terrible reason, of course. We're supposed to be smart people." Alex took the full trash bag from her and pulled the top closed, tied a knot. "Thanks for helping. You didn't need to do that."

Maya leaned against a peeling eucalyptus trunk, gazed out at the distant clouds. "Your new interns seem good. I like them."

"We're having orientations all month. Hey." A thought occurred to him. "Most of them are from out of state. Would you have time to give a talk on public health issues in Phoenix? You know, valley fever, heat illness, snakes and scorpions. And mosquitoes, of course." He raised his eyebrows. "Your little buddies. You could do it on a Thursday, when you'll be at the clinic anyway."

She considered a moment. "Sure. I could throw something together. And I'd better include rabies. About an hour long?"

Alex nodded. "That would be really helpful. They get tired of just listening to us."

They settled on a day. Alex wanted to ask about Whit, why he didn't come, why she never brought him. But he held back since the last time he mentioned Whit, Maya went cold. Now she dawdled, in no rush to leave, helped carry soda cans to the recycle bin.

Alex hardly dared think what this meant. He quickly searched his mind, trying to remember the last time Maya mentioned Whit. Certainly often in the past, all the times she'd said things like *Whit is so busy this week* or *Whit and I are taking a little trip to the Grand Canyon soon*. But not lately. Was he being pathetic?

"Well." Maya brushed off her hands. Only a few people remained, chatting, picking up. One resident sat at a picnic table on his phone, a serious expression, talking to someone about electrolytes. The tops of far thunderheads shone pink in the dusk, and she pointed. "They look like cotton candy."

Alex wiped the sweat from his face. "It's got to rain soon, right? I'm tired of waiting."

"So am I," she replied. Her cheeks rosy. Her gray eyes felt warm, comforting like flannel, and Alex was pretty certain she wanted to reach out and touch his arm, but she didn't. Instead she said, "See you tomorrow?"

"You bet," he said lightly.

Enough questions to keep him wondering all the way home.

26

Whitaker called Maya.

He had poor timing. She just saw a frustrating new patient, an indignant middle-aged woman who wanted oxycodone for her chronic back pain. Oxycodone, better known as Percocet.

Maya's morning ran well until then. Twice, she embraced her favorite task, explaining the female cycle and contraception, helping patients select their best method. She described how an egg emerged from the ovary each month and traveled blindly to the uterus, and how to prevent sperm from finding it. Maya prescribed birth control pills for one and arranged an IUD insertion for the other.

The new patient, Tina Gimble, sat uncomfortably in the exam room chair, shifting frequently. Injured years before in a car accident, Tina said her pain required as few as two or as many as eight tablets of oxycodone each day, and she requested a month's prescription for two hundred pills. Maya's intuition tingled when Tina could not remember her last physician's name, even though she had been seeing him for a year.

Maya explained the narcotic policy and Tina's face changed. Before writing a prescription, Maya must review Tina's previous medical records, check the pharmacy database, order a urine drug test, and screen for depression. Perform a thorough exam. See what treatments and medications were tried before, what helped and what failed. Find what X-rays or scans had been done, which specialists were consulted, and the impact of physical therapy. Treating chronic pain was no simple undertaking.

While exasperated by the process, most patients understood. The policies were designed to provide the best, safest treatment and to prevent diversion—obtaining drugs to sell. Maya's established pain patients followed the rules and remained stable. Some had decreased their opiates through biofeedback and antidepressants.

"It will take me weeks to get all those records," Tina moaned. She ran both hands through her stiff bleached hair. "My pills run out tonight."

"It's not only our policy—it's everyone's policy," Maya apologized. "You'll run into the same problem wherever you go because the state has new rules. I'm really sorry, but the guidelines are changing rapidly because of the opioid epidemic. Usually your last physician will give you enough meds for another month, if they know you're getting established with me."

Maya didn't mention the newest regulation about to take place, that all opiate prescriptions would become electronic. No more handing over a paper prescription that could be sold or altered: a few small marks with a pen changed an order for ten pills to forty. Or a prescription pad could be stolen, the physician's signature forged. Instead, all prescriptions flew straight from the doctor's computer to the pharmacy, a huge step in halting illegal access. Those physicians without computerized systems, the ones Mel called dinosaurs, could no longer prescribe such drugs.

"So I'm just supposed to go through withdrawal?" Her heels thumped loudly against the exam table. "Is that what you want?"

"Of course not. If your last doctor won't help, I can send you to a community center. You can go there every day, and they'll monitor you and give you enough to prevent withdrawal."

"I'm not a goddamn addict." Tina's voice rose.

Maya shook her head. "I never said that. But if you're having withdrawal, that means your body is dependent on the narcotic." She wrote the address on a notepad and handed it to her. "I'll call them now, let them know you're on the way. If you contact your previous doctor's office, they can fax us your records quickly. Or if you give your permission, I'll be happy to call them myself, talk with that doctor. We could handle this much more quickly."

"I just told you, I don't remember his name," she spat. She didn't say the word, but Maya practically heard it in her head. *Bitch.*

"It's on your prescription bottle. Or the pharmacy will know. Or you can just go to his office." Maya had to give her a chance. Maybe this was the moment things could shift. "Tina. Once we get you properly established in a few days, or by next week at the latest, we can really work on this. There are some treatments you've never tried. I think we can control your pain better. Maybe you're a candidate for suboxone."

Tina waited, as if considering. Maya imagined she would ask more about suboxone, a prescription narcotic that prevented withdrawal and controlled dependency.

"You know what? You suck!" Tina yelled. "You're a terrible doctor. I'm going to file a complaint with your company and put it online. I'm going to report you to the medical board."

"I'm really sorry you feel that way." Maya's pulse quickened but she forced herself to act calm, even though these confrontations always felt terrible. Every physician faced it, over and over. And would continue to face it until the frenzy of opioid overuse improved.

Tina jumped from the exam table and stomped out, slamming the door and cursing loudly down the hall.

In the nursing station, Connie glanced at Maya. "That got ugly."

"I wish I was better at this," Maya said unhappily.

"Well, I think you helped her. She ran out of here a lot faster than she limped in."

Maya's phone buzzed…Whitaker. Noon seemed an odd time for him to call, and she felt frazzled from the patient. But she didn't want to make him leave a message, because what if he didn't? Enough of this waiting. Maya stepped back into the empty exam room for privacy and answered.

"Hello, Maya," he said. Formal, guarded.

She felt blunt. "Did you try to call me a few days ago?"

"No. I mean, yes." He hesitated. "I've been…I miss you."

"Really." She hadn't anticipated that. She expected defensiveness, expected him to justify his behavior. Or to ask her to justify hers.

"I kept hoping you would call," he said. "When you were ready."

"I kept thinking I might call."

"But you didn't…" He sounded sad.

"No, I was still angry." The new Maya, forthright.

"Are you now?"

"I don't know." Maybe the new Maya wasn't as forthright as she hoped, because she still felt angry. Only now she grappled with his admission, that he missed her. It sounded like a confession.

She heard Connie in the nursing station, asking *Has anyone seen Dr. Summer?* Someone down the hall laughed, and an old man's reedy voice loudly thanked his doctor for helping him. A cart wheeled by.

"Listen," Maya said, distracted. "Can we talk later? It's noisy here, and I'm wrapping up seeing patients."

"Of course. I forgot this is your patient day. I need to go, too. How about we talk tonight?"

"Yes, perfect."

They disconnected, and Maya exhaled slowly. So this was good, right? He apologized, sort of. Not exactly. *I miss you.* It seemed like code. She felt she should know what that meant but could no longer tell.

JOURNAL

It's stunning how many people in my high school were surprised when I became valedictorian. I mean, I knew no one liked me. That was obvious. I never really hung out with people. I didn't play their games, didn't gossip about others. I never put anyone down, and I never pretended to fall in love. I never went to their tedious football or basketball games or acted like a Neanderthal. All that hysterical cheering and booing, so senseless.

It's as if they actually thought I was stupid. Maybe it sounds trite to say they were judging a book by its cover, but that's what happened. I know I should let this go, but it still bothers me.

They were sorry later.

I'm slowly getting better at this. No one has any idea.

27

Last night after the picnic, Alex dreamed about Maya. She wore that long striped skirt, and he knelt beside her and slowly raised the hem to expose her leg, the one with the recurrent limp. He awoke with an erection… which, he reminded himself, was common for any man on any morning.

Despite the heat, he biked to work. Between Jim Barrow and Maya Summer, he felt constantly disquieted and he craved the physical release of exercise. Besides, his weight was up a little. Once at work, he showered in the call room and changed into the fresh clothes he kept in his office. He wondered if maybe he should have seen Wendy Jones again after all, should have slept with her. Nothing wrong with having fun if everyone is on the same page. But too much time had passed since then, and he didn't want to anyway.

The afternoon in the attending office with Maya ran hot and cold. She behaved amusing and warm one moment, preoccupied and distant the next. Her mood kept shifting, so variable that he gave up trying to read her. Reluctantly, Alex began to wonder if she might be too erratic, too inconsistent, to ever really know.

Between staffing with residents, he ate through a boxed salad for his late lunch.

"Just a salad?" Maya teased during one of her lighter moments.

"Hey. I have to keep my boyish figure. Healthy food and more biking." He noticed she periodically glanced at her phone, as if expecting something.

"With a helmet," she emphasized, looking back up.

Alex grinned. "Of course."

Veronica slid into the chair. Alex realized he had never seen her staff a case with Maya.

"How are you doing, Dr. Reddish?" she asked, a wide smile, producing the dimple at the edge of her mouth. She leaned toward him and looked closely in his eyes. "It seems I haven't seen you much lately."

"I'm good," he said lightly, sensing Maya's attention on them. "I've been right here, like always."

"Of course." A crease of concern between her honey-colored brows. "I've got one of those depression cases we talked about. You said you can show me how to be quick—I'm getting behind."

"Very good. Tell me about it." How to be more *efficient*, not quicker, Alex mentally corrected her. But he thought she would not appreciate the subtlety right now and let it go. She came to him with this willingly, not the time to criticize.

Veronica described a highly depressed man, a forty-year-old plumber who had been fighting the blues for months. He slept poorly, his appetite floundered, and he no longer enjoyed his golf league. His wife insisted that he snap out of it, but he couldn't. His mother and his brother both struggled with depression, and they urged him to see his doctor.

"Pretty thorough history," Alex said. "Anything else you should be worried about, ask about?"

"You mean…" Veronica paused. "Whether he wants to take medication? If he's interested in counseling?"

"No. I mean, those are good questions, but are you worried about his risk for suicide?"

Veronica shrugged. "He doesn't seem suicidal."

"But did you ask him?"

She stared at Alex. "Not in those exact words."

"You really should." Alex thought she would know that; he knew the curriculum covered it. "Patients may be reluctant to bring it up themselves, but if you ask they're likely to respond. More than half of them will tell you."

Veronica amazed Alex by glancing at her watch.

"Let me meet him," Alex said quickly. "Let's go see him together."

He rejoined Maya fifteen minutes later. Her eyebrows arched in question.

"Well, was he suicidal?" she asked.

"He'd thought about it." Alex rubbed his face. He had taken over the interview because Veronica went silent. "He'd even thought about how. But he denied he would really carry through. So we need to stay on top of it, in case something switches."

Jim Barrow entered, brushed past Alex without a glance, and asked Maya to help evaluate a hand injury. Then everyone had questions, Alex and Maya constantly in and out, barely interacting the rest of the day. Alex finished his salad, which now tasted warm and a little off.

He felt weary and wished he'd eaten more protein. Or maybe that wasn't it at all, maybe he was disappointed that today's Maya was no longer the appealing last-night-picnic Maya. Last night they seemed connected, that new energy. Today seemed business as usual, or less.

Maya sat engrossed at her computer, finishing her encounters from the morning. He didn't want to bother her; he just wanted to leave and stood to go. She turned and looked him up and down.

"Are you really biking home in this heat?"

"I'll soak myself first, then I'll soak again at a gas station halfway. I'll be bone dry in about fifteen minutes, but that gets me through." His eyes closed unexpectedly and he sprang them open. Wake up.

"Are you sure?" She squinted at him. "I can take you home. My car's got a hatchback for hauling hay—your bike would fit."

Alex declined. He wanted to go, not wait for her, not have her do him a favor. Her variable moods discouraged him. He changed clothes and strapped on his helmet, took a long drink of water and filled his water bottle. Had he slept poorly last night? Probably—that dream about Maya. What a sap. At the spigot in the parking garage, he drenched himself head to toe and took off.

Summer traffic remained light, schools and colleges out of session, tourists gone. Within ten minutes a dull headache gripped his skull and he wobbled, nearly hitting the curb. He straightened, pumped hard with new determination, then it happened again. What the hell. Perturbed, feeling fuzzy, he dismounted and pulled his bike under a tree, to sit for a moment in the shade. Maybe it was hotter than he thought, maybe he should have eaten more and hydrated better. He took his pulse, expecting it to be high, but found it only eighty. Strange. He would relax a few minutes here, then go again. Downing a long swig of water, he leaned back against the tree.

He felt worse—no way could he keep riding. He tried to think, but knew no one available with a car that could carry his bike except Maya. And she had offered. Weaker, now nauseated, he pulled out his phone and called her, hoping she had not yet left the clinic. She answered on the first ring, and he somehow managed to tell her that he was sick and where to find him.

Propped against the tree, Alex dropped his head back and stared up into the branches. Sunlight shone around the leaves in blue halos, fell through in glowing shafts, and smoldered about the limbs in a greenish blur, as if the tree itself wore an aura. What the heck.

28

Maya drove past Alex at first because he gave her the wrong location, off by several blocks. She circled around and found him, slumped below a thorny ironwood tree, his bicycle lying beside him. He opened his eyes as she hurried up.

"Hiya Maya," he mumbled, waving his fingers. "Hey. That rhymes."

She knelt beside him. He looked utterly depleted. "Alex. What's going on?"

"I'm just really tired." His eyes closed.

"Come on." She stood and took his hands, tugged. "You can't stay here."

He nodded and staggered up, made a small step toward her car, then held back. "Wait. I have to get my bike. It's almost brand new."

"I'll get it in a minute. Come on," she insisted. He must not have slept much last night, she guessed. Combine lack of sleep with poor nutrition—maybe all he ate was the salad she saw—and add dehydration and heat, and that could account for his condition. The air hung heavy, humid, the sky cobbled with clouds, which made overheating more likely. She realized how little she knew about Alex Reddish. Whether he had family in town. If he had any medical issues, took any medications.

He sat heavily in the car, slowly pulled in his legs.

"Take off your helmet," Maya suggested, "so you can cool down quicker. I'll get your bike."

First she started the car, put on the AC, and turned all the vents toward him. His bike weighed almost nothing, and she hoisted it easily into her hatchback. Sliding behind the wheel, she saw he had not removed his helmet. So she reached over and released the clasp, pulled it off his head.

"Thanks. That feels better." His eyes still closed.

Maya handed him his water bottle and instructed him to drink up.

She knew where he lived because last fall they held a faculty retreat at his home, an old adobe-style house by a city park. A small, charming place. Maya only vaguely remembered the interior because they'd sat in the park for the retreat, a lovely autumn day, cool and sunny. Perfect Phoenix weather, still months away.

Alex collapsed on his couch. Maya brought him a wet towel and sat beside him to check his pulse, looked at him with surprise.

"Your pulse is only seventy-five," she said. Though clearly fit from biking, his leg muscles ropy, his stomach flat, the dehydration and heat should have his heart racing. "What's your normal resting rate?"

He looked at her, bleary. "Huh?"

"Your normal resting heart rate," Maya repeated. He still held the wet towel, limp in his hand. She picked it up and slipped off his glasses, wiped his face. "Alex. Pay attention."

"Mm?" He squinted, shifted his head.

Something seemed off. Maybe she should have taken him to the emergency room. Maya shook his arm, made him listen, took his history. No medical problems, no medications. No marijuana or street drugs. He threw her a wounded look.

"Maya. Maya." He shook his head. "Maya. You know me better than that."

"No, actually I don't." Why didn't she? He knew much about her, always listened so well. So supportive whenever they saw each other. She felt like she hadn't kept up her end of the friendship.

His hazel eyes sharpened and looked straight into her. "I feel like I've known you forever."

"Alex, please. Concentrate."

She pressed him about his symptoms. He felt dizzy, weak, nauseated. He kept blinking, kept screwing up his face and tilting his head, as if to see better.

"Everything looks weird," he complained. "It's all greeny-yellow. Blurry. Glowy."

"Glowy? That's not a word." She couldn't help teasing him, it was second nature. And Maya couldn't place it, those visual symptoms, too distracted to recall what they meant. She insisted he keep sipping water, put the fan on. He leaned over and lay down, put his head on the pillow.

"You doing okay?" she asked.

"Mm hm." He fell asleep.

Maya sat there, observed his breathing. Deep and regular. Well, now what? She couldn't leave, not convinced he was stable, but she didn't want to wake him either. He probably needed sleep as much as anything.

She went out to her car and unloaded his bicycle. Kids played in the park across the street, calling out in the dusk. Thunderheads mounted far in the north, an occasional sputter of lightning. She thought of the horses, the mirrored tank, perhaps under that very storm right now. Maya brought the bike inside and propped it up by the front door. Alex still slept deeply.

It came to her…halos around lights, yellow-green visual discoloration. That old heart medication digitalis, rarely used now, could cause those symptoms. *Digitalis purpurea*, derived from the foxglove plant, had been used for centuries. But it made no sense, for newer and better cardiac drugs had mostly replaced it. And he just told her he had no heart problems.

Maya checked her phone, checked her email. Nothing important. She went online and starting searching, looking to see what other drugs or substances might cause visual halos. She only found digitalis or chemicals related to it.

She began to wander the house, hoping she might find a clue. Don't snoop, she thought sternly, but she convinced herself it might be important, especially if his pulse dropped further. Which made her go back, place her fingers gently on his wrist without waking him. Sixty. Though low, still a possible healthy pulse for a fit person.

Not much in his medicine cabinet, just ibuprofen and the usual sundries. The house was neat and fairly clean, pleasant landscape prints on the walls and a large stunning photo of a nebula in space. Nothing revealing in the refrigerator.

Maya debated, then opened the door to the spare bedroom. She caught herself walking on tiptoe and made herself stop. Set up as an office and lined with bookcases, a futon spread with a colorful serape and bright pillows, the space felt warm and inviting, and Maya knew instantly that he liked to read and study here. A desk faced the large window overlooking the backyard, a graceful jacaranda tree, a hummingbird feeder, and a hedge of oleander along the back wall. A glint near the floor caught her eye where a metallic cluster lay heaped on a bottom bookshelf.

Trophies, all sizes, maybe a dozen. Piled crookedly, as if shoved there and forgotten. Maya sat on the floor and picked through them, straightened them. All chess championships, all first place. She spied a photo album on the shelf above. Should she look? Of course not. She should stop.

Not exactly a photo album, but more like a nicely bound scrapbook, with photos and newspaper clippings of sweet young Alex Reddish, thick plastic glasses slipping down his nose. Always holding up a trophy, much bigger trophies than the ones here. A little chubby, a pile of brown hair down his forehead, always serious, sometimes a somber smile. Never a grin, nothing ecstatic. And in many photos there stood an intense, beaming woman with teased platinum hair who must be his mother, leaning over him and clutching his shoulder with dark red fingernails. Bronze facial foundation, wine-colored lipstick, dark eyeliner. She looked unnatural. It didn't take long for Maya to notice that the solemn smile on little Alex's face only appeared when his mother was not there.

Fascinated, Maya kept turning the pages. She saw Alex become a teenager with over-large aviator glasses and mild acne, saw him slowly mature. Occasionally an adult man stood by the mother, two separate men at different times. Alex must have been about nineteen or twenty years old when the scrapbook abruptly ended.

Maya's phone rang. Whitaker.

She completely forgot they were supposed to talk tonight. Guilty, she closed the scrapbook and shoved it back before answering, keeping her voice low to not wake Alex in the other room.

Considerate and solicitous, Whit asked if he could come over to see her right now.

"Not tonight." Maya heard herself stammer, took hold of herself. "I've just got to finish this project I'm in the middle of." Basically true, for Alex was sort of a project. She should simply tell Whit the whole story, but it felt too complicated to explain.

"I understand. I've been there." Whit being the epitome of thoughtfulness. "Let me take you out properly, okay? Saturday night?"

"That would be good," Maya agreed, relieved.

"I can't wait." He paused. "I've missed you so much."

"Me too."

Maybe things would be better now. Maybe they learned not to take one another for granted. Maybe they could take up where they left off, caring about each other, helping each other out. No—some changes were needed. She would not wait around for him as much, and she would see her friends more. While she would be careful about her promises to him, he should be willing to join her more often with her people, too. They could iron it out Saturday.

Alex stirred in the other room. Maya hurried out and found him sitting up, more color in his face.

"You look better," she commented.

"Wow." He wiped his eyes, peered around.

"Does your vision still look funny?"

"No. It's just about normal. But I still feel pretty weak. How long have I been asleep?"

Maya checked her watch. Eight-thirty. "A few hours."

He looked about, saw his bicycle by the door. "Geez, thanks Maya. It was so nice of you to get me. *Really* nice, above and beyond. I don't know what came over me—I don't know what I would have done."

"No problem. I'm glad to do it. Are you hungry?"

She made them peanut butter and honey sandwiches and watched Alex become more and more normal. They chatted and even laughed. Maya kept turning it in her mind, wondering when she should say something. Now, or later. But later might be too late.

"Excuse me for a second. I think my fluids caught up." Alex stood and moved toward the bathroom.

"Wait." Maya hurried to the kitchen, opened a few cabinets, and found what she wanted, brought him back a small clean jar. She made a face, apologetic. "This is going to sound strange. But I've been researching your symptoms, especially the visual symptoms, and the only cause for that I can find is digitalis. Or chemicals like it. And your pulse was slow when it should have been fast. Digitalis does that, too." Alex squinted, and she hurried on. "What I'm saying, is that maybe you should see if you've somehow been exposed. You know, get a urine test."

"Are you serious?"

Maya grimaced. "Maybe."

He stared at her. "But really—digitalis? That's pretty far-fetched."

"I know." She had nothing better to say.

But Alex nodded and complied. They discussed whether he should take the sample to his own physician and request the test, or if Maya should simply run it at the state lab.

"You take it. It's just easier," Alex said. He put the jar in a paper bag before handing it to her, apparently so she wouldn't have to look at his urine. Maya suppressed a smile—she would have done the same thing.

He thanked her profusely again when she left.

"I'm just glad you're better now," Maya said, heartfelt. This time when they hugged, she hugged him back, and it felt natural.

Before she drove away, though, sitting in her car, she took out the jar and held it to the light. His sample looked pale yellow, the urine of a well-hydrated person. Well, she had to know if he needed more liquids. She was a doctor, after all.

29

Alex left his bike home and drove to work the next day. Not quite recovered, he still battled mild lethargy. By afternoon, though, the physical fog had cleared.

Scott Sherman stopped by, flopped into the chair by Alex's desk.

Alex hoped to complete a draft of his bike helmet project so he could send it to Maya for feedback. He kept wondering about his urine test, when it would be done, although of course it would be negative. Maya's concern seemed implausible. He worried more about food poisoning, maybe from that salad left out too long, maybe the dressing. All those boxed lunches yesterday were catered, so no telling when his food was actually made or when it was last refrigerated. The symptoms didn't support that, though.

"Hey." Scott nudged his elbow, waited for Alex to stop typing. "How'd it go with Wendy? Still seeing her? And I do mean, *all* of her."

Alex sat back. "No, I'm afraid it didn't work out. She was nice, though. We had a pleasant dinner."

"Nice?" Scott made a derisive sound. "Yeah, she's nice. Are you telling me you only saw her once?"

"Yeah. It just wasn't a good match, for some reason." Alex shrugged. "You know how that goes."

"Alex. My man," Scott said sadly. His tan deeper since summer began, his hair more pale. Alex noted little crows' feet and suspected Scott would not age well. Scott went on. "I'm trying my very best to de-nerdify you, but you've got to work with me. You can't worry about things like who fulfills your so-called dreams. I doubt you know what you want. You've got to ride a bunch of fillies, you know, to find the winner."

Enough of that, Alex thought. "How's Jim doing?"

"Jimbo? How would I know?" Scott rolled his eyes.

"He's your advisee. I assume you talk with—"

"Yeah, don't assume anything. One day he's falling asleep, the next day he's mad at me. The next day he seems fine. It's like working with a yo-yo." Scott sighed dramatically, then a smile crept across his face. "He likes you, I think. You're all touchy-feely, aren't you? You sure you don't want to trade? Jimbo for V?"

"No." Alex twisted his mouth. "He'll hardly talk to me. That meeting didn't go well."

Scott stared at Alex as if he was hopeless. Then he laughed, his face lit up. "I know who you like. You like that lively little piece from the health department. Mayo. No, Maya. Maya what's-her-name."

"Summer," Alex said coldly. Scott could be such an ass.

"More like winter. I can't get much out of her. Guess I'm too charming—probably throws her off." Scott batted his eyelashes. His eyes looked green, too green to be natural. Likely tinted contact lenses.

"You're way off," Alex said dismissively, disgusted. "She sees Whitaker Thicket. And show some respect, for god's sake. She's your colleague. Don't be such an ass."

Scott pulled a long face. "Thicket? Sorry, man, but that's out of your league. Let her go—you've got no chance. He's handsome *and* smart *and* rich. Not necessarily in that order. But hell, have you seen the car he drives? *I'd* date him, if I was into that."

Alex turned back to his computer. "Sorry, I've got to get this done. Thanks for all the romance advice."

"Any time." Scott stood to go, then sat back down. "Hey. Seriously. How do I talk to Jimbo? I don't really think he's a bad guy. His last patient surveys were actually pretty good—they like him. But he's refusing drug rehab because he says he's not using. He actually wants to take a lie detector test. Talk about denial, right? Or defiance—maybe he thinks he can beat the test. I guess some people can."

Scott reached across the desk and helped himself to a cookie sitting on a napkin, broke the cookie in half, making a mess. Dr. Agatha Mercer, the older attending who often baked them goodies, was there staffing this afternoon.

Alex turned back to him, brushed the crumbs off his desk. "What does the psychiatrist say?"

"Not much. You know how those shrinks are. Needs more time with him, blah blah blah. She says he's depressed, not sleeping well."

Alex pondered. He hadn't talked much with Jim lately, not since Jim started dodging him. "But she says he can work?"

"Yeah. As long as his work quality is acceptable. Which it is, more or less. It's weak, but acceptable. Barely."

Alex nodded, agreed with that assessment. "I would just encourage him. Give him positive feedback wherever you can. Show him you're worried about him."

"Sure. Right. In between telling him all the things he gets wrong or forgets to do. There's just something weird about that guy. And just my luck that I have to be his advisor. Talk about a time-suck, reviewing all his charts, meeting with him all the time to go over his mistakes. Burns better give me some normal residents next year, that's all I can say." Scott pushed up and took the rest of the cookie. "Okay, I'll try what you said. But I'm betting he doesn't make it to Christmas."

Alex winced. "Well. One day at a time, right?"

"What are you, the local AA chapter?" Scott laughed and left.

Alex stared at his computer screen, at the note he'd been writing to Maya. Scott was right, of course, about Thicket. Next to him, Alex was pretty much plain potatoes. He saved the message as a draft and went home.

A stifling evening, the air dense, a fifty percent chance of storms. Beefy clouds clumped overhead, and a cumulonimbus churned in the eastern sky, slowly roiling knobs of gray, a milky dome. Once home, he felt weary again, discouraged. Alex dialed down his AC and dropped on the futon in his study to read. Through the window, the jacaranda branches swayed in the freshening wind…maybe it really would rain tonight.

He noticed the change. The jumble of trophies on the bottom bookshelf stood neatly upright. He thought a moment and figured it must have been Maya last night, poking around, killing time while he slept. What did he expect? Alex felt both violated at her prying and a little rewarded by her interest. Then he saw the scrapbook tilted at an angle, as if hastily shoved away. He recalled all those photos, him alone and him with his mom. His mom with his father, then with his chess coach, who later slept with her.

Sometimes he could barely stand to look at those things. He could hardly imagine what Maya must think.

128

30

Why, Maya thought crossly, can I never get anything done? Theoretically, she had all day to work on her projects, create action plans, and answer calls and advise interventions. Sometimes to require interventions. The time to study the true impact of policy on health, analyze data, and decipher conflicting results.

"I've got other things to do," Maya complained to Sheila. "And besides, nothing about fluoride has changed. We've done the same things for years. There's no such thing as a fluoride crisis."

"There is now." Sheila ran her fingers through her hair, sprouting like a corona about her head. A hint of gray at the roots. Even her green curl bristled. "Have you heard about this guy? He's all over social media."

"No…" Maya sighed.

"It's so stupid. He apparently joined the paranoids who think fluoridating public water is a government plot to take over his brain. Well, someone needs to, because his brain doesn't work so well. I guess he saw a dentist a few weeks ago and found out he had a mouthful of rotten teeth. Turns out he's been drinking distilled water and using non-fluoride toothpaste for years. Maybe decades."

"Sheila. I don't see why I need to know about this." Fluoride added to drinking water had long proven worthwhile at reducing dental cavities, especially in children.

"Bear with me." Sheila grinned. "So he panicked about all his cavities and tried to make up for lost time. Long story short, he overdosed on fluoride supplements and almost died."

"Good grief," muttered Maya, stopping her work and switching computers to look up fluoride toxicity. Nausea, bloody vomit, spasms, and convulsions. Low calcium and high potassium, chemical derangements that made heart muscles spasm, could cause cardiac arrest. "So he's okay now?"

"Apparently. But now he's using his 'brush with death' to show he was right in the first place, to prove how dangerous fluoride can be."

"No. That's completely convoluted." Maya threw up her hands. "He did it to himself, by taking too much."

"Right. And now your old buddy Bluff Barrington from KTAN wants to interview you about fluoride and whatever else we might find in the water."

"It's Friday afternoon," Maya protested. She saw the new blinking light on her message queue—that must be Bluff. It would be a slippery discussion because lately more and more pharmaceuticals appeared in drinking water. Hormones, antibiotics, antidepressants…people flushed their drugs, or simply excreted them into sewage as waste from their bodies, and not every single molecule got filtered out during water purification. Carcinogens, plastics. While only trace amounts of drugs crept into the water supply, she needed more facts, even though not much data had surfaced and much more research was needed. Good luck with that, she thought with dismay, as research budgets across the country kept being gutted at alarming rates.

"He'll have to wait till Monday," Maya went on. "That will give me time to check out a few things, make sure I have all the data correct."

"Got your back. I'll let him know." Sheila returned to her desk.

"Tell him I have laryngitis and can't talk right now," Maya called after her in a mock whisper.

The vote for motorcycle helmets drew closer. Maya received many requests from newspapers and radio stations, wanting her statistics and comments. No one complains about seatbelt laws or the safety glass in windshields, she pointed out. No one rails about the painted no-passing zones on highway curves. Many lives had been saved. Could be saved.

In the last year alone, five thousand Americans died from motorcycle accidents. Nineteen states enforced strict helmet laws for all motorcycle riders, while three states had no laws at all. Arizona belonged to the remainder, those that mandated helmets up to age eighteen. Yet no one else seemed to care as much as Maya, overlooking the massive healthcare costs to taxpayers because—curiously—injured motorcyclists were less likely to carry health insurance.

The threats toward Maya accelerated again, suggesting she might want to watch her back. Saying that accidents could happen in cars as well as on motorcycles, so maybe she should wear a helmet when she drove. Last night, arriving home late after helping Alex, she found the patio furniture on her back porch rearranged.

She called Alex that afternoon to see if he had recovered, and to tell him his digitalis test would be ready Monday. He thanked her profusely again, reporting that he felt good now. Relieved, Maya wondered if they would ever know what happened.

And now she needed to research fluoride and the water supply. Sure, why not add another project to the weekend? Tomorrow night she would see Whit for the first time in several weeks, and her emotions skidded back and forth: relief and eagerness, then caution and uncertainty. She felt giddy one moment, queasy the next.

On Sunday morning, Mel would bring the new horse. Such poor planning—she should have asked Mel to come another day. Because if all went well, she might stay at Whit's Saturday night, so the next morning she would need to rush home to meet Mel. But it was too late to change plans now, and she already asked Rafael to come greet the pinto.

After work that evening, Maya joined Rosa and Rafael for supper. Before Whit, they often teamed up at night, throwing a meal together, the adults sitting with a glass of wine as sunset roasted the sky into coals. When Maya suggested that, Rosa looked surprised.

"Where's Whitaker?" she asked.

Maya's mouth crimped. "We've been on pause for a few weeks. Sorting things out. I'll see him Saturday."

Rosa's face stayed carefully neutral and she said nothing. Maya reminded Rafael about Sunday morning, the horse coming. He regarded her for a long moment with serious eyes.

"What's his name?" Skeptical, as if another horse could not possibly replace Luna. Not exactly angry, but close.

"I don't know. I don't know if he even has a name," Maya admitted. "Sometimes ranch horses don't get names. Mel just calls him the pinto."

Rafael narrowed his gaze.

Rosa gently placed her hand on his head and thanked Maya for including him.

31

On Saturday evening, Maya prepared for Whit. She had not exactly been lonely without him because she busied herself refreshing old friendships, but something felt missing. Maybe it was just physical, just sexual. Maybe she was that shallow.

No, she reminded herself, you miss his conversation, his energy. And she knew he truly worried about her, about her hip pain, her inevitable future with surgeries yet to come. He would always take care of her, he said, a thought both comforting and disquieting. She didn't need a caretaker after all. But she shouldn't resist his impulse, either—that didn't make sense.

Maya stared in her closet, trying to find the right look. Something appealing, but not going too far—not actually seductive. In case things didn't go well.

She wondered again how it must feel to pull on a short skirt, showing all that leg. After the accident, Maya tried it now and then, said the hell with it, and wore shorts or a miniskirt in public. She tried to ignore the looks, the murmured comments, saw people stare and point. Their curiosity, their pity. Not just because of the thick incision scar than ran down her thigh, hip to knee, but also the damage below, the off-color slightly puckered skin graft that wrapped around her calf, the muscle crushed and torn away. But she found it impossible to relax with her leg exposed and eventually quit trying. Maya discovered she craved obscurity more than abandon.

She chose a pair of wide-legged palazzo pants and a sleeveless shirt that showed off her arms and just a hint of cleavage. Good enough.

Whit tapped quietly on the door, then swept through and circled his arm around her, a firm kiss on her lips. "You look great."

"You look pretty darn good yourself." That spill of dark hair across his forehead, those lively blue eyes, now avidly searching her. His narrow handsome face. She thought he would be more cautious, more tentative under the circumstances; his boldness was unexpected.

She imagined they would go to his favorite steakhouse, but he chose the organic café she treasured, in a small plain cottage with simple appetizing dishes, local wines and craft beers. Maya felt pleased and gratified. He asked her advice on the menu and complimented the food she recommended. He listened attentively to everything she said.

They talked about work, laughed about Bluff Barrington and the fluoride man and Whit's latest challenge with his personnel, a manager who wore four-inch stilettos and fractured her ankle when the heel broke. The woman claimed disability, insisting she couldn't work for two months, even though her job entailed making phone calls while sitting in a chair.

His work was going well, he reported. No recent disasters or failures, most patients' hearts behaving as told. Their conversation faltered only once, when Maya mentioned the horse coming the next morning, that Mel was bringing the pinto from his ranch.

Whit's brow furrowed. "Do you really want that commitment again? Won't that tie you down, morning and night?"

Maya shrugged. "I miss it. I like having a horse around. And my neighbors help. Rafael is so reliable, and he enjoys the responsibility. It's good for him. Besides, if I decide I don't want the horse, if he's too much trouble, Mel will take him back."

Whit's lips tightened at Mel's name and Maya braced herself, but he said nothing and the moment passed. She likely imagined it, oversensitive.

Driving to his house after dinner, Whit turned affectionate, his hand never leaving her except to shift gears, stroking her arm, her knee, her thigh. At a stoplight he kissed her, his fingers drifting down her throat and under her shirt. Maya had never seen him so hungry. They barely made it through the door and he dragged her to the bedroom, pulling at her clothes. Gasping, intensely aroused, Maya gave way to this unusual passion. She became so heated, this lust so unlike their usual measured lovemaking, that she hardly knew herself.

Early at breakfast, Maya realized they never talked about their quarrel. Perhaps last night spoke for itself. But the path forward still felt unclear and she could not brush it aside, although that seemed Whit's intent. If he harbored any aggravation toward her for saddling him with an awkward dinner, they should air it now. She speculated how the conversation must have gone that night, what excuses he made for her, how the other woman responded. And while Maya would not have done differently, she felt badly because it was so important to him.

"So, I never asked you." Maya sipped her coffee. "How did that dinner go, that night? When I had to ditch you. Was the wife upset I wasn't there?"

Whit's eyes raised to her, then away. His tousled morning hair looked young, sensual. He started to smile, then seemed to think better of it.

"She didn't show up," he admitted, sheepish. "I guess something came up. So it was just us guys, after all."

Maya stared at him.

"Kind of ironic, huh." He rolled his eyes.

Maya found her voice. "What the hell, Whit. Were you going to tell me? I've been feeling so bad about this. I mean, don't get me wrong— I had to do it. But it's been hard, knowing how angry you were."

He exhaled, cautious. "I just want to move on, leave that behind. Get back to how things were. I didn't think it mattered anymore."

Maybe he was right, maybe it didn't matter. Or maybe he was full of crap. Maya felt deceived, as if their reunion had been based on a lie. Which made no sense, since he never lied about it. But she repeatedly imagined him talking with the wife, trying to be cordial, making excuses for Maya as he fumed internally. Maya felt almost dizzy, as if the past had changed without warning.

She looked at her watch.

"We need to get going or I'll be late for Mel," she said coldly.

"Maya." He hesitated. "I'm sorry. I didn't think we needed to rehash that. I apologize if I was wrong."

He had never expressed regret, not so openly, and she found herself mostly mollified. She leaned over and kissed him. "I really appreciate you saying that."

When he drove her home, he kept picking up her hand and squeezing it, kept looking at her fondly. Maya's thoughts wandered, random, noticing the excellent air conditioning in his car. Instantly cold, even too cold. She shivered and took her hand back, rubbed her fingers to warm them.

"Are you chilly?"

"No, I'm fine." She turned her vent away. Whit would always have things like this, which cost a great deal and worked very well. Nothing wrong with that, was there? And here they were, a couple again. She suspected things could move quickly now, if she wished. Maya Summer-Thicket. Thicket-Summer. It sounded like a duck pond. A rabbit warren.

He stopped in her driveway and hurried around to her door, unusually attentive. Maya couldn't help but smile at how hard he was trying.

"You should stay," she suggested. "You can meet Mel, and visit with Rafael and Rosa again." Whit only met them once before.

"I'd better get back." He didn't say why. His hand rested on her shoulder and his eyes shone in the harsh sunlight; he seemed downright misty with romance. He kissed her cheek, then gently her lips. Not too long, not to short. Just right. Maya thought of fairytales and worried for her sanity. He gripped her hands, squinting in the sun. "Maya. I…This makes me really happy. To have you back."

"Me too." She smiled, relieved. He had rarely shown her this softer side.

Her phone chirped as Whit settled into his car. He looked up quizzically.

"It's nothing," she assured him, seeing the text from Alex. As he drove off, she looked back at her phone.

Hey. Stewart wants me to attend that valley fever symposium in Tucson coming up. I think you said you're going. Maybe we could drive together?

Valley fever was one of Arizona's most unique and fascinating diseases, one of her favorite topics. Maya planned to go alone and did not look forward to the long trip back and forth. Now it would be fun.

I can drive, she offered.

No, your car has too many miles. It's too hot out to risk a breakdown, he replied.

How do you know how many miles my car has? She supposed that her car, with far more than a hundred thousand miles, did harbor an increased risk of mechanical mishaps.

I rode in your front seat. I was sick, not dead.

Maya would have wagered a fair amount that Alex could not possibly have noticed her mileage, as ill as he was. She didn't think he even opened his eyes during that trip.

Okay, you drive, she conceded.

Bring your foster mosquitoes if they need an outing. I won't judge.

Maya laughed out loud.

32

The pinto horse clattered down the trailer ramp, snorting and blowing, tossing his head to glare about with a nervous eye.

Now in daylight, Maya saw the damage, why the horse needed a break. Bite marks broke his smooth hide, ragged crescents on his flanks and neck. A deep gouge from a kick oozed along his ribs, and his white ear showed a small tear near the tip, crusted with scab.

"He's all beat up, isn't he," she remarked. The horse trotted back and forth, testing the space in the enclosure, building up speed; his gait reached long and he floated with each stride, suspended, before striking ground. He avoided the humans and kept to the far side. "But kind of fancy. Look at that trot."

He stopped abruptly and stood gazing out at the desert.

"Is he broke at all?" asked Maya. She offered him carrots, then a pail with oats, but he shied away from her and ignored the bribes. Most horses would have been thrilled.

"Green broke," Mel said. "Gelded late, still thinks he's a stud. After he settles in, I might have a guy come by, work with him. That okay?"

"Of course." Maya looked at Rafael, who wore a baseball cap and sat on the top rail, watching with tight lips. "What do you think, Rafael?"

Rafael switched his eyes from the horse to Maya. "I think he's mad at everyone."

Mel moved over, put his hand on the boy's shoulder. "I think you're right, son."

Rafael blinked and looked back at the horse. "What's his name?"

"Why don't you come up with something, okay?"

The boy nodded slowly. "Why is he like this? Why don't the other horses like him?"

"No one knows. Something must have happened to him."

Maya fixed a snack and soft drinks, called Rosa over. They sat on the back porch, even though it was too hot, and watched the horse roam. Sunlight pierced the mesquite tree, fiery slivers on their skin. Rafael sat on the ground with Twinkie, rubbed his rough head and offered him apple slices. Mel drummed his fingers and studied the boy.

"Listen, son," Mel finally said. "Maya could use your help here, and I think you're up to it. But you mustn't go inside that pen with him, you understand? Not until he's broke better."

Rafael sat still a long moment, gave Twinkie another apple piece. A tiny sound of munching, the tortoise's mouth sticky with fruit.

"Sure," he said finally.

The cicadas began calling, escalating quickly. Maya glanced up at the tree: *Diceroprocta apache*, the Apache cicada. The insects spent at least three years underground, nibbling blindly, until emerging and seeking a mate, filling the air with their strident clacking buzz. A startling and insistent love call, a sound more metallic than alive. Sometimes the noise grew deafening.

The horse finally relaxed under the shade screen by the shed, although his ears remained pointed toward the humans. Maya handed Rafael a carrot and asked if he wanted to offer it again.

"No." Rafael seemed vexed. "He doesn't want it."

The adults traded glances. Rosa changed the subject and asked Maya about her Saturday night out. Maya smiled and said it went well.

"You still with that cardiology guy?" Mel asked, gruff. "I thought you were done with him."

"I never said that," Maya protested.

"Guess I just surmised it." Mel raised his chin, acted sage.

"No, we ironed out a few things." Even as she said that, though, Maya was not certain they had. She wished now they had discussed their quarrel instead of letting it go. That Whit had either showed frustration or explained himself. Or asked her how she felt. Then she reminded herself that he apologized, and she worried she was too needy. Move on.

"Anyway," Maya announced, "I've got to get going. I'm driving over to see my parents."

"Too hot out anyway," Mel agreed.

After Mel left, hauling away the rattling trailer, Maya and Rosa cleaned up. Rosa mentioned she would spend the afternoon making jewelry, one of her side businesses, and Rafael would be on his own for a few hours.

"He can go with me." Maya thought how little family he had, no father, no grandparents, no cousins. "Do you want to meet my parents? They would love that. And they *habla español*."

"Really?" He looked unbelieving.

"*Verdad.*" Maya smiled. "It's true. And anyway, I should work on my Spanish. So you can come with me, but we have to speak Spanish while we drive. Except I'll need a lot of help."

"Are you sure?" asked Rosa.

Rosa ran home to wrap up fresh tortillas for Maya's parents, while Maya asked Rafael to toss a flake of hay into the corral. The horse waited until they were in the car before he lowered his head and began eating.

"His name is Manchado," Rafael said, staring back as they drove away.

"I don't know that word. What does it mean?"

Rafael looked somberly through his dark lashes. "It means he's spotted."

"That works."

Her parents were delighted with Rafael. Happy to be the center of attention, lavished with treats and compliments, Rafael chatted in Spanish about school and his favorite books and sports. They even asked about his fears, the limbo of a Dreamer. Coming to Arizona when he was six months old, he now found himself caught in the exhausting dilemma of citizenship. Maya promised to bring him with her more often.

On the way home, when they spoke about the horse again, his mood retreated.

Later that night, after Rafael fell asleep, Rosa appeared at Maya's door with a small pitcher of sangria and a thin silver bracelet for Maya. They sat outside to watch the storms approach, twisted towers. Thunder crept across the sky and lightning skipped between the stacks, flashing the desert in and out of darkness.

Rosa explained that Manchado was a complicated name, that it had other interpretations besides *spotted*.

It also meant stained. Or damaged.

"Do you think Rafael understands that?" Maya asked, startled.

Rosa couldn't quite hide her sorrow. "Yes."

The hot wind picked up and tree branches clashed, but the storm moved eastward. They could see a thick downpour below the cloud bellies, drenching the distant suburbs. Maya sighed and hoped for rain again. Maybe tomorrow.

33

Stunned, Alex stared at the phone after he hung up with Maya.

Surely there had been an error. His urine sample contained digitalis, or rather a form of digitalis. When the lab investigated further, the report became quite specific: oleandrin. A chemical found in the oleander plant, highly toxic.

He knew that plants evolved their own methods for self-preservation. Some wielded wicked thorns, or grew impenetrable bark. Some carried toxins. Oleanders thrived in Phoenix, well suited to the dry, salty soil. They grew in dense hedges up to twelve feet high, could be fashioned into trees or used as accent bushes. Alex's own yard had a low decorative oleander hedge along the back wall, masses of pink flowers nodding in the sun. But he had not trimmed them in a month.

Nerium oleander, Maya said. She couldn't seem to stop herself from latching onto Latin nomenclature—a trait he found oddly appealing. No, she insisted, there were no errors. They checked it twice. Somehow last Thursday, Alex ingested oleander. Besides his scrambled egg breakfast, all he ate that day was the boxed salad, the one he snacked on through the afternoon. Other people consumed salads from the same kitchen but no one else became ill.

They cautiously discussed what it meant. If the oleander came from his salad, someone had chopped it up and mixed it in.

"You mean intentionally?" Alex said, unbelieving. He remembered, though, how the greens tasted bitter at the end of the day. He thought he'd left it out too long.

"It's hard to imagine it happening accidentally," Maya remarked. She paused. "Alex. This is going to sound dramatic, maybe crazy. But do you have any enemies?"

Alex was flabbergasted. "Of course not. I mean, I'm not sure everyone around here thinks I'm the best teacher. I can be a little weird, you know."

"Oh, come on. Everyone there likes you," she objected.

Alex ignored that. "But do I have real enemies? Who wish me harm? No. I can't imagine."

"I know," she agreed. "It's bizarre. I just don't know what to think. But your symptoms fit the positive test, and that's hard to ignore. If we want to rule out random contamination, we'll start with the catering company and inspect your clinic. We'll send someone out." She hesitated, and he heard concern in her voice. "I'm also going to ask some people what you should do. Whether you should talk to law enforcement."

His mind swam; he could hardly finish the conversation. Now he stood up, paced his office, sat back down. It all seemed absurd—this was real life, not CSI on television.

Calm down, he told himself. There must be an explanation.

His mind dove into the past, that chess tournament in high school where one of the boys put emetics in the water cooler—drugs that made you vomit. Some contestants withdrew, too sick to continue. They found the culprit, who Alex knew from his advanced math class, a scrawny boy in a wrinkled T-shirt whose father often hung at the edge of parent groups. The father unfriendly and the boy hangdog. He actually had a good mind for chess and sometimes Alex wondered what happened to him after that, after he was banned from further games. Suddenly curious, Alex now searched for him online and found a photo, some sort of work announcement in Dallas. He looked remarkably like he did in high school. He looked a bit like Jim Barrow.

No. Don't even think it. You're supposed to be working in the attending office in a few minutes. You need to get your head straight.

Alex went and talked to Stewart Burns. He didn't know what else to do.

Burns was appalled. He promised to personally call the caterer, regardless of Maya's investigation. He insisted Alex visit the employee health center and get tested again, to make certain no chemical persisted. The exposure almost certainly happened at work, after all. Burns sent an email to all clinic staff and physicians asking about symptoms, then called hospital security and requested an enquiry.

Alex felt better with plans in place and hurried to the attending office. The morning was busy as usual. First-year resident Cameron Bowen got bogged down in alcohol counseling. A kind young man, he commiserated too much with his patient, why she couldn't slow her drinking right now, so Alex went in to show Cameron a motivational approach.

Second-year resident Janet Miles jubilantly presented a healthy baby she delivered last week, after guiding an anxious mother-to-be through a difficult pregnancy. Welcome to the rollercoaster, Alex thought.

Veronica glided in next to Alex, a worried frown, rested her palm on the back of his hand. Her wrist bangles clicked against his watch and her fingernails pressed lightly into his skin. It felt intimate.

"I heard you were sick. Are you all right now?" Her golden-brown eyes wide, startled.

"I'm good," Alex said, too brightly. He wondered exactly what Burns said in that email and wished he'd seen it. "How is your plumber doing, the man with depression?"

She glanced at the door. "I don't know. He's probably better. He hasn't come back for follow-up."

Alex nodded. "That happens, I'm afraid. But V—you can't necessarily assume he's better. You might want to call him, check up on him."

"Sure, Dr. Reddish. I mean, Alex."

"Let me know how it goes," he said, worried that she would not. He jotted himself a reminder as she watched. "I'll be here all day, all week."

"Of course."

He wanted to end this conversation more upbeat. "How's the career planning going? Have you explored anything?"

Her smile appeared, the dimple. "I've decided to take some time off first. Maybe travel."

"That sounds nice. How much time?" Most graduating residents had immense school loans to pay off and could not afford to indulge in much of a break between leaving residency and starting their practices. Some began their new jobs almost immediately.

"Three or four months, I think. Maybe six." She studied his features haphazardly.

"That's a long time." Alex doubted it was wise, but why should he judge? Maybe Veronica felt more stressed than she behaved, maybe less composed than she acted. Maybe her finances were better than most.

"I decided I deserve it. I've worked hard for so many years. Don't you ever want to escape, just run away? Throw caution to the wind?" She leaned forward, lips parted, eyes alight. "You should let go sometime, Alex. Live it up."

"Not really my nature." He laughed, standing abruptly, as if he had something to do. Her boldness made him uncomfortable. "Maybe someday. Give me a few decades."

Veronica smiled and left. Stewart Burns stuck his head in the attending office.

"Come see me as soon as you're done," he said brusquely.

Alex nodded. Maybe Stewart found something, something obvious they overlooked. Maybe this would be quickly resolved. He hustled through his work.

"Shut the door," Stewart said. "I'm not sure I handled this well. It all happened really fast."

"What?"

"I was talking with Barrow. We have these weekly meetings, to discuss his progress." Stewart ran his hand down his face, his eyes dark. "I asked him if he'd seen my email, the one about oleander, and he asked who got sick. Maybe I shouldn't have told him it was you, but I did. I wanted to see his reaction."

"And did he react?" Alex caught himself holding his breath, blew it out.

"Yeah. He seemed really upset. Then he looked me straight in the eye and said he wanted to take a month off, take a leave of absence. Like I've been suggesting all along."

Alex sat back, his heart beating strangely. "Do you honestly think it could be him?"

"Hell, I don't know. I sure hope not. Maybe he's afraid he'll be a scapegoat." Stewart squinted. "What do you think?"

Alex thought about Jim, all their cases this year, all their discussions. How Jim used to come to him readily, but now acted hurt. "I don't think so. I mean, he's having a hard time, but I just can't see it."

"I sure as hell hope you're right." Stewart's phone rang and Alex rose to leave. "We'll work on this more tomorrow."

That night the storm struck with fury, bending the trees, lightning knifing the ground, thunder cleaving the air. Rain violently pounded his roof and yard, a fearsome roar for thirty minutes. After it stopped, Alex checked outside for damage. Jacaranda branches strewed the muddy lawn, while the supple oleander hedge sparkled with water drops, intact, uninjured.

Alex did something he'd never done before, and double-checked the locks on his doors.

34

Maya breathed easier after a week went by, a normal week. No one became ill, and everyone at the residency seemed more relaxed without Jim Barrow around.

Items in Maya's yard started moving again.

A large contingent of bikers demonstrated in downtown Phoenix, snarling traffic, making claims about freedom. Freedom from helmets. KTAN interviewed one, a man on a huge rumbling motorcycle who complained of "these meddling public health busybodies."

Maya found a hummingbird feeder hung from a different tree. One day she came home to find a *For Sale by Owner* sign in her front yard; the phone number posted there went to the main office at Arizona Public Health. Maya pulled up the sign and threw it in her garage, much to Rosa's relief, who panicked when she saw it. These nuisances seemed childish, silly pranks, and Maya tried to ignore them. It would all be over soon enough.

Anyway, the polls did not look favorable for the new law to pass. Maya felt let down and tried to imagine what else she could do.

Three more patients contracted West Nile virus. Yet the public talked most about Zika, as cases climbed in Central America. Maya felt the inevitable approach, wondered how long it would take for those tiny wisps of flying infectivity to find their way across the wide stretches of Sonoran Desert. Monsoon storms aggravated the spread, leaving behind puddles, shallow breeding ponds for mosquitoes. Maya redoubled the mosquito education campaigns because, Zika or not, it would help with West Nile.

Nothing turned up in the oleander investigation. The catering company was incensed about being questioned.

"Don't get mad, okay?" Sheila stood in the door, not happy.

"Now what?" This occurred far too often, Sheila at her door, something urgent and new that Maya was unprepared to manage. She felt constantly inept and off balance.

"The newspaper is doing a big story on opioids for the Sunday edition. About opioids in Arizona, that is. They've already talked with Mel, got most of the story done. But now they want to add a little information about medical marijuana. So you need to meet with them."

"Marijuana? There's no such thing as 'a little information' about marijuana," Maya objected. "It's not my field, not at all. And that data is a swamp. No one wants to believe how little we know. Besides, that's Mel's baby."

"Yeah, well. Mel's out this week." Sheila looked apologetic, then smiled brightly. "But the reporter's not coming today. You've got until tomorrow."

Maya groaned. "There has to be someone better than me."

"Not really. And anyway, these people are nice to work with. They said they'll email their questions today, so you can be efficient."

Maya put her head on her desk. "Where's Mel, anyway? Someplace far, far away, like Hawaii?"

Sheila burst out laughing. "Can't you just picture that? Mel in swim trunks and cowboy boots? No, he's up at that ranch, helping his brother with the yearling foals. Groundwork, he said." She made a funny face. "I gave him a hard time about it, how he was getting too old to break horses, so he said I should come up, ride the fence with him. Crazy old man."

"Old man? Let me point out how he's probably younger than you. Do you even know how to ride?"

Sheila stuck her nose in the air. "I used to ride dressage, smarty pants. Back in my youth. Half-passes, pirouettes, tempi lead changes, all that fancy jazz. Mel calls it foo-foo riding."

Maya's jaw dropped. "And why don't I know this?"

"Never came up. I'd kind of forgotten about it, to tell you the truth. It's been forty years. You'll see what happens to all your bits and pieces after you've lived a longer life."

"What else don't I know about you?"

"A lot of things," Sheila replied mysteriously and left.

Maya brought up the state guidelines on medical marijuana and began searching the scanty evidence. Maybe she could find new data.

The best studies showed that marijuana helped with certain seizures and with the muscle spasms of multiple sclerosis. Sometimes it reduced nausea caused by chemotherapy. Maybe useful for nerve pain, but long-term outcomes were unclear. The benefits for other conditions remained questionable; standard treatments might be better. The research simply hadn't been done. Being federally illegal, yet legal in many states, the ability to perform studies bogged down.

People did not want to hear this. They craved a simple fix for difficult problems.

Was marijuana better than opioid addiction? Most likely, for people didn't suddenly die from marijuana. While marijuana might trigger anxiety, memory loss, and many trips to the emergency room, people tended to relax and stay home. If they drove, car accidents increased. But that data was nothing compared to what happened with opioids and alcohol. Of course, with increased marijuana use, statistics could change. Even at legal weed shops, dosages were often vague and impossible to measure. Marijuana varieties and doses were art more than science, often myth more than reality. The names were entertaining, if nothing else. Pineapple Express and Super Lemon Haze. Sour Diesel and Blue Dream.

By the end of the day, Maya had gathered a reasonable sheet of marijuana facts and fictions and the very wide gray zone in between. She closed up and went home, for Whit was coming over for supper.

Manchado had learned the rhythms of Maya's life. He waited for her or Rafael now at mealtimes, not eager and demanding like some horses, but quietly anticipating. He grew used to her moving about the large corral as she mucked, talking and singing to accustom him to her voice. She could approach him now if she put aside the rake. In the last few days, he let her lightly rub his neck. He flinched the first time, then slowly accepted her touch.

Maya often found Rafael sitting on the rail, heels hooked, watching the horse. Sometimes Manchado stood off, sometimes near. If Rafael spoke to him, the horse moved closer, listening. Rafael never offered treats, never extended his hand.

"How's he doing?" Maya asked Rafael one evening. A hot wind tugged against them, the sky agitated with curling clouds. Manchado stood ten feet away, his mane and tail floating up in the breeze. The bite marks on his hide had faded, nearly gone. "Are you getting to know him?"

Rafael flicked a glance at Maya, then went back to observing the horse.

"He's afraid to have a friend," he said.

When Maya looked out the window later, Rafael had moved further down the rail and the horse had moved, too, although he still kept apart. Rafael's lips moved.

When Whit came over, he showed no interest in the horse.

"Seems like a lot of work," he commented.

Maya couldn't decide at first if that bothered her. Then she decided it did, while wishing it did not. The logic felt perverse, and she could not gauge if there was a right or wrong answer.

She and Whit chatted in the kitchen, cleaning up after dinner, when Alex called.

"Are you busy?" he asked cautiously.

"No. What's up, Alex?" Maya clamped the phone against her ear as she put dishes away.

"I thought you'd be interested in this about Jim Barrow. He's been out on leave for about ten days now, you know. Well, he called Burns to say he's feeling better, and he went and repeated his urine drug screen. And guess what?"

"Um, it's positive for marijuana?" Suddenly contrite, Maya rushed on. "Sorry. That's not funny. It's just that I spent hours today on marijuana. No wait, that sounds wrong—for the record, I am *not* on marijuana. I meant I spent the time reviewing marijuana data."

Alex laughed. "No. Jim's test is completely negative. Nothing."

They tried to figure out what it meant. Worried by recent events, maybe Jim was scared straight. Then Alex switched to the real reason for his call and arranged to pick her up in two days, bright and early, for the trip to Tucson.

Whit spoke up briskly as Maya disconnected.

"Why does he call you all the time?" he grumbled, putting his arm around her.

Maya felt surprised. "He doesn't. Just every now and then, about work at the residency."

"Maybe it just seems like it, because you talk about him so much." His arm tighter.

"No, I don't," Maya objected, pulling away. "What are you saying?"

He softened, drew her back. "Nothing, forget it. I'm being silly. Let's go to bed."

Journal

Datura just started blooming in the desert. I discovered long vines of it down deep in a wash and I filled my backpack. If you walk around out there, explore a little, you'll find it. Most people go right past it, have no idea. It's astounding how almost no one knows about datura, what it can do. How powerful it is.

The Natives knew, and they understood how to use it. They knew how to be careful, because it's a fine line between outcomes and demise.

Nowadays people don't even go outside, don't know a daisy from a rose. They just shove their faces in their phones and read about politics, as if any of that matters.

Clowns.

35

A strange July dawn, the air thick. Clouds elbowed against one another, threatening to claim the sky. Usually monsoon storms gathered late in the afternoon, so the day seemed off. Alex hoped it wasn't an omen. He barely allowed himself to think how much he looked forward to this day.

Alex would never admit his small deception, for Burns did not actually ask him to attend this conference. Instead, Alex suggested it, after learning Maya would be there. Well, he thought, someone from the residency needed the latest updates on cocci. It might as well be him.

When he arrived at Maya's, he noticed movement out back, curls of dust where a horse roamed. Striking color, black and white. The last he'd heard from Maya about horses was when the old mare died.

"What's with the handsome horse?" Alex asked as Maya came out. Carrying a large messenger bag, she wore a long slender black skirt and silky gray top, a style both relaxed and classy. The gray fabric shimmered, a soft sheen that made him want to touch it, a disquieting impulse.

"My difficult new guest," Maya laughed. "He's staying here to get used to people in a positive way—he may have been abused when he was a horse child."

Alex walked to the fence as Maya stowed her bag. He reached out toward the horse, who eyed him suspiciously and backed away. Something compelling about this animal, he thought. The large dark eyes held a kind of despair.

"He's touchy with strangers," she warned, appearing beside him. Maya smelled fresh, like mint soap, and her dark hair gleamed with copper. She tugged Alex's arm. "We have to get going before my makeup melts in this heat."

Alex imagined saying something clever about how she didn't need makeup, but it felt trite. He tried to create a funny quip, then realized he had taken too long and let it go.

As they took off, Maya explained about the horse, about Mel. She spun a good story, funny details about cranky Mel and her wild drive alone one night to get Mel's horses to water. Alex laughed and prodded her on. Eventually they cleared Phoenix and the road to Tucson unfurled before them, flat and uninspired, spooling across miles of crusted sand. He felt unshackled, leaving the city clutter behind and flying over the bleak terrain with spiny plants and burning rock.

The sky flowed in motion, transforming. The clouds swelled and collided, fusing and blotting out the sun, the air going dim.

"This is so odd." Maya craned her neck and peered up. "An early morning storm? That never happens this time of year."

"Look." Alex pointed south. "Is that smoke? Could that be a brush fire?"

A long smudge of rusty haze blurred the horizon. They both stared, uneasy, as the distant brown vapor ascended and spread.

"Crap," Alex exclaimed, his eyes widening. "I think that's dust."

"At seven in the morning? No way." Maya stared again, then turned back and poked his arm. "Hey, quit looking at the sky. Watch the road."

"Good lord, that's getting huge. And it's coming right at us. Fast." Despite Maya's reproach, Alex could hardly keep his eyes off the blooming mass. A burgeoning *haboob*, Arabic for a vast dust cloud. Triggered by winds rising before a storm, a large haboob could develop quickly and rise a mile into the sky, spread dozens of miles wide, and travel over fifty miles an hour. He instinctively sped up, as if he might outrun it, realizing the foolishness of his impulse even as he pressed forward. Bulky clumps of dirt-colored powder stirred within the approaching bank, revolving shades of brown and buff as distant hills disappeared. Then it swallowed the nearby landscape, and the bronze fog enveloped them.

Alex slowed and flipped on his headlights, barely able to see fifty feet. The danger of a highway dust storm was gauging distance—the taillights ahead might be two hundred feet away, or maybe much closer. Someone barreling up behind you might be driving too fast to stop in time, with deadly results. Alex needed to get off the highway, pull over and wait it out.

A sign appeared in the murk—an exit only a few miles away. They crept along, tense, braced for an impact they would hardly see coming, until reaching the ramp. Alex edged onto it and emerged on an old two-lane road with wide gravel shoulders, and he parked as far off as he could.

"Whew." Alex leaned back to relax. He switched off the car and the headlights, took his foot from the brake. Wind buffeted the car, rocking it, swirling dust around them. The floury grit drifted onto the windshield, piled up on the wipers, no signs of letting up. He could taste it inside the car, sifting through tiny spaces.

"Kind of ironic." He smiled, looking over at her. "We're on our way to a cocci conference, and now here we are, in a cloud probably full of cocci spores."

Maya sat silent, chewing her lip, her face stony. Something was wrong. She turned and took a long look over her shoulder to see behind them, then ducked her chin. Her hair swung forward and hid her face.

"Maya?" He wanted to touch her hair, pull it gently back, but checked himself.

"I'm fine," she said quickly, too loudly.

"Really?"

She started to say something, then didn't.

"Maya. We're safe here. We're well off the road." He felt at sea. She had just been great, upbeat and talkative.

Her eyes bounced off his and returned to the window. "Just give me a few seconds. Please. Talk about something, anything. Tell me about your chess."

"Okay…"

Alex started slowly. He had trouble concentrating, keeping an eye on her. He rambled, telling how he discovered his talent for chess when he was five years old. How as a boy he loved the game, delighted in the strategy, the wily pieces and how they navigated the board. He practically felt like those pieces were alive, as if they were people he knew, traveling about. Then he realized that might sound unbalanced and stopped.

Maya gave a tiny smile, nodded. "Keep going. It helps."

Her shoulders relaxed a fraction, and she no longer stared out the glass, so he shifted and went on.

He hadn't meant to, but somehow he talked about his mother, how she pushed him, her devotion to his chess. The best coaches, the toughest tournaments. How proudly she claimed center stage after his wins when he was small, shoving him to shake hands with everyone, beaming too much. Her incessant prattle about him becoming a grandmaster. By his teenage years, embarrassed by her, he forbid her to talk at his matches. He said she distracted him, worrying what she would say or do. That she had to remain silent, or simply not come. And he grew to hate himself for that, her crestfallen look—so he walked it back, thinking she had learned, and before long she started again. And then he grew to hate chess itself because it consumed his life and he barely knew how to talk to real people.

So he quit.

He could hardly believe he told Maya all that. He never talked about it.

"What did your mother say? When you quit?" Maya asked. Absorbed, she seemed to have forgotten the storm, her gray eyes sharp, searching his. The sky lightened and the hills began to reappear, like ghosts.

Alex removed his glasses and rubbed his eyes, gritty and irritated. He wanted to stop talking about it and kept it brief.

"She got really depressed. And angry. Not a good combination."

"But then she felt better when you decided to go into medicine, right? Then she felt proud again, right?" Maya leaned toward him, eager.

Alex laughed. "Sort of. Briefly. She wanted me to be something big, someone fancy, a neurologist or plastic surgeon. Her idea of fancy. When I chose family medicine, she gave up on me. She still thinks I ruined her dreams." He rubbed at his eyes again. "We're not very close anymore. I mean, we never were."

Maya sat back. "That's too bad, Alex. I disappointed my parents, too. In a different way."

"Maya." Questions crowded his head. He felt strangely unfettered now, oddly bold. "I want to hear that story, for sure. But what just happened? One minute you were fine, and then you were—I don't know. Gone. Was it me? Did I say something stupid? I'm so sorry. I know I can be clumsy. Did I—"

He could not describe her look.

"No, of course not. It's not you." She looked away, looked back. "It's a long boring story. You don't want to know."

He could not imagine anything he wanted more. "You're wrong. I really do."

36

Maya studied his earnest face. This seemed the wrong time for her saga.

They sat only a few hundred yards from that very spot, her accident with the motorcycle. Usually when she drove to Tucson she saw it coming, knew the bend in the road past Casa Grande, just before the off-ramp. She learned to divert her memory and look away, glance across the median at a stunted saguaro that appeared exactly the same year after year, never growing larger, never changing. A desert survivor—the same scarred upward limbs, a bellwether of poise. By the time her eyes skipped back to the highway, the place was behind her.

Today caught her unprepared, no big deal. She recovered quickly.

"Maybe later," she said, checking her watch. Sunlight filtered weakly through the dust, still suspended. "Maybe on the way home. We're going to be late."

"No, now," he insisted. Then he seemed abashed by his boldness. "Please."

Alex was so considerate. Quick-witted, insightful. She always looked forward to working with him, sometimes the highlight of her week. And just now, when she momentarily faltered, he somehow understood. He got it, or at least he got it enough to roll with it. With hardly a hesitation, without flinching, he shared a most vulnerable past. Incredible, really, that he would disclose so much.

It shook her from her own battered history into his. At some level, she owed him an explanation.

"All right." Her voice stern. "But only on one condition. You can't act all sorry for me. You can't say *how awful for you*, or any sap like that. And don't you dare say that I'm brave, or strong, or any sentimental crap. And I hate the word *resilient*. Okay?"

He nodded solemnly, his eyes huge.

"And you only get the condensed version because we have to get going," she continued curtly.

He nodded again, mute. Probably afraid to say anything, Maya thought. Well, he wanted the truth and it was not a story she liked to tell. She could barely remember the last time she recounted it. Probably to Whit, long over a year ago.

Maya spoke quickly and didn't mince words. The slamming collision. The terrible ripping agony, the paramedics bent over her. The dead man sprawled bloody in the road. The surgeries and transfusions and a long painful year of rehabilitation. The doubts that still haunted her, that if maybe she had reacted more quickly the man might have lived.

Her inability afterward to work in remote places, where a similar accident meant death.

Maya took a deep breath. "So. When you keep asking me what's wrong with my leg, that's what. My right hip is wrecked—it's all scar tissue and traumatic arthritis. One of these days, I'll need a joint replacement."

Alex stared at her. "Jesus, Maya."

"You promised." She frowned. "No pity."

His mouth switched back and forth, as if deciding where to go. Then he pushed his glasses up his nose and his eyes lit.

"Can I see your X-rays?" he asked.

Maya stared back. No one ever said such a thing. No one would dream of asking such a thing. She felt something crack inside her, and she suddenly laughed.

"My *X-rays*?"

"Or your CT, or MRI, whatever you have," he replied. "I mean, I assume you have some films. Probably a lot of them."

"Yes, I do," she said slowly, trying to read her own mood. But it was actually funny and astute, she had to admit, in a startling sort of way.

"Well?" He waited.

"What?"

Alex peered over his glasses, hair falling in his eyes. "Can I see them?"

"Of course you can, you weirdo." Maya buckled her seatbelt. "Just hurry up and start driving before we miss half the conference."

37

The conference began an hour late because the dust storm delayed so many attendees. Which made Maya and Alex right on time. The first lecture covered basic background material about coccidioidomycosis, which Maya knew well anyway. Although she listened, she kept processing what happened with Alex, thoughts zipping around her brain like hummingbirds.

Pay attention, she told herself.

Coccidioides immitis lurked in southwestern desert dirt, a tiny patient fungus remarkably adept at invading lungs. Any activity that disturbed the soil—digging, construction, a dust storm—liberated the organism. Called valley fever or "cocci" for short, the spores wandered the air wherever dust floated, waiting to be inhaled. An unlucky human who breathed it in could develop cough, fever, and exhaustion. While many patients endured only mild symptoms and recovered on their own, others deteriorated into pneumonia and occasionally meningitis. The fungus sometimes found its way into bones and other organs. Occasionally, the infection turned fatal.

Annually, thousands of humans in the Southwest contracted cocci. Around five hundred died, especially people with weak immune systems—those with HIV and AIDS, people on chemotherapy, geriatric patients. People with transplanted organs. As the mild desert climate drew more inhabitants, more contracted cocci. At least ten percent of all pneumonias in Phoenix and Tucson were caused by the fungus. Some experts said more.

Maya studied her syllabus, but her subconscious slipped back to the dusty car with Alex. She thought of Whit's accusation, that she talked with Alex so frequently. Well, wasn't that natural? Whit talked with his associates all the time, never a problem. Something else they needed to discuss.

Alex was drawn to the horse. Went immediately to the fence and reached out, even though he admitted he knew nothing about horses. In that one moment Alex gave more attention to Manchado than Whit ever had, not only ignoring the horse but seemingly annoyed at his existence.

And that story about chess, his mother. It must be the tip of an iceberg, a huge cold chunk of his past. Still a raw slab of ice that might never melt. No wonder he deflected questions about it.

Pay attention. A new speaker lectured about cocci outbreaks, unexpected clusters. Over two hundred cases and three cocci deaths followed a California earthquake that triggered landslides, which generated dust clouds. People who spent more time in the dust were most likely to become ill. An older man in England got diagnosed with cocci after returning from a model-airplane convention in a dry southwestern town. A group of Navy SEALS, training for the Middle East in the desert, contracted acute valley fever; many suffered severe symptoms. Construction crews, farmworkers, anthropologists digging for artifacts—all at risk. The resident doctors at the clinic would love these stories.

That morning she left her own cocci story untold, warning Alex she wouldn't tell him everything. But two weeks after her accident she turned feverish, grew weaker. At first her doctors suspected a surgical infection, ran more scans and labs. Then the cough began and her chest X-ray revealed a thick cloud in her lung. Apparently when her car plowed off the highway at seventy-five miles an hour, it dislodged great gouts of dirt, laden with cocci spores. Maya took antifungal medication for months, depleted and weak, limp as a rag. Her lung films would forever show a white knot of scar tissue.

Sometimes she hated her own story.

It was difficult to listen for hours without her mind drifting…sitting at long tables in a chilly hotel ballroom stiffened her hip and dulled her mind. The topic switched to treatment, something she needed to hear, and she sipped her cold coffee to stay alert. Mild cocci cases did not require medication, just the serious ones, so it was important to know the guidelines for starting drug therapy.

She noticed Alex's arm.

He sat on her left, plenty of room, but he just placed his right arm oddly close to her. It didn't even look comfortable. He seemed absorbed in the speaker, intently studying the graphs, yet his arm lay there, practically touching.

Maya felt silly, but she edged her arm over, two or three tiny milli-meters, and barely contacted his. A moment passed, then he pressed back. Or maybe she imagined it. That miniscule push somehow felt private, and she stole a quick glance at him. He looked straight ahead, then the corner of his mouth deepened.

Maya leaned back in her chair and moved her arm away.

You are really going nutty, she told herself.

38

As they drove back toward Phoenix, Alex shifted restlessly, a nervous energy from sitting all day. He did not know how far to tempt fate. The storms had vanished. The delayed conference ended late, and now a quarter moon rode the twilight before them, a curved ivory tusk.

"That was good," Alex said. "I learned a lot. You probably knew most of it already."

Maya shook her head. "Not at all. The treatment guidelines have been changed. And that new test looks promising."

Alex felt more daring, for they had shared much. Maya responded to his experiment, and subtly touched his arm. And not once had she mentioned Thicket.

"So…" she was saying, a little impish. "Your chess pieces were like real people?"

Alex taunted her back. "Hey. Think about it. Everyone you know is probably like one. I mean, look at you."

"No. I can't possibly remind you of any one chess piece." She pretended to be offended. "I'm far too complicated."

"Ha. You are totally wrong. You're a knight."

"What, because I like horses?" Maya scoffed. "That's pretty simplistic."

"Not because you like horses—give me a break. You're a knight because it's hard to know which way you'll move next. You're skittish and might go any direction. You're creative and unpredictable."

Maya stared at him. "Then what are you?"

"Nope, that's not how this works. You have to say what you think I am."

She folded her arms, checked him up and down. "You're a bishop."

Alex laughed. "I think I know why, but go ahead and tell me."

"Because you move obliquely. You act oblique. You *are* oblique." She looked thoughtful. "And by that I mean you're careful, guarded. You come out of leftfield, at an angle, but you're almost always correct. If you ever let on what you're really thinking."

Alex nodded.

They assigned other people. Stewart Burns was a rook, tackling everything straight and true—you knew what to expect. No nonsense, no drama. Agatha Mercer, the older part-time physician with a penchant for baking, was also a rook, honest and transparent. Alex claimed Scott Sherman to be a bishop like him, but that Scott was the opposing color and worked against him, devious. Jim Barrow felt like a sad pawn. Then Alex made a mistake and asked Maya who her king might be. She turned silent and he wanted to kick himself, since it was obviously that bastard Whit. Or maybe he wasn't a bastard…maybe Alex was simply jealous. Either way, he quickly changed direction.

"Don't worry about the king—kings aren't important until they are." He winged it now, making that up, but didn't care. "Who do you think is the queen?"

"Who do *you* think is the queen?" she fired back, grinning again.

They both spoke at once. "Veronica!"

"You mean V, of course," Alex corrected.

Maya looked sideways at him. "You know what that V really means, don't you," she said, making the peace sign. Her voice lowered dramatically. "Lady parts."

Alex felt himself blush. "Maya!"

"You know it's true." She vigorously shook out her hand, as if her fingers had done that unbidden. "It's all part of her flirting."

Alex reluctantly agreed. And thought to himself that Maya's capacity to astonish him seemed endless. Absolutely a knight. He glanced over, suddenly curious about her observations.

"What do you think she wants?" he asked.

"From you? Do you have to ask?" Maya clucked. "Alex. You may be sort of a quiet guy, but you're not that innocent."

"I don't think that's it. It's more complicated. Like she's playing some kind of game, testing me. Seeing how far she can go. Trying to make me react. I don't think she's actually interested in me."

"Hm. I guess some women do that, don't they?" Maya frowned. "They like the power."

Alex thought of Scott Sherman. "Men, too."

They talked about everything. About the dead-end oleander investigation, how Alex began to relax as time went by. About Jim's upcoming return to work in a few weeks, how that might go. About parents and expectations. About Maya's work on the helmet law, a likely disappointing loss. Alex now understood her passion about helmets, and he thought of her accident and the biker's death with a surge of compassion. But of course he said nothing. He wasn't stupid. At least, not that stupid.

His car ate up the miles, sailing through the hot night as the moon crept toward the horizon, and all too soon Alex pulled into Maya's driveway. He wished he'd driven slower, taken detours, gotten lost. They passed dozens of places where he could have suggested an evening snack or dessert—why hadn't he thought of that? Never mind that they ate supper before leaving Tucson. Not the point.

Maya climbed out and her step faltered, that little catch. He picked up her messenger bag, heavy with syllabus and laptop, as she dug for her keys.

"Does that make your hip worse," he asked, "when you sit for so long?"

"Usually." She finally fished up the keys from her bag, then made a face. "You learn to live with it."

Her front porchlight shone dimly, spattered with bugs, and a large moth circled, erratic. The tusk of moon touched the dark hills, about to withdraw. Alex felt tenderness spill over him, both hopeful and hopeless at once.

"This was great," he said slowly. "Thanks."

"No, thank you. For driving." Maya paused. "For putting up with me. And for sharing your story. That meant a lot to me."

"Maya." His arm circled her, drew her to him. She fit perfectly, her head under his chin. He expected her to sidestep, to flee, but she stood there tucked against him. He took the chance.

"Can I kiss you?" he asked quietly.

A long silence. The moth batted the light. He felt her exhale.

"Alex. I—I can't. It's not right. I'm still seeing—"

"I'm not asking you to kiss me. I asked if I could kiss you. Big difference."

She huffed, a tiny breath. He hoped it meant she was amused. She looked up at him, a crinkled smile. Then her hand rose and one finger tapped her cheek, showing him where.

"As friends," she said.

"Absolutely." He bent and pressed his lips on her skin where she'd pointed. She still smelled like mint.

He planned nothing more, but his hand followed its own agenda and moved to rest on her hip. Laterally, where the scar must be. Years ago,

Alex worked moonlighting shifts with an orthopedic surgeon, assisting in the operating room. He knew the anatomy of hips—from skin to muscle to bone—had been inside the joints. Now his fingers lightly touched there, as if seeking the mark through the thin fabric of her skirt.

Maya motionless.

"Does that hurt if you touch it?" His lips still against her cheek.

"Not really," she said, very soft. "It just aches. A little numb."

Alex stepped back. He felt torn into small pieces, afraid he'd gone too far, had been too strange.

"I care about you, Maya. That's all." Then he leaned to her ear and whispered loudly. "I would say more, but your horse is watching me."

They turned to look. Only a small corner of the pen could be seen from where they stood. In that corner, Manchado stared at the humans.

Maya laughed, Alex laughed. She took her things from him, then stretched up on her toes and quickly kissed his cheek.

"Alex," she said. Then she went inside.

39

When Stewart Burns called Maya on Tuesday night, she didn't recognize his phone and did not answer right away. Plagued by too many marketing calls lately, she rarely bothered with unknown numbers.

She and Whit prepared to watch a movie. They were celebrating the cooler weather, highs of "only" one hundred five degrees, after a brutal three-day spell of one hundred eighteen. The air scorched lungs and cracked skin. Trees split and birds clung to broken branches with their beaks open, panting, eyes glazed. The sky stood dazed, a feeble ruined blue.

People posted videos of frying eggs on sidewalks, on car hoods, on skillets set out in the sun. The health department issued stern warnings to stay inside, stay cool, and be smart. Then more warnings, about not eating those half-cooked eggs and risking salmonella.

Wanting to be inventive, Maya brought Whit an indoor picnic that night, chicken salad and corn-on-the-cob. Everything between them flowed smoothly these days. That moment with Alex had been a fluke, misplaced feelings of companionship. A chaste kiss, each way. His hand on her hip felt odd, but she'd piqued his curiosity and he perceived her pain. She cherished her friendship with Alex and hoped he would find a good partner sooner or later.

Whit loved her picnic, and he supplied wine and dessert. Maya often remarked how his modern house lacked hominess, with its long spare lines and gray tones, so she spread a red checkered tablecloth on the floor under a ceiling fan and pretended it was November with a balmy breeze. Whit smiled and alluded to the future again, how he wanted to take care of her.

Alex had said something different: *I care about you.* She caught herself thinking about knights and bishops; she harbored no doubts about Whit being the king. What did Alex say, that the king didn't matter until he did? Whatever that meant. Then she wondered why Alex was in her head.

"What are you thinking about?" Whit asked.

"Games," she answered without thinking.

"What kinds of games?" He wiggled his eyebrows, suggestive. He took her bare foot, stroked it with his thumb. "We don't have to watch the movie."

"No, let's watch it first. We've got time for everything." She looked forward to the movie, wanted that escape. Then she saw her phone flashing and realized she had a message—uncommon for a marketing call. "Maybe I should check this."

Stewart Burns's voice sounded upset. He wanted to know if she could change her schedule, if she could possibly come staff the clinic tomorrow, on Wednesday, instead of her usual Thursday. Maya called him back immediately. Whit withdrew his hand and rolled his eyes, helped himself to more chicken salad while she talked.

She listened to Burns with dismay. There had been an accident: Alex crashed on his bike riding home that evening. Yes, he would be all right, pretty banged up, but no fractures. They scanned his head in the ER, no damage there, and they sent him home. Of course he'd worn his helmet. While he didn't know the details of the wreck, Burns insisted that Alex take tomorrow off to see his physician, which left them short in clinic supervisors. At the height of summer, many faculty members were on vacation. Everyone left Phoenix when they had the chance.

Maya agreed to the switch, fairly certain she had no immediate demands tomorrow, knowing she could count on Sheila to fix any conflicts. Once again, she thanked her stars for Sheila.

Whit waited impatiently.

"Sorry," she told Whit, wincing. "But Alex is hurt—his bike crashed on his way home from work. They asked me to cover for him tomorrow."

"And that couldn't wait until morning?"

Maya shook her head, puzzled. "Well, no. Because if I couldn't do it, they would need to find someone else."

"Whatever. I'm sure they would figure it out." He seemed peevish for no real reason.

"Whit. I really think I should call Alex and make sure he's all right. He lives alone." She looked closely at him, trying to sift his attitude.

"Seriously?"

"Yes, seriously. Maybe we should drop by, check on him. Would you be up for that?" She took one glance at his expression and rushed on. "He's a nice man, a good man. You'd like him."

"You're kidding, right?"

"Just let me call him really quick. It'll only take a second." She grabbed her phone and tapped his number, Whit staring at her. Her pulse quickened and she looked at the floor. "Alex, are you all right? I just heard from Stewart about your accident."

Maya knew he would minimize his injuries. He never drew attention to himself.

"I'm fine," he said slowly. "Everything just hurts. Well, almost everything. I think my toes feel normal."

A short laugh escaped her, but she quickly sobered. "Good god, Alex. What happened?"

"It was so strange. My handlebars cracked and broke…they just collapsed and I pitched to the pavement. And I was going pretty fast. I mean, that's a new bike, with carbon fiber handlebars. Must be some kind of design flaw, some factory defect. Luckily there wasn't a car in the lane next to me."

Maya glanced at Whit, his face dark. She held up a finger, signaling him to wait, and said to Alex, "Do you need help tonight? Should you be home alone?"

Whit scowled and leaned far forward, his mouth inches from her phone.

"Hurry up, Maya. I'm waiting for you," Whit said loudly.

Silence from Alex. Then quietly, "I'm good."

Alex hung up.

Maya looked sharply at Whit, taken aback. She set down her phone and watched him. Not certain what she should say, not sure what she was feeling. Some kind of dread building inside her. She remembered the conflict over Mel, those accusations Whit made, and her stomach slanted.

"Don't be so nice," Whit finally said. His jaw moved sideways.

"That was pretty rude. Saying that so he could hear it." She spoke carefully, slowly. "He's a friend. Normally you try to help your friends."

Whit stood abruptly, gathered up dishes. Clattered them, noisy. "I'm sick of hearing about your friends. Especially all your fucking male friends. What the hell, Maya. How come I never come first? Now help me clean up."

Maya felt herself turn to glass.

She became like thin crystal, as if the merest touch or word would fracture her.

Or maybe she had already shattered, sat there in shards. Maybe that was why she felt no pain, her nerves gone numb.

"Maya!" he called from the kitchen. Silverware clashed into the sink.

She stood, pocketed her phone. Though barefoot, her flip-flops must be in the kitchen and she wouldn't go there, not now. Maya picked up her bag and turned her back and walked out the front door, across the burning gravel to her car, tiny hot pebbles sticking to her feet. The pain felt good. She heard him exclaim something, but couldn't make out the words.

She was backing the car when he surged through the front door, holding her flip-flops. Maya looked quickly around at him, his contorted face, and backed faster into the street, shifted into drive. One flip-flop struck her windshield, one bounced off the hood. Then she flew away down the street.

She made herself slow down. Her mind blank, anesthetized. She drove aimlessly through the neighborhood, got lost in the winding lanes. The evening nearly dark now, she wandered through the luxury development, no streetlights, expensive homes set far back from the road. Porchlights twinkled through manicured desert yards. She didn't worry about him coming after her—he was too proud for that.

Eventually she focused and worked her way back to the main road, headed toward Alex's place. But she shouldn't just show up without warning. She pulled into a supermarket parking lot and called him.

"Maya?" Alex sounded cautious.

"I want to come check on you," she said firmly. "I'm so worried about you."

"No, please. It's not necessary."

"But I want to." She felt petulant. He shouldn't deny her this after what she'd just done. Of course, he had no idea.

"Really, Maya. I'm perfectly fine. Just bruises and scrapes, all superficial. Besides." A long pause, cautious. "Aren't you with Whit?"

"Not anymore."

Another long silence. "It's okay, Maya. I appreciate the offer, but I don't need anything."

"All right then, if you're sure," she said, subdued. She could hardly guess how he must feel after Whit pulled that stunt. How Whit demeaned Alex. Mortified her. "But please let me know if you need anything, okay?"

"Of course. Thanks, Maya." He still sounded wary. As he should.

When Maya reached home, she didn't go inside right away, couldn't face four walls.

She walked barefoot through the stones and dirt to where Manchado waited. She leaned against the poles, rubbing one foot against the other, feeling the dust caked between her toes. She chided herself—she knew better. If a scorpion nailed her, she deserved it.

She almost craved it.

A bright half-moon listed in the dull sky, casting shadows across the corral. Half-empty moon or half-full? Did it matter? Maya shut her eyes and the foul scene replayed in her head, felt even worse. When she opened her eyes Manchado stood before her. He put his black nostril against her face and she touched the sensitive velvet arc, breathed into him. She waited, and he inhaled her air. His eye gleamed, and he rested his head on her shoulder.

They stood that way a long time. The stars circled, going nowhere, and the half-hollow half-gorged moon slunk through the sky like a fraud.

40

Alex looked in the mirror the next morning. What he saw wasn't good.

Raw scrapes crossed his chin and cheek, starting to crust but still oozing if he moved his mouth. His jaw stiffened overnight and he didn't dare yawn. He would need to grow a beard for a while because shaving appeared impossible. One eyelid swollen, purple. A short laceration on his right cheek sprouted three nylon stitches.

That was just his face. When the handlebars collapsed, he rolled and then skidded across the pavement. Bruises bloomed on his back and limbs. One knee abraded, puffy. Thank heaven he wrecked beneath an overpass, in the shade, because if he'd been in the sun the blazing road would have burned him as well. Every movement hurt. He appreciated Stewart for insisting he stay home, even though Alex had protested initially. No one wanted to look at him today.

Plenty of work I can do at home, he thought. And he would take his bike to the shop. See what they thought, check for other damage. He'd bought that bike less than six months ago, so maybe a guarantee would cover the handlebars. Fortunately, one of the ER nurses he knew drove her pickup truck to work yesterday and was ending her shift, so she took Alex and his bike home.

You are one sorry creature, he told himself. He looked frightening… he should avoid small children. His face hurt, his head ached, and his twisted back made it difficult to stand up straight. He limped on the bad knee.

You'll be fine, he argued with himself. Quit feeling sorry for yourself. None of this is serious. Your injuries will heal.

Which made him think of Maya, and her wounds that would never truly heal. She still had pain years later, still needed more surgery. She still harbored guilt, whether warranted or not. Still fought a morass of emotions that she channeled into action, like the helmet law.

His thoughts went subterranean. Maybe that's why she stayed with Whit. Lack of confidence, fear of her future.

No, that didn't feel right. She seemed quite confident when they taught together. And the way she eschewed pity, did not act fearful at all, except for that one brief spell during the dust storm. As faculty, the residents sought her. She tolerated public criticism, engaged well in debate, put up with those bikers. She managed difficult interviews like the one on KTAN and came out on top.

What really defines us, he speculated—how we act most of the time, or how we act at our worst moments? He thought of his own past and decided not to go there.

Now he questioned what she meant last night, that she wasn't with Whit. *Not anymore*, she said. Did she mean just at that moment, or for the rest of the evening? Surely she didn't mean forever. He'd let himself feel hopeful more than once and look what happened. Put down by that bastard over the phone, of all things. The humiliation made his skin crawl.

Maybe Maya was simply too damaged, too neurotic. Maybe his attraction to her threw off his judgment. His thoughts ran back and forth. She called him last night, on her own, worried. Then called him back again, after that insult from Whit. She seemed disturbed when Alex didn't want her help. Perhaps he should have let her come by.

No. She took care of him once, when he was sick and had no option. If she did it again, he would feel like her needy child. A convoluted dynamic, unhealthy. He felt trapped in the worst chess game ever, unable to read or anticipate her moves, her moods. Maybe he should concede the game and walk away.

It's not a chess game, you miserable chump, he countered. He felt like Sméagol, arguing with Gollum. Quit thinking so much. Quit analyzing. You're running in circles and going nowhere. He made a milkshake for lunch, gingerly sipped it down, and tried not to move his jaw. Then he shoved the bike in his car and drove to the shop.

Randy, Alex's favorite bicycle mechanic, looked like an old burnt-out hippie in filthy khaki shorts. Two long gray braids hung to his waist, and a black bandana circled his forehead above bright aqua eyes. His skin ruined from too much sun, darkly wrinkled and splotched, a shriveled peace sign tattooed on one skinny bicep and a faded dove on the other. Mellow to a fault, Randy never expressed alarm or surprise; Alex suspected he worked stoned half the time.

"Dude." Randy's eyebrows climbed up under the bandana as Alex limped in. For Randy, that amounted to absolute shock.

While Randy examined the bike, Alex waited on a grubby sofa. He laid back his head, knowing that Randy—meticulous and slow—never hurried his assessments. He must have dozed off, for when he opened his eyes Randy leaned on the counter watching him, a wrench in one stained hand and the broken pieces in the other.

Randy shook his head, doleful. "Not good, man."

"Some kind of defect?" Alex asked. "Is there a warranty?"

"There's no warranty for sabotage." Randy dropped down next to Alex. He pointed a blackened fingernail at faint marks on the carbon fiber tubing, alongside the break. "This here's been tampered with. By some kind of rasp. Maybe a little saw. See those scratches, those grooves?"

"What?" Alex bolted upright. His heart pulsed strangely.

"Someone messed with this, dude. Made it weak, so it would break. You'd be surprised how fragile carbon fiber can be sometimes."

Alex speechless. Horrified. Randy patted him on the shoulder, then went to the back of the shop and rattled around, searching for something. He returned and held out an offering, a small joint of weed.

"Take this—you sorta look like you could use it," Randy said kindly. He discreetly asked no questions. "Give me about a week to get your bike ready."

Alex drove home in a stupor.

First he called Stewart Burns. Then he called the police. Much later, Alex realized he had absently slipped the joint into his pocket, but fortunately that was after the detective had left.

41

Maya tried to keep her mind off Whit while at work, no easy task. He felt like a red-hot poker jabbing her brain. Alex's accident scared her to death, and now he kept distant because of Whit, which made it worse. Feeling sad and alone, Maya questioned every move she made.

Although she decided not to involve Bluff Barrington from KTAN in her helmet campaign, Bluff got wind of it himself. He started grilling Maya via emails, and when she dragged her feet on a live interview, he found the data on his own. The information was public knowledge, after all, and not difficult to capture for a determined person with a computer. The latest statistics estimated that a thousand lives might be saved every year if bikers wore helmets. Some years more, some years less. He wore Maya down and she finally responded to his persistent calls.

"A thousand lives!" Bluff screeched in her ear.

"I'm aware of that," she said calmly. "That's why I want this law."

Scattered stories ran on television and radio, in major newspapers and minor newsletters. She hesitated now with Bluff because the publicity fire seemed fueled enough, and the fallout wearied her. The incidents at home, the midnight bikers blasting her street, the threats online. She wanted it over, and she hardly wished to further antagonize her opponents with Bluff's high-strung drama.

"I need to make this good, really engaging," he said. "Tell me something that everyone worries about but shouldn't. You know, like we did with Zika and West Nile."

Maya couldn't deny that many neighborhoods actually reported better mosquito control since Bluff began his tales of mosquito terror.

"How about scorpions?" she asked.

"Ew. I hate scorpions. They can kill you, right? How many people in Arizona die from scorpions every year?" He gagged. "And they look so gross. Those nasty little see-through bodies and those creepy stingers up in the air. Horror movie stuff."

"No. They don't kill people, almost never." She described the small venomous bark scorpion, *Centruroides sculpturatus*, a creature only one or two inches long yet bearing a potent nerve toxin in its little stinger.

Although one of the most poisonous of all scorpions in North America, no Arizona deaths had been attributed to them in decades. "It's very painful to be stung, though, and it makes you pretty sick. Especially bad for babies and small children—they can even have seizures."

"Whoa. Whoa. Let me get this down." Papers rattled. "Here's what. I'm going to tell people how scary scorpions are, with that nerve toxin. Then I'll point out that riding a motorcycle without a helmet is hundreds of times more dangerous. Brilliant, right? It'll blow their minds."

Maya smiled. The analogy didn't quite make sense, but his energy entertained her. "And scorpions are usually nocturnal, so tell people to be extra careful at night. And you know what's the coolest thing? They're fluorescent. If you shine a black light on them in the dark, they glow green."

"Whoa. This is awesome, Dr. Summer. Thanks! And what about rattle-snakes? Are they safer than we think?"

"No. Rattlesnakes are very dangerous. Stick with scorpions." *Crotatus atrox*, the western diamondback, flourished in Phoenix. While not always fatal, the venom caused devastating damage to victims. Flesh rotted, black and swollen, and blood quit coagulating. Getting treated quickly with antivenom was critical. "I mean, if you want to do a separate story on rattlesnake dangers, that would actually be great."

"Thanks! I'll keep that in mind." He hung up quickly.

Maybe she could learn how to channel his zany enthusiasm.

Maya hadn't seen Alex since he crashed last week. A few days ago he texted her, briefly explaining the bike sabotage and warning her that everyone he knew would be contacted by a detective. An amusing text, assuring her she wasn't a suspect. Maya appreciated the notice, but felt stung that he didn't call her. Clearly, he had decided to avoid her.

The detective bore a tiny black moustache, distracting because it re-minded her of Wild West villains. She imagined him before the mirror each morning, combing those little wings. A dour man, he asked many clipped questions and offered nothing. She couldn't help but wonder how his interview went with Jim Barrow.

Between the bike wreck and the oleander, her fears about Alex sky-rocketed. Maya worried herself sick about him. No one knew why, but someone had a grudge.

Finally seeing Alex in the flesh made it worse.

"Holy cow," she exclaimed, staring at his scabbed cheek and jaw, at the red laceration where sutures had been recently removed. A short thick beard, dark blond, fringed his face.

Alex looked rueful. "I know. So much for my modeling career."

"Oh, Alex." Filled with concern, Maya reached up, gently touched the rough skin. "You look awful."

"Gee, thanks. That makes me feel better."

Veronica materialized in the doorway and cleared her throat. Maya quickly withdrew her hand as Veronica slipped her a cold glance, then entered and sat by Alex.

"Dr. Reddish. Alex. Should you even be working?" Veronica crooned, leaning forward to study his wounds. Finally she sat back. "Have they found who did it?"

"Thanks for asking, V. No, these things take time. But let's not talk about it while we're in the middle of work, all right? Now, what's going on with your patient?"

He acted measured, careful. But who wouldn't? It made Maya's brushes with the bikers seem like nothing. When Alex left with Veronica to see the patient, Maya saw how Veronica managed to jostle against him as they exited through the doorway.

She hated this distance from Alex. It was her fault, because of Whit, and she had to fix it. The next time they were alone in the attending office, she whispered to him.

"I think she's getting worse."

Alex suddenly grinned and whispered back. "You might be right. What should I do?"

"Well. You tried disfiguring your face, but that hasn't worked." She lowered her voice, encouraged by his playfulness. "You may have to take it to the next level."

He nodded solemnly. "I was afraid of that. I'm going to have to quit my job and join the circus."

Maya laughed. "You can be a carny! The beard is a good start. But you're a little too neat and clean."

Alex pretended to look dejected, lowered his head. His hair in his eyes. "All right. I'll quit bathing and start sleeping in my clothes."

Maya took a chance. She put her hand on his wrist, leaned close.

"Dr. Reddish. *Alex*," she said quietly.

Alex grinned and snatched his arm away. Maya was delighted that he responded.

Veronica walked past the open door, a line between her brows, staring at them. Maya felt a little bad and vowed to be a better person.

Then the remarkable happened. Alex became busy with another resident, and Veronica needed to discuss a case. She loitered by the door, waiting for him, checking her watch.

"Can I help you?" Maya asked. Veronica had never staffed with her.

"I guess." Veronica barely met Maya's eyes, pushed her flaxen hair back from her face. "This woman wants me to refill her birth control pills. But she's way overdue for a Pap, so I don't want to or she'll never come back for that. I can't do it today because she's on her period. I told her to use condoms till she gets her Pap. Does that sound right?"

Maya chose her words. "Actually, that's an outdated concept. Contraception and cancer screening should not be linked. That's like telling a man you won't treat his blood pressure if he doesn't get his prostate checked." Maya smiled to soften her feedback. "As long as she doesn't have contraindications for taking the pill—you know, like high blood pressure or blood clots or smoking—I'd absolutely give it to her."

"That doesn't seem right." Veronica's citrine eyes narrowed. "The gynecologist I worked with last year wouldn't do it. He seemed pretty determined about that."

Maya checked her tongue, didn't ask if he was an older physician, still following invalid guidelines.

"Don't get me wrong," Maya said. "You should recommend the Pap. Along with everything else she needs, like her vaccines and a healthy diet. And condoms. But nearly half of pregnancies are unintended, so we want to avoid that. The incidence of cervical cancer is way under one percent."

"Sure, Dr. Summer." Unhappy, Veronica left abruptly.

Such a peculiar person, Maya thought, surprised that Veronica espoused such an archaic notion of Paps and contraceptives. Maya expected someone young and smart like Veronica to advocate strongly for access to birth control. Many countries in Europe did not require prescriptions.

Ten minutes later, Alex reappeared. "Everyone's done," he announced.

He shut down his computer and had one foot out the door. "I'll see you next week, okay?"

Maya jumped up, distressed at his quick exit, his persistent reserve.

"No. I mean yes, of course." She took a breath and plunged. "Alex, this isn't right. We have to talk."

42

Alex felt good. Really good.

Just calm down, he ordered himself. Remember, someone is trying to hurt you. It's terrifying, and you have no idea why. So you have no business being happy, not even a little bit.

Alex still felt good.

Maya touched his arm at the end of the day. They retreated to his office, her face stricken.

"I'm so, so sorry, Alex." Those gray eyes rimmed with black, stormy.

"Well, I'm just going to carry on," he said. "Maybe it's all a fluke. The cops think it must be a patient, someone upset about their diagnosis or treatment, blaming me. I know a few hospital cases that might have seemed that way, things that couldn't be controlled. You know how that goes. There's just no—"

She shook her head. "Not that. I mean, that's awful. I don't know how you can even think straight. But I'm talking about me, about Whit. What he did last week. Saying that on my phone, so you would hear it. That was inexcusable."

Alex shrugged, uncomfortable. "Look. I don't know what was going on between you two. Obviously something, and obviously not my business. Please just forget it."

"No. I owe you—"

"Maya. You don't. Your relationship is not my concern. To be honest, I'd rather not be involved with this." There, he said it. It was both the truth, and not true at all.

She looked distraught. "I just think you—"

"Maya. Please. It's really awkward for me to talk to you about your boyfriend." He debated how far to go. "I care about you. I'm afraid I'll say the wrong thing."

She sat back, exasperated, folded her arms. "That's what I'm trying to tell you. We've broken up. For good."

He stared at her. She stared at him.

"Huh." Now there were a dozen things he wanted to say. None of them felt wise.

"Yeah. So." Maya stood, seemed relieved. "I just thought you should know, that's all. After last week."

Alex leaped up, blocked her exit. He felt clumsy, as if he'd never talked with a woman before. He wanted to tell her he was sorry. He wanted to tell her he was thrilled. And he knew it wasn't even reliable—though she just said she was done with Whit for good, they might get back together. He thought they had split once before, and then they hadn't.

But now he was taking too long. Say something, you idiot.

"I'm sorry. I'm not sorry. I don't know what to say." Maybe if he tried really hard, he could come across as more blundering.

Maya actually laughed. "You're so honest. I can always count on you for that, can't I?"

"Yes, you can." What an amazing thing for her to say. It made him daring. "Do you want to talk about it more? Go somewhere?"

Her face twisted. "Maybe soon. Give me a bit more time."

He told her he was traveling to Las Vegas that coming weekend, to visit an old friend from medical school. A male friend, he clarified. He needed a break from Phoenix, from all this stress. He and Maya agreed to have dinner together the following Thursday after work.

Quit grinning, he told himself as he drove home. You'll make your face bleed. And with his luck, she could be back with Whit by then. Think about something else.

The oppressive afternoon sunbaked his car, made the pavement wiggle with heat. He thought about his bike. Because Jim Barrow was no longer at work and had no access to Alex's bike, Alex assumed that exonerated him. Then Randy explained that the tampering could have happened any time—maybe recently, the very day of the crash, or maybe weeks ago. All the doctors' fingerprints were on file, for you couldn't become a resident physician without passing major security checks. But no fingerprints were found on the bike except Alex's and Randy's.

Barrow would return to work next week. Stewart reported that Jim felt better, stronger, seemed on top of things. Alex began to think the detective was right and it must be an unhappy patient, or maybe a patient's family member. Not exactly reassuring, but better to be someone he didn't know.

He thought of Maya.

Quit grinning.

43

On Friday, Maya hoped for a quiet weekend.

Alex flew to Las Vegas for a few days of lighthearted entertainment, so he should be safe. One less thing to worry about. Maya felt relieved he decided not to drive, those bleak three hundred miles, many on a two-lane highway. The soaring new bridge at Hoover Dam, a beautiful and frightfully high architectural wonder, shortened the trip considerably from what it used to be, but it still took hours.

Whit remained silent. Maya suspected they would simply never speak again. She preferred that—it felt cleaner, crisp. The few items left at his home were replaceable, and she wanted no artificial sentiments like *let's still be friends*. Impossible.

Heat clamped the city in a ruthless vice, no sign of letting go. Thunderstorm cells wandered the nights like restless hulking gods, flashing and gusting, sparking fires in one place and deluging another with rain and hail. Now early August, they all crouched under the heat and dreamed of cooler weather in October. Rarely, a hurricane struck Mexico and sent heavy wet clouds fanning across the Southwest. A short respite.

Because monsoon storms raised fatal lightning strikes, Maya created new programs for lightning safety. Never shelter under a tree, a common scenario for being struck. In fact, stay away from trees—get wet, not lit. Lowering your height by sitting or lying on the ground did not always make you safer, because it exposed you to more ground current from a nearby strike. Get inside a building or vehicle, but not a convertible. Administer CPR immediately to a victim. Young white men seemed more likely to take risks and more likely to die from lightning.

That morning, Mel caught up with her in the parking lot as they both arrived. With the temperature in the high nineties and headed upward, Maya wilted already.

"Haven't seen much of you lately," he complained. His morose gaze scanned her, as if inspecting for trouble.

"Haven't seen much of you," she fired back. He could decipher her mood in seconds, so she tried to distract him. The last thing she wanted to discuss with Mel was Whit. In the blazing light, she saw that Mel's hair had turned whiter.

"How's that pony?" He still watched her, probably knew she was off.

"Better. He comes to me now. He hangs out with Rafael, follows him, lets him groom him. Rafael is patient…I think he spent an hour brushing him the other day. Manchado nudged him for more."

"That boy know how to ride?" Mel looked thoughtful.

Rafael used to sit on Luna's back as she moseyed around the corral, but Maya doubted he'd ridden more than that. "I don't think so."

"Huh. Come fall, maybe he ought to come up to the ranch and learn."

"Mel, that would be wonderful. I'll check with Rosa before we say anything." Maya knew not all parents embraced the dreams of horse-obsessed children. The potential injuries, the real injuries. Constantly begging to ride, craving their own horse—it could be exhausting. And expensive.

They entered the welcome relief of the building like slipping into a cool cave. Maya waved hello to Sheila as she moved by while Mel stopped to talk. Maya saw Mel lean toward Sheila, saw Sheila beam and laugh.

Interesting.

On Saturday afternoon, Maya started painting her bedroom, a project delayed too long. The entire house cried for paint, inside and out, so she might as well start there. The exterior had to wait for cooler weather. She turned on the ceiling fan and lost herself in the process, rolling creamy sand-colored paint across the walls, obliterating the dated brown tint her parents had used. The room slowly transformed into a fresh, lighter space.

Rafael tapped on her door, wanting to know if Manchado could eat watermelon.

"You bet. Rind and all," Maya said. She watched him run out to the corral, then hurry back.

He looked at her spattered arms, paint smeared on her cheek. "Can I help?"

Maya assigned him to a wall, put on music, and they worked together for the next two hours, finishing the job much sooner than she expected. She sent Rafael home with money in his pocket and to invite his mom over for supper, extra payment for a job well done.

Later that night, peacefully tired, Maya tried to sleep. But the house stank of paint fumes, so she turned off the AC and opened the windows to air the room. Waiting outside, she watched a small thunderstorm drift by at a distance, a fine spectacle of spindly lightning and sulky clouds. The breeze picked up and the air cooled slightly, and Maya lay on her backyard lounge, enjoying the sky.

In her dream, shadowy men talked about her. She heard their low voices but could not make out the words, could not see them. Uneasy, she kept trying to find a light, kept fumbling in the dark for a switch. Everything felt wrong—she should wake up.

"Don't she look like an angel, sleeping like that?" someone said.

Maya breathed deeply and slowly opened her eyes.

She jerked up and cried out.

A man sat on each side of her, grinning and staring. One skinny, one heavy. Black T-shirts, dark pants, heavy boots. Tattoos and sweat stains. The heavy one raised a stained finger to his lips.

"Sh. You'll wake the neighbors."

A feeling like a thousand crows flapped inside her chest, beating her lungs, taking her breath. She clutched the chair and looked frantically about.

"Easy, easy," the other said, soothing. A sly look toward his friend. "We ain't going to hurt you. Much."

Her thoughts raced in circles while the crows flailed inside her. She felt desperate, faint and ill. Her phone must be inside. She wanted to leap up and try to run but she knew that was insane, there was no way could she escape. Paralyzed, any movement at all felt hazardous.

A hand reached out, touched her hair. Rubbed the strands between his fingers.

"That's mighty pretty hair. So shiny." His hand smelled like gasoline.

Maya grimaced and leaned away. He let go, let her hair fall.

"Please. Can we talk?" she said. A tiny shaky voice that didn't seem hers. But she forced herself to look up, connect with each man's cold eyes.

"Aw, honey. Talk? You like to talk a lot, don't you? Yak yak yak. All you do is talk. Helmet this and helmet that." Angry at first, then he smiled. "Well, maybe I don't like to wear a helmet. Maybe it ruins my looks." He flipped his fingers through his limp hair and flashed his eyes, then turned to his friend. "What about you? You like wearing a helmet, Slat?"

"Hell no." Slat stood up and she saw a glint, a long knife at his belt.

"And I can't stomach a bitch like this telling me I have to, neither. She should shut her damn mouth up." He kicked her lounge chair, made her jump. Her heart pounded, a wild drum.

"Babe. You obviously need some kind of education. We don't want to, see? We've been trying to warn you, but some people don't take a hint." His lip curled and he put his hand on her bare foot, circled her ankle, squeezed. Rough skin, ragged nails. He slid his hand up her leg until he reached her knee, and a slow smile warped half his face. He licked his lips, dug his fingers in.

The crows attacked her lungs. She might vomit. Her breath tore in and out, hyperventilating, and she went dizzy and thought she could really pass out. She wanted to yank her leg away, but feared that a quick movement might trigger him, sudden violence. She told herself to stay alert, pay attention, think of something to say, anything to distract them, but dread overwhelmed her. She heard a sound like a whimper that must have come from her own throat.

"Okay, boys." A new voice, deeper. "That's enough."

The knife man released her knee as a shadow moved beneath the tree, where a third man emerged.

"Hey, Boss. Didn't see you sneak up. You're just in time for the fun."

The new man strolled over. Maya sank into utter despair, saw his eyes glide over her, then shift to the other men. She wanted to fold up, put her arms over her head, hide. She should scream, kick, run. But she couldn't move.

"You've had plenty of fun," he growled. "Look at her—you've scared her nearly to death. Go on, get out of here."

"Aw, come on, Boss. Just let me—"

The new man stiffened. In the dull light Maya made out a scorpion tattoo on his forearm, lizards crawling up to his shoulder. The man at the stoplight last month.

The other two mumbled and backed up, shuffled away. "He just wants her for himself," one complained. "That ain't fair."

He stood there, hands on his hips, watching them go. She heard the cough and spew of engines, heard the motorcycles recede. He turned back to her then, a stony sneer. Snarled hair writhed about his head, a jutting beaked nose and pointed chin, a raptor.

"What's your deal, anyway?" He flung the words at her.

Maya struggled to find her voice, still gulping air. "I—I don't know. I don't know what you mean."

"I mean why the hell do you care if anyone wears a fucking helmet? So what if we die? Why can't you just leave it alone? Christ, lady."

Maya stared. Behind him she saw Manchado pacing, looking her way.

"Well?" He picked up a chair and turned it around, sat straddling it and leaned over the back. His face in shadow, a spark of eye. "Come on, tell me. I want to know what the fuck your problem is."

Maya straightened, overwrought, suddenly savage with adrenaline. *The hell with you*, she thought fiercely and let it spill in a rush. "There—there was an accident. I almost died. A biker without a helmet did die. He—I—it might have been my fault."

He stared at her, incredulous, then threw his head back and laughed. Kept laughing, eyes closed. He finally stopped himself and grinned, delighted. "You mean you killed him?"

Maya couldn't stand to look at him, watched the horse instead. "Yes. Probably."

His eyes ran over her. She wore little, a tank top and shorts. Now her bravado fled and panic came flooding back as he considered her, the crows starting to flap again. He studied her damaged leg, the graft and scars, and his mouth skewed.

"You might as well give up. Your law won't pass."

"I know," she said softly. He kept eyeing her leg and she wanted to pull it up under her.

"But it might pass next time. This damn state's getting downright liberal, I'm sorry to say. People are listening to you. Pisses me off."

Maya stayed silent. Nothing felt safe.

He pushed himself up, chuckled. "Okay. That was a good laugh. I needed that. What a hoot, you trying to protect all us losers, for your own salvation. Save us, save your soul. Deliverance, right? That's rich. Here I thought you were some kind of goody-goody, who likes to tell everyone how to behave. But it turns out you're just crazy, aren't you?"

He laughed again, a short yap. "Don't worry. No one will bother you anymore. You got my word on it. Just do me one little favor and don't call the cops right now, okay?" He saw her dire expression. "Hey. I got those filthy animals off you, didn't I?"

"Yes," she whispered.

"Did anyone hurt you?"

She shook her head, a tiny motion.

"So don't call the cops, okay?" A little menacing.

Maya drew a shaky breath and nodded.

"Good girl." He stood, looking about, pointed at the corral with his chin. "Nice horse."

"Please don't harm him," she pleaded. It would be so easy.

His expression darkened. "You don't know me at all, sweetheart. I'd hurt you way before I'd ever touch a hair on that fine animal."

He scowled and left.

Maya sat frozen, shocked. It was over. Was it over? She stood and staggered, nearly collapsed, as if she had no blood pressure, no bones. She stumbled inside the house and grabbed her phone—it seemed a miracle that it sat there, waiting for her.

But who could she call? She didn't dare turn to Rosa, would never put Rosa and Rafael at risk, in case the men returned. Whit? Unthinkable. Alex was in Nevada, trying to relax—he couldn't help her from there, and she would ruin his trip. Mel couldn't do anything himself, but he would most certainly call the police. Mel would insist she stay somewhere else, and she didn't want that. Sheila? Sheila would tell Mel.

Calling the police felt extremely foolish and would accomplish zero. She wasn't hurt, like he said.

Maya heard a small crackle and dropped into a crouch, crept to the window. Nothing. Maybe a packrat, foraging outside. Suddenly she felt trapped inside the house, too confined, and she rushed out, clutching the phone. She stood a long time, listening and watching, legs braced for flight and her body throbbing. Nothing. Just Manchado, alert, gazing about as if on surveillance.

The shed behind the corral drew her. Along the side of the shed stood a wooden bench, black in shadow, unseen. A hideout, well away from the house and yard. Maya grabbed a cushion and hurried over, brushed off the dust. She gripped her phone and sat, rigid and motionless for an hour. Vigilant, invisible, a clear view of the road and house. The night stood still around her, hot and deep, the stars faint as ghosts. A far storm flicked in the north, barely seen.

After another hour, her pulse slowed and her adrenaline dropped. She lay down to wait for dawn. Stared at the impassive sky and watched it revolve. Forced herself not to think about scorpions that might be prowling nearby.

The laugh came back to her. *You're just crazy, aren't you?*

Manchado stood beside her all night. Eventually the sky tinged gold and pink, soft colors streaking over her, unfurled streamers proclaiming day from horizon to horizon. Maya rose stiffly, went back inside, and could not imagine that she would ever sleep again.

44

Alex never considered himself a Las Vegas sort of person. That inescapable glare of lights and incessant jangling of slot machines made him feel edgy, a little unhinged. He didn't mind taking risks—chess took risks, too—he just wanted it quieter, no droning dealers or clanging machines with predestined electronic algorithms. It's not like he took big chances, anyway.

But he enjoyed his friend Marley, a chunky cheery emergency doc who was thrilled to have Alex visit and took him out both nights. They went to a show, a comedy club, and a nightclub. They laughed and drank too much, enjoyed watching all the eccentric people and inventing backstories for them. Marley insisted Alex needed a topless revue to distract himself, but once there, what Alex marveled at most was the identical size and shape of the women's breasts. He wondered how they selected so many young females built exactly the same. Did they advertise for a certain size, or send everyone to the same plastic surgeon? Was there a modeling tryout, or measurements? His imagination reeled.

He tried not to think about Maya. She needed time. He tried not to hate Thicket but wanted to throttle him—Thicket clearly had been awful. He tried not to wonder what Maya saw in that selfish prig, even as he knew that all relationships were more complicated than they appeared on the surface. He tried not to project when he should approach her at the next level. He tried not to think about someone trying to hurt him, about how to protect himself.

He realized that he was trying not to think about quite a lot. Then he tried not to think about not thinking about it. Be in the moment, he insisted, and enjoy your little vacation. Quit calculating everything five moves ahead.

Ha. Good luck with that.

His plane landed back in Phoenix early Sunday evening, dropping into a hazy inflamed landscape as the burning ingot of sun struck the horizon. He planned to put his feet up and relax, watch some television, figure out where to have dinner with Maya later that week. His bruises were fading rapidly and soon he could shave again, hopefully by Thursday. He hardly dared admit how keenly he wished to kiss her, even as he promised himself prudence. In case she wasn't ready. In case she wasn't actually interested. Stay real.

He couldn't settle. Restless. Preoccupied. Should he call her, just for fun? No, he would look overeager, insensitive. Maya mentioned looking forward to her quiet weekend, nothing planned, a chance to sleep in late and forget about work. He suspected she really meant to forget about Whit. By Thursday she should be calmer, unwound.

He found his phone in his hand. You're pathetic, he thought, looking at her number. He set the phone down, then picked it up. Then quickly tapped her number.

Maya sounded tired and subdued.

See? It was a bad idea to call. Some people never learn.

Too late now to back out. He entertained her with Vegas stories. How anytime he sat down at a poker machine he was joined immediately by a roving cocktail waitress who brought him free drinks, who could glide about on high heels as easily as most people in running shoes. The all-you-can-eat buffet, brimming with mediocre dishes from marginally accurate ethnic stations. His advice: start with dessert. He nearly said *We should go there some day* but managed to keep that to himself because her responses felt so anemic.

"So how was your weekend?" he asked, about to wrap up. "Nice and relaxing?"

"No, not really." She spoke slowly, offered nothing more.

"Um. Maya? How come?" He had a bad feeling.

"I…" She faded away, came back, then her voice cracked. "I'm sorry. I'm trying to figure this out."

What the hell, he thought. Surely not. But he had to say something and simply blurted it. "Are you back with Whit again?"

"No! Heavens no. Never."

She sort of laughed. She sort of huffed, and then her words cascaded, piled up and crashed. Last night, bikers, threats, everything is fine, I'm good, I'm good. They won't come back, he promised, everything is good now. Alex tried to interrupt, to understand, but she tore on, reassuring him, it was just so scary you know, of course who wouldn't be scared, the way they touched me, so creepy but now it's okay and maybe I can finally sleep tonight and—"

"Maya," Alex said loudly, stopping her. He might be confused with the details, but he understood enough. "Stay put. I'm coming over. Right now."

"No. No, don't do that," she said, calmer. He heard her inhale. "You just got home. I'll be okay. I just had to tell someone, just let it out, you know. I feel better now. It's over and done. It's—"

"On my way." He hung up and rushed to his car.

45

Maybe this is what lack of sleep does to you, Maya mused. You start channeling ancient Romans. Like all physicians, Maya was no stranger to exhaustion, but Roman philosophers had left her alone in the past.

Lucius Seneca said it. A victim of Caligula. She did not look up the exact quote, but knew he remarked something like *If you want to escape the things that bother you, what you need is not to be in a different place but to be a different person.* Although she learned that phrase from ancient literature over a decade back, here it came, returning, as if it knew where it belonged.

And now Alex approached. Maya would invite him in for a few minutes, give him some iced tea and a snack, send him home. He must be tired from traveling, and she herself had not slept at all. While puny with fatigue, she suddenly felt safer just knowing he was coming. What the heck. She shucked off her shorts and halter and slid into a full-length summer shift, washed her face, then started picking up.

Remarkable, really, how much better everything seemed in the last few minutes, after telling him. As if it just needed the light of day. Somewhere a lesson hovered there, something about transparency, but she couldn't focus—too hard to think straight. The house looked disorderly from painting yesterday and dishes sat stacked by the sink, so she hastened to put things away.

Alex barely paused to knock. He wrapped both arms around her before she could say a word. His unexpected force derailed her resolve and she sagged into him with relief. He simply stood there, clutching her even tighter against him.

A moment passed.

"Alex," she whispered.

"What?" he whispered back.

"You're kind of smashing my face."

"Sorry." He loosened his grip. "But your story scared the hell out of me. And I couldn't even understand what really happened."

"I told you—"

"Maya. You were barely making any sense."

"So you just dropped everything and came over?"

"I heard you say *bikers* and that someone touched you. I kind of quit listening after that."

She took his hands, squeezed. "Thank you."

"Jesus, Maya." He seemed to be sorting what to say. "Am I the first person you've told? What the hell. Can we start at the beginning? Is that all right?"

They sat on the sofa and he gripped her hand as if she might float away. It anchored her, solid, and she needed only a little prodding to share every detail. Something about his wide hazel eyes, his riveted attention, his warm steady fingers, made it easy.

"Come home with me," he insisted. "Don't stay here alone."

She shrugged, filtering her feelings. "I actually sort of believe him. The boss, whoever he was. I wasn't sure last night, but now that I'm reliving it with you, I don't think they'll be back."

"Jesus, Maya. You don't have to be so tough all the time. Let me help." Alex frowned.

"I'm not tough," she retorted. "I completely froze up. And quit saying *Jesus, Maya.*"

"You were powerless. You were smart to freeze."

"It wasn't a decision. I wanted to move—to run away, to fight back—but I couldn't. So don't give me credit." She sighed. "I have to stay here. Don't you see? If I run and hide, they win. Maybe I should get a big dog."

"Like, get a dog tonight?"

Maya laughed. Which felt good, since she thought she might never laugh again.

"No, silly." She paused. "Alex. Thank you so much for this."

He pulled her comfortably against him. He smelled like Las Vegas, a complicated mix of fried food and cigarette smoke and coffee, of airports and money and aftershave. Maybe a trace of tequila. She knew she was losing it, as if all those scents could possibly be real.

"I'm glad you feel better, because I don't," he grumbled. "I'm furious and I'm frightened for you. I want to kill those guys. I think we should call the cops. I think you should come home with me."

Maya said no. She turned drowsy, warm and relaxed, his arm around her. "Remember what I told you?" she mumbled, slurring her words with weariness. "What that guy said? I'm just crazy."

Alex rubbed her shoulder. He slid his fingers along her jaw, under her chin, and tipped her face up.

"We're all crazy," he said quietly. "You've got no monopoly on that… you have to share the title."

Maya shifted to see him better, his clear brown-green eyes, the brows faintly gathered. Lucius Seneca was right, two thousand years ago. She should be a different person…she had been so passive with Whit. No more of that. Maya touched his wounded cheek, then gently pressed her lips to his.

Alex seemed to pause. Maya imagined the chessboard, his fingers over the piece. She hoped she had not made a mistake, that this was the right different person she should be.

"You are *such* a knight," he murmured. He started kissing her softly, taking his time. Then not taking his time, suddenly urgent. Maya responded, flushing, fierce with heat. Then Alex gradually backed down, braking, braking, departing her mouth, kissing her cheeks and forehead and eyelids. Stopped.

Maya felt his arms go around her, his chin on her head. She knew he was right.

"We can't. Not right now," Alex said, still breathing a little hard.

"I know." Too stressed, too exhausted. Everything was wrong. "I'm sorry. I never should have—"

"Are you kidding me?" he said, amused.

"I just—"

"Maya." He gave her a tolerant look.

"Alex." She gave the look back.

"Sh. Try to sleep."

Maya curled against him. "It's getting late. You should probably go home."

"I will. Soon."

She fell asleep.

46

The week flew. Alex took comfort that nothing bad happened. His bike stood back in his house, new handlebars, all tuned up, but he hadn't summoned the fortitude to ride to work again. The weather was too tyrannical anyway, completely intolerable with high temperatures and high humidity, an overbearing bully. Storms came and went, elusive, cruel either way—too brutal when they pummeled you with hail, too heartless when they passed you by. August always became the worst month, the relief of autumn too far in the future, and Alex's resolve to endure melted away. Phoenix hunkered down, waiting. Those who couldn't leave the city withdrew inside with their air conditioning.

Alex laughed, though, when people from northern climates derided him, wondering how he could stand those summers. So inhumane and confining, they said. Alex pointed out they put up with months of bitter cold and ice, equally or more restricting. At least in Phoenix your car never got stuck in the snow, you never skidded on ice into an intersection. You just had to remember not to leave canned drinks in your parked car because they might boil and explode. You learned not to leave meltable items like lip balm, deodorant, crayons, chocolate, most foods, some plastics like CD cases—the list went on. You wore light cottons and always kept water handy, and you learned not to touch anything, inside or outside your car, without testing first to see if it would burn you.

By Thursday, Alex chose and discarded at least four restaurants for his dinner with Maya. He wanted an intimate place, not too fancy, with simple food, but really excellent. Not too bright, not too dark. He drove himself batty. While no one ever needed reservations this time of year— in August you could stroll into any restaurant and find a table, places you couldn't touch in winter—he took no chances.

Earlier that morning, before patients arrived, Jim Barrow appeared in Alex's doorway.

"Come in, come in." Alex tried not to act guarded, but also not be too warm, not overdo it and seem insincere. "It's nice to have you back."

Jim looked better, much better. Professional. He had a nice haircut, a crisp blue button-down shirt, a striped yellow tie. His skin more tanned, traces of a sunburn, so he clearly had been spending time outside. He stood tensely before Alex, his brown eyes troubled but direct.

"Dr. Reddish. I just want you to know it's not me. I would never do anything like that."

"I know that, Jim." Alex felt almost certain Jim told the truth, even though a tiny voice inside Alex's head chirped that a guilty person would say exactly those words. "Can you sit down?"

"No, I'm going to prep my charts. I'm trying to be more efficient." Jim's jaw set, determined. "I'm exercising, eating healthy. I quit drinking coffee and soda. I feel so much better."

"Good for you. I'm impressed. Let me know if I can help you, okay?"

"You bet. Thanks, Dr. Reddish."

Maybe Jim really could turn over a new leaf.

That afternoon, Maya barely made it to the attending office in time for the afternoon session.

"Tough morning?" Alex asked.

"The worst. I was almost an hour behind." She sat down and spread out her papers, looking stressed. "One of my favorite patients, Gloria Gonzalez. She's ninety, and she has another urinary infection. A stroke patient, years ago. I want her in the hospital because she doesn't look good. Her blood pressure's a little low and her pulse is a little high. But she won't go."

She frowned with worry. He loved how her hair curved onto her shoulders, the tips brushing her throat. Alex wanted to reach up and rub the lines from her forehead. He wanted to touch her so much it almost hurt.

"Does she have anyone to help her? Family?" he asked.

Maya shook her head. "I asked her to return here tomorrow, to make sure she's stable. Jim Barrow has an opening, so he'll see her. I already told him and introduced them." Maya sighed. "These stubborn old women."

Alex laughed. "You'll be just the same. Fifty or sixty years from now."

"Ack. Let's take one year at a time."

"I'm just looking forward to one night at a time. Like dinner tonight." His eyebrows raised.

Maya smiled warmly and Alex felt his heart flop. In a very good way.

A typical staffing afternoon. A fractured wrist. A broken heart that kept its human from sleeping. Sugars too high and potassiums too low. A patient with a virus demanding antibiotics, a patient on antibiotics developing diarrhea. A crampy gut, a swollen leg, lumpy lymph nodes. A cancer follow-up. Alex made himself focus and nearly ignored Maya in order to function. She wore beige slacks with a wraparound cream top that looked amazing next to her toasty-tan chest, and he caught himself wondering how to undo it. Pay attention to your work, you degenerate, he told himself.

Jim Barrow sat with Maya, talking about inflammatory bowel disease. Jim spoke clearly, asked good questions, making Alex wonder if they would ever understand his slump. Was Jim himself clueless, or being crafty, hiding it? Alex cleaned up the work area and moved an untidy stack of medical journals.

"Hey, Jim," Alex said, seeing Jim's old coffee mug. The one with the Superman logo that rarely left Jim's hand before he took his leave. It must have been hidden behind that pile of journals all month.

"Huh." Jim took it and unscrewed the lid, peered inside. "Ick—all dried up. Man, I drank a lot of coffee in those days." As if it had been another lifetime. Jim tipped the cup so Alex could see dried scum in the bottom. Then Jim brought the cup to his nose and sniffed. "Nope. Just smells like dead coffee."

"What were you expecting?" Maya asked, curious.

"I don't know." He glanced at the doorway to see if anyone else was near. "I keep trying to figure this out. What happened, that stupid drug test. How much better I feel now, after getting away. I mean, maybe I was just really depressed and needed a break, right?"

Unbidden, Alex remembered that party with the tainted punch. The nurse's positive drug test and how Alex felt that evening, his strange lethargy. Maya took the cup and gazed inside, a focused expression. Probably remembering the same things. A strange foreboding stirred inside him.

"Jim," Maya said carefully. "Would you like me to have this tested? For substances?"

Jim sat back. "Are you serious?"

Maya shrugged. "Up to you. It's rather preposterous, I agree."

"Can testing even work?" Alex asked. "After it's all dried up?"

"Just add water, I think," Maya said. "Molecules are molecules. I'd leave that to a chemist."

"Yes, please." Jim stood up. "I've got to get back to my patients."

He gave them an uncomfortable look and left.

Although intuition told Alex that Jim was not the problem, it bothered him that he could not quite interpret Jim's expression.

47

Alex peered up and down the hall, wondering where Maya had gone. He hadn't seen her for at least thirty minutes, and he staffed the last few cases with residents by himself. Her papers remained scattered across the desk in the attending office, an uncapped pen, her half-open bag on the floor. The computer dimly gray, gone to sleep from inactivity.

He strolled along the hall, looking for a closed door where Maya and a resident might be with a patient. But all the rooms stood wide open, the medical assistants nearly done as they chatted and cleaned up, restocking drawers and countertop items, cotton swabs and alcohol wipes. He poked his head in the residents' room and scanned for her there—just a few residents finishing notes, talking on phones. Someone laughed at a joke. Someone waved at him. No Maya.

She must be nearby. Alex checked the back hall, peeked in the empty procedure room, the little casting room, the storeroom with liquid nitrogen and supplies. Rounding the corner, he passed the restroom when he thought he heard a sound. A scrape, a muffled word. He looked self-consciously about and put his ear to the door. Another little noise.

He tapped on the door. Nothing. He tapped louder.

"Maya?"

A hand fumbled with the latch and the door cracked open.

"Alex? Oh, thank goodness."

Maya leaned against the wall. Alex touched her arm, her skin red and warm. Her clothes rumpled, a stain on her thigh, maybe vomit, the way it smelled. His nose wrinkled.

"I'm sorry," she mumbled, embarrassed. She abruptly bent over the toilet and retched, spit out a trace of mucus.

"Jesus, Maya," Alex said. He closed the lid and sat her down, then wetted a paper towel and wiped her scarlet face. "I think you've got a fever. You're really hot."

She nodded weakly. "Maybe gastroenteritis?"

"I guess." Alex propped the door open for better air, tried to make a plan. "Can you sit here a few seconds? I'll get your things."

"Sure." Maya leaned back.

The staff were gone, the halls quiet now. Alex stuffed Maya's papers into her bag, shut down her computer, then went to the linen closet for a towel. When he returned, Maya still sat propped against the sink. Her head twitched up when she saw him, eyes glittering.

"Come on," Alex said, helping her up.

"I'm really thirsty."

"Not yet. You just threw up," Alex reminded her. "You can have some sips when you get home."

He walked her to his car, avoiding the halls and the residents' room, holding her arm. Once she bowed over, retching again, but nothing came up. He eased her into the front seat and gave her the towel.

"In case you vomit again," he explained.

"Brilliant. But I think I'm empty."

"I noticed." Likely some stomach bug—those viruses struck quickly. Two nurses left with similar symptoms yesterday, and he remembered Veronica complaining of nausea and aching muscles early in the week. Maya shifted restlessly, tugging at the seatbelt.

"How are you feeling?" he asked.

"Pretty awful. Hot. Thirsty. I'm so sorry."

"Don't be ridiculous." A horrible suspicion swept over him. "Maya. What did you eat today?"

Silence.

"Maya?"

"I'm thinking." She spoke slowly. "I brought my lunch from home, a sandwich. I took it out and ate it during the conference. No one could have messed with it. Then later I had a muffin, one of those commercial wrapped pastries they keep in the employee lounge. Ever since your oleander thing, I quit eating food at the clinic. Just the prepackaged stuff."

"Nothing else?"

"No. I'm sure."

"Good." Alex breathed a sigh of relief. He saw her hand go to her stomach and she pressed the towel to her mouth, but nothing happened.

She moaned. "Just a spasm."

He drove up to her front door and helped her out. She stumbled and he hooked his arm around her, practically carried her inside, put her on the sofa.

"I'm getting you some ice chips," he said, heading for the kitchen.

"Hurry," she called faintly. "I'm burning up."

He returned with the ice and stopped short, eyes wide.

"*Maya.*"

"It's okay. We're all friends." She waved dismissively.

She had peeled off her shirt, dropped it on the floor. Now she stood, stepping out of her slacks. Tripping, catching herself. Alex felt uncomfortable enough to see her in her underwear, a satiny blue bra, matching bikini panties that stretched around her hips and dove between her legs.

But the damage caught him cold.

A thin rope of scar started below her sternum and ran the length of her abdomen, detoured around her navel, then branched out across her right pelvis. He imagined how it must have been in the operating room, her body unzipped, splayed open on the table, blood welling in the cavity, and the suction apparatus slurping and humming full speed as the surgeons frantically searched for the torn veins.

Another wide scar traveled the outside of her right thigh, hip to knee, indented and dark. And her right calf muscle partly gone, misshapen, bound with a pale wide graft of skin, slightly wrinkled. Along the front of her other thigh, a large faint rectangular mark, discolored, where the skin graft had been harvested.

"Jesus, Maya," he whispered. He thought of her long skirts and slacks with a wrench—it was much worse than he'd imagined.

"Quit saying that," she complained. She weakly raised her hands and her fingers formed tiny air quotes. Exasperated, she repeated, "Jesus, Maya."

Alex almost laughed, but it wasn't funny. She seemed too out of it—her fever must be high. Maybe he could find some acetaminophen or ibuprofen. He quit staring, turned and hurried to her bedroom, returned with a large T-shirt and pushed it over her head, helped thread her arms through. Trying not to look at her bareness.

For the next hour he sat with her, brought her ice chips. She crunched them almost desperately, held some against her face. Restless, she kept trying to stand, and he kept pulling her back. Alex couldn't find any acetaminophen. No thermometer, either—he really wanted to check her fever. Typical doctor home, Alex thought, no basic medical equipment. Yet he would bet that somewhere nearby she had a thermometer for a horse.

Once she startled, looked across the room. She blurted out *Why is he here?* Then she shook her head. *Oh, he's gone.*

Slowly, the flush faded. She hadn't retched in a long time, so Alex brought her water, gave her small sips.

"Thanks," Maya murmured, frail but better. "Now you've rescued me twice."

"Yeah," he smiled, relieved. "You've only rescued me once, so you owe me one. I'm holding you to it."

"Raincheck," she mumbled. She drifted asleep as he sat there.

Déjà vu, Alex thought. What the hell. It hadn't been a week, and here he was again, watching her fall asleep. First the bikers, now this. He debated carrying her into the bedroom, tucking her in, but didn't want to wake her.

Instead, he went to the bedroom himself and napped there, getting up frequently to check her. She had rolled over and he gently tugged down the T-shirt to cover her better, even as he studied her scars again. He felt her resilience, that intangible notion she had forbidden him to express. She never complained and few knew her story.

And while he was wondering, he also took some time to wonder what the hell had happened to his once-quiet life.

48

When Maya woke, she heard the bubbly warble of quail outside the window. She figured it must be nearly six in the morning, judging from the slant of light. Some days before rising she would lie there and count how many sounds she could identify: the drone of an airplane, a carping dog, a silvery whinny. A faint hum of traffic out on the main road, over half a mile away.

Never voices. Only now she heard voices, the cadence of conversation.

Maya sat up. Why was she on the sofa? Her clothes lay crumpled on the floor. Good lord—why was she wearing this crappy old T-shirt from the discard pile in her bedroom? Her brain pounded, her mouth like sand, and she had to pee in the worst way. Strange notions crowded her head, dreamlike and vague. Moving weakly to the bathroom, she emptied her bladder, then changed into cotton pants and a sleeveless shirt. People were actually talking on her back porch, so she hadn't imagined that. She felt feeble as a kitten, not certain what day it was.

She remembered that cruel nausea, her stomach ripped inside out as she vomited again and again. Her skin on fire.

Maya looked out the kitchen door. Alex stood on the back porch holding a skillet, dishing out pancakes for Rosa and Rafael. Butter and syrup on the table, glasses of orange juice. Still early enough in the morning that sitting outside felt borderline tolerable. Alex saw her and came quickly inside.

He set the skillet in the sink. "You look better. Much better."

"Um. Alex. What's going on?" She sat down, overwhelmed.

"How much do you remember?" Alex glanced outside, then sat with her. He reviewed her illness: the bright red flush, her vomiting and fever, her mild confusion. How she gradually improved and slept.

"It's coming back." She pressed her temples. "But how did I get that old shirt on? I hate that shirt—I meant to throw it out. And why are my clothes in the living room?"

"Hm. That." He looked away.

"Alex?"

"Well. You sort of undressed while I was in the kitchen, getting you some ice. You kept saying you were burning up. You hardly knew what you were doing…your fever must have been really high, but I couldn't find a thermometer." A little accusatory.

Maya closed her eyes, wanted to escape. "Please tell me I left something on."

"Yes, of course. Your underwear." Alex looked out the window.

Mortified, her hand slipped over her mouth. Not only did he see her nearly naked, but that meant he saw the rest of her, too. Her leg, all the scars. She had planned to prepare him for that.

Alex carried on. "So I got you a shirt from your bedroom. I just picked up the first thing I saw."

It was too much to process right now. Maya realized it was Friday and she should get ready for work.

"But why are my neighbors here? Why are you cooking?"

Alex seemed happy to move on. In the kitchen earlier, making her tea, he saw Rafael with the horse and went out to say hello. He suspected Rafael was actually checking things out, what with Maya's car missing and a strange vehicle at her door. Then Rosa, who also kept watch, joined them, and before he knew it, he offered to fix them breakfast. He admitted to Maya that he loved breakfast, and he was pretty hungry after missing dinner last night.

"What great friends you have," Alex said warmly.

Maya kept struggling. "What did you tell them? I mean, about who you are, why you're here?"

"Why, I told them the truth. That you were sick, and I brought you home."

"Oh." That seemed too obvious. Then it caught up to her. "Oh, Alex. I'm so sorry. Our dinner."

"Come on out and visit, and I'll fix you something." Alex held the door open, took her arm. "You're still a little shaky."

Rosa and Rafael made room and Maya took a plate, reached for a pancake.

"Nope," said Alex, taking it away. "You can't have rich food so soon. Sit still and I'll make you toast. And the tea. Don't even think of drinking that orange juice."

Rosa caught Maya's eye, amused. She forked a bite of pancake and smiled her approval. Rafael sat quietly, eating his food and watching the adults.

"What a nice friend you have. And such a good cook," Rosa said, then she frowned. "You look bad. Pale like a ghost."

Maya nibbled her toast and sipped the tea, then checked her watch. "I've got to get ready for work."

Alex glared at her and went inside. He returned with her phone, handed it to her.

"Call in sick. You can't work today." Something else shadowed his face, she felt certain. "I mean it, Maya."

"But I—"

He shook his head. "You can't get there, anyway. Your car isn't here because I drove you home."

"You can take me and—"

"I won't. We can all see how weak you are."

Rosa crossed her arms. "I'll make her stay. And later on, if she's better, I'll drive her downtown for her car."

Maya gave up. They were right, anyway. She felt limp, mentally fuzzy. Rosa and Rafael left and Alex rushed about, straightening the kitchen.

"I've got to get going," he said. "I'll call later and see how you are. Just rest and push fluids, okay?"

"There's something else. What aren't you telling me?"

Alex sat down, took her hands. "I don't know. I mean, a high fever might explain everything, so maybe that's what it was. And other people have been sick with stomach symptoms this week. But your pupils were a little dilated. And there was one weird moment, where you thought you saw someone. Who wasn't there."

"You mean, like a hallucination?" She quailed—she almost remembered that.

"Yes. Exactly."

"That could be from high fever."

"Certainly."

Maya's heart clunked. "You're worried that maybe I was drugged."

He leaned forward and kissed her forehead. "I don't know. I sure as hell hope not. I'm probably just paranoid."

"I certainly hope so," Maya agreed.

After he left, she realized that was not a normal thing to hope.

49

Alex had a rough Friday at all levels. He only slept three or four hours at Maya's house. He'd endured worse, had functioned on much less when he must. Residents in training followed strict rules on how many hours they could work without sleep, but attending physicians had no rules at all.

No one else at the clinic turned sick yesterday, but earlier in the week there were three. If caused by a stomach virus, Alex had been closely exposed to Maya and might turn ill himself at any minute. If caused by a drug, he worried he was the actual target and Maya somehow got in the way.

This fear tore him in half. On the brink of intimacy, he considered distancing himself to protect her. And although he tried hard to avoid the association, he knew that Jim Barrow was present all afternoon and spent considerable time staffing cases with Maya.

Maya called Alex halfway through the day. She asked him for a list of her symptoms, her own memory unreliable.

"Every little thing you can remember," she insisted. "It's pretty hazy to me. I'm sending it to our toxicologist."

She sounded better, still improving.

Then midafternoon a clinic receptionist suddenly succumbed, vomiting and flushed. Probably the same virus, Alex thought with relief. Then he felt bad to be pleased that someone was ill. You're all twisted up, he told himself. Good things are bad and bad things are good.

Jim Barrow appeared in the attending office.

"I heard Dr. Summer got really sick," he said with concern.

"How do you know that?" Alex sounded sharper than he'd meant.

Jim's eyes narrowed. "Because you were asking around all morning if anyone else had stomach symptoms."

"Oh. Right." Alex told himself to pay attention. He needed some sleep.

Jim pursed his lips, then went on. "I'm seeing Gloria Gonzalez, that older patient of Dr. Summer's with the urinary tract infection. She's not any better, a little dehydrated. I recommended that we admit her to the hospital for some fluids and IV antibiotics. But she won't go."

"Do you know why?"

"I asked her. She's pretty neurotic about it." Jim's brow wrinkled. "She said she doesn't like being closed up in those rooms. Makes me think she's claustrophobic, you know?"

"Interesting." Decisions in medicine never came as straightforward as they ought, Alex knew. "That adds a difficult angle."

"Will you see if you can talk her into it?"

Alex tried, but Ms. Gonzalez remained adamant. She smiled and agreed with everything Alex said, and then declined his advice. Alex wished for Maya to be there, suspecting she might be the only person who could convince her. As it was, he helped Jim construct a list of precautions for the patient, including when to call for help. They always had a doctor on call over the weekend, and she should phone for anything. Finally, Alex asked Jim to notify Maya.

"Will do," Jim said.

"I'll get her number for you." Alex looked for any hint that Jim acted off, but he seemed just as he should, engaged and concerned.

"She already gave it to me."

Of course she did, Alex thought. Jim returned, saying Maya planned to call the patient herself and convince her.

Of course she will, Alex thought. He kept trying not to admire her, and kept failing. He saw Jim's coffee mug on the desk and remembered that Maya meant to take it to her lab, before she got sick and everything derailed. Since he would certainly fall asleep if he attended the lunch lecture, he decided to drive to her office instead and drop it off there. It would be waiting for her Monday morning. His good deed for the day, to make up for snapping at Jim.

JOURNAL

I found a dead jackrabbit along the trail when I went hiking at South Mountain.

Some friends said they'd meet me there and hike with me, but one cancelled at the last minute and the other just didn't show up. I call them friends, but they're not.

I was glad, because I prefer walking alone. I don't know why I asked them in the first place—it was a mistake.

Once when I was young I had a pet rabbit. My mother said it would teach me responsibility. It had ears soft as silk and big black eyes, blank as buttons. Depending on what you feed it, a rabbit doesn't last very long.

The jackrabbit at South Mountain was torn almost in half. Maybe a coyote, or maybe an owl dropped it. The eyes were hollow and black and the ears were chewed off. I saw maggots squirming in the belly. I'm going back again to see how much it's changed.

50

By Saturday morning Maya had recovered. She sat under the mesquite tree with Rafael and Mel, watching Mel's trainer work with Manchado.

Brad Farley looked like a youthful version of Mel, lanky legs in denim, creased and cracked cowboy boots the color of dirt, a plaid cotton shirt. He wore a sweat-rotted buff-brown Stetson, his young skin already toughened by sun. Brad's steady voice fixed the horse's attention as he rubbed a saddle blanket over his haunches, his back, his neck. Manchado stood alert and skeptical but willing, so far, to tolerate the stranger.

Rafael observed intently, sitting on the low stone wall. He reached down now and then to stroke Twinkie's head, who stood by his foot. Sometimes Rafael's lips moved silently, as if talking to the horse. Sometimes his fingers twitched, as if touching the horse himself. Mel regarded Rafael, then glanced over at Maya.

"Looks like someone wants to do this himself," Mel said. Rafael never heard him, too focused on the scene.

Brad finished up and came over. "He's a good horse…he's got a good mind. But he's suspicious."

"When will you ride him?" Maya asked.

"After one more session. We'll saddle him up next time. You can tell he knows most of this—he's just not sure it's a great idea." Brad wiped his face and Maya handed him a glass of cold water.

After Brad left, Rafael drifted to the corral, sat on the rail in the shade. Manchado came to him, rested his head on his knee.

"Hm." Mel squinted at them, then turned to Maya. "You okay now?"

"Good as new. Dumb virus."

"You've never called in sick before." He sounded almost reproachful.

Maya shrugged. Physically she was good. But the possibility of being drugged gnawed at her, especially if Alex had been the target. The investigators still looked for a disgruntled patient, someone off in the head. But other workers developed similar symptoms, Alex told her. Her thoughts ran back and forth like mice, hunting for crumbs.

Mel considered her. "How's your cardiology boyfriend?"

Maya tried to look neutral and well-adjusted. "Gone."

"Ha. You finally got rid of him? For good?"

"Don't look so happy," she complained, irritated. "It was traumatic."

"Sorry to be insensitive." Mel clapped her back, not seeming at all sorry.

"Right." Maya made a face at him.

Mel grinned, then shifted his eyes to Rafael, who now copied Brad's pattern with his hands, running them over Manchado's neck and back and hindquarters. The horse stood with his eyes closed.

"I have a feeling there's a good man out there. Someone who's right for you." Mel still watched Rafael. "That boy's going to sit on that horse soon. When we're not looking."

"No," Maya protested. "He knows he's not supposed to do that."

Mel looked sour. "Guess you were never a young boy, were you?"

Maya doubted Rafael would defy them and changed the subject. "Did you happen to talk with Sheila yesterday? I hope it wasn't too much trouble to fix the schedule without me."

"Sheila's a wizard. There's not much that woman can't do." He sounded downright proud of her.

Maya smiled and wondered just how fond of Sheila Mel was becoming.

After they left, Maya found herself at loose ends. A good man, Mel said. She could hardly admit she already teetered on the brink with someone new, so close on the heels of Whit. Did that make her needy? Or smart? Maybe she finally saw what she wanted. Maybe she was impulsive and foolish. Besides, Alex had turned cautious. When they talked last night, he confessed he feared for her, felt responsible. When she offered to see him tonight, he said she should rest and recover.

"I'm fine," she assured him.

"You always say you're fine, even if you're not."

Maya didn't press it but felt let down. Then she recalled everything Alex had done for her lately: driving to Tucson, the night after the bikers, her illness, and wondered why he hadn't run away from her. Maybe he should.

The bikers stayed away. No more motorcycles at midnight, and nothing moved in her yard.

Alex was right. Take it slow, ease into this.

I'm not going to lie down and let trouble walk over me. The quote came out of nowhere, from Ellen Glasgow, a little-known novelist of the early twentieth century. Hey, Maya thought, at least her literary memories were getting closer to the present—no ancient Romans this time.

Listen to Glasgow. Do something, don't wallow.

Maya decided to paint her bathroom. But after she gathered her supplies and masked off the fixtures and baseboards, covered the floor and draped the sink, she felt weary. Perhaps she was not quite recovered. Now early evening, she helped Rafael feed Manchado and chopped some veggies for Twinkie, watching the sun go down in neon flames. She scanned for promising storms but the sky held nothing, clear and empty. The monsoon had paused.

Maya decided to get some reading done. She would finish the bathroom tomorrow.

Maybe she should call Alex.

51

Saturday at dusk, Alex took his bike out. It was a stupid time to cycle, the air still baking, but at least the sun stood low in the melting sky, almost down, and he simply had to do something. Just a short ride, mostly to check on the repairs and make certain everything worked right. He doused himself with the garden hose, slapped on his helmet, and took off dripping down the street. The asphalt made a hot sticky sound under his tires.

He accomplished some of his best thinking while he biked. And he really needed to think.

Maya clearly wanted to see him tonight. But he put her off, afraid. Though better, she was not quite herself. The ways he wanted to touch her, the things he wanted to do with her, required her full alert assent. His thoughts no longer fixed on her scars but her soft bareness, the swell of her in that silky bra, the curve and slope of her thighs, bisected by that slip of satin. He nearly ran through an intersection without looking.

Focus, man—this is not the thinking you need to do. The bike felt great, smooth and oiled, gliding sweetly through the gears. Shadows lengthened, striping the road, and he finally turned around, for his bike had no light and he should get home before dark. His shirt was nearly dry now anyway, and he would start to overheat. Time to be done.

Yesterday at lunch, Friday, Alex took the twelve minute drive to Arizona Public Health with Barrow's coffee mug. The security guard handed him a temporary badge and showed him to an office where an older woman and man stood talking.

"Now, how do you know Dr. Summer?" The woman took the mug, studied it dubiously. Late sixties, he guessed, she had a lively face and short brass-gold hair, except for one strand that curled around her ear, dyed green. The man straightened, craggy, wearing jeans and a blazer, cowboy boots. His eyebrows a jumble of gray and white, a lancing gaze.

"I work with her at the residency," Alex explained, as they all introduced themselves. "I was there yesterday when she got sick—I took her home."

"I don't think she's ever called in sick," the man said abruptly. Dr. Melvin Black.

"She's better now." Alex oddly felt a need to measure up, as if meeting Maya's parents. It seemed he shouldn't mention spending the night, like that was somehow inappropriate. "She was quite ill, though. Probably a stomach bug. She wanted to come to work today but I told her she couldn't."

"Good for you," Mel said shortly, still scanning him with a chary eye.

Alex had asked Sheila to leave the mug for Maya on Monday and left quickly, although he caught himself smiling as he exited the building.

Now here it was Saturday night, and Alex wanted to kick himself for being overly cautious. You're always your own worst enemy, he thought. He could be out with Maya right now. Over and over he thought about calling her, but hated giving such mixed signals. The earliest he dared call her should be tomorrow, Sunday afternoon. A civilized hour.

Alex showered and flopped down with a book. Unable to concentrate, he turned the television on, then off again. He wandered into his study and stared at the chess trophies, the scrapbook. He felt good about how he'd reinvented himself, but had no idea if he was right for Maya.

He tried to imagine what she must be doing tonight. Maybe just sleeping. Maybe visiting her neighbors. Maybe out by the corral, stroking that strange and striking horse.

Alex longed to be that strange and striking horse.

52

Her cheeping phone woke her. Nearly ten o'clock at night, she had dozed off and on, a medical journal in her lap. Maya recognized the hospital prefix and answered quickly.

"Dr. Summer? This is Burt Rogers. I'm one of the family medicine interns working in the ICU this month, and we just admitted your patient. Gloria Gonzalez. Do you remember her?"

"Of course. Is she okay?" What a stupid question, because obviously she wasn't. Wake up.

"Not really…there's a lot going on. I guess Barrow saw her yesterday in his clinic. He thought she was dehydrated and wanted to admit her then, but she refused."

"I know," Maya said. "I talked with Jim, then I called her. I couldn't convince her either." Maya worried she should have been more forceful, but truthfully she'd been very blunt. "I told her how dangerous this was. I told her she could die."

"She told me you said that." He gave a short laugh.

Maya met Burt at the picnic in July, a large gentle young man who planned to practice medicine in his rural hometown near the White Mountains. He caught her up on Gonzalez's story.

That morning, Gloria felt weaker. Her heart skipped and skittered, and she knew she should call the doctor. But on her way to the phone, pain slammed through her chest and she went down, landing on her hip—on the good leg not affected by her stroke. She heard the crack, like an old tree limb. Lying on the floor, stunned with agony and unable to rise, she called out for hours until a neighbor girl happened to walk by the window and heard her.

"She asked me to notify you," Burt finished. "So that's it. Possible sepsis from the urinary infection. A hip fracture and a heart attack. And her cardiac rhythm is deteriorating. Right now she's in atrial fib, with big pauses. Probably needs a pacemaker."

Maya's breath caught at the devastating diagnoses. At Gloria's age, a hip fracture alone often marked the beginning of the end. Add the cardiac problems, and her marginal prognosis took a nosedive.

"She's tough as nails," Maya said. "I'm going to come see her, okay? Have you consulted cardiology yet?"

"I'm just writing the order. Have to see who's on call."

They disconnected and Maya changed clothes. Gloria had no family left, and Maya knew her medical history better than anyone. It's not like Maya had other things to do tonight, except worry about Alex and think about work. Maybe she could help Burt and distract herself at the same time. While Maya no longer managed the care of hospitalized patients, especially not in the ICU, she nevertheless kept courtesy privileges, precisely for times like this. She could talk with the patient, write notes in the chart, and contribute to the team's decisions.

Halfway to the hospital, Maya's phone rang again, another call from Burt. Even though it was after ten-thirty, the night hung heavy with heat. The cooled air streaming inside her car tasted dusty and alkaline.

"Dr. Summer. Um. Sorry. I talked with the cardiologist—he'll be here in about an hour. But he said I should check with you to see if you wanted to consult someone else." Burt sounded uncomfortable.

Maya's stomach sank. Millions of people lived in Phoenix, and hospital rosters carried dozens of cardiologists. What were the odds? It felt like poor form not to use the physician on call, especially since she had no real authority in the hospital.

"Of course it's okay," she said brightly, too brightly. "Who is it?"

"Dr. Thicket. You know him, right?"

Inevitable. "Yes. I do."

53

Maya walked into the unit, relieved that Whit had not arrived. She harbored a tiny hope that he might be delayed and maybe she could leave before he got there.

Burt Rogers greeted her warmly. He had a large soft body and big soft fingers that felt like friendly bear paws when he shook her hand.

"She's not doing well," he warned, inclining his head toward the monitors.

The wiggling line of Gloria Gonzalez's heart rhythm hopped and hesitated, rushed then rested. For a moment they both held their breaths when the beat stopped altogether, a long flat stretch, then it resumed in a flurry of quick steps as if making up for the gap.

"Not so good," Maya agreed.

She listened to the erratic chorus of bleeping monitors, marking minutes relentlessly, more ominous than a clock. Each tick of the heart, another step toward the end of a rough road. It sounded like a ragged choir, a crooked peeping tune, like a disjointed, high-pitched Gregorian chant of the body. She shook herself out of that reverie and went to see her patient.

"How are you feeling?" Maya asked quietly, not certain if Gloria was awake. She lay sunk in the bed, deep in a pillow. A braid trailed down one shoulder, her usual gray bun undone. Then her papery eyelids flew open and she looked silently at Maya.

"Any chest pain now?" Maya asked.

A slight shake of her head.

"Any trouble breathing?" Maya took her limp hand.

Another small shake. The dark eyes watched her.

"Is anything bothering you?"

A barely visible motion, negative, as the woman took a deep breath. Reacting slowly because of the morphine, Maya thought.

"Nothing like that," Gloria said softly.

Maya's eyebrows rose, a question.

"My heart hurts, *mi querida*, but not your kind of pain." A smile touched her withered lips, her mouth caved in without her dentures.

"You know—my soul, my spirit—whatever is in there." Her eyes closed for a long moment then fluttered open, up and down a few times like faulty shutters. "I don't want to be here. I can't do this…I'll never walk again. I should have stayed home and died."

"I don't think your neighbors could leave you lying there on the floor till you starved to death."

"They could have dragged me to my bed and let me starve to death there."

"Right." Maya studied her fondly. "I have to ask you something, although I think you just told me." Maya squeezed her hand, a thin cage of bones and blue veins. "Just in case something happens. So far you're hanging in there, but you did have a heart attack. And your heartbeat is pretty unsteady. And you're not as young as you used to be."

"I'm old. Really old."

"Well, yes. You are. So." Maya stroked her hand. "If something bad happens, like if your heart stops, or if you stop breathing, we need to know what you want us to do. I'm not saying it will, because knowing you, you'll get through this and live another ten or twenty years. I know we've talked about this before, but I need to be sure. I need to know if you want us to resuscitate you or not."

Gloria shifted. "What would you do to me?"

"Try to get your heart going again. Thump on your chest. Give your heart an electric shock. Puff air into your lungs. A breathing machine."

Gloria's eyes closed. "No, I don't want any of that. But thank you for offering." As if she were declining dessert.

"Okay. I'll make sure everyone knows. And there's a cardiologist coming to look at your funny heart beats."

Her eyes closed again.

Maya returned to the nursing station and sat down. A nurse she knew, Susan, handed her a cup of coffee.

"Haven't seen you in a while," Susan remarked. About fifty, Susan had pale eyebrows and sun-beaten skin. Endlessly efficient like every good ICU nurse, she always looked harried. "Sorry about your patient. She's a sweetie."

"Thanks." Maya took a sip and choked. "Jeez, Susan. How can you drink this stuff? It's like oil sludge. No, like toxic waste."

"It's too strong?"

"Toxic," Maya repeated, rinsing her mouth with cold water from the tap.

"I can make another pot," Susan offered, amused, her wrinkles deepening. "It's the only way I can stay up all night."

"Don't bother. I got enough caffeine from one sip to last for hours."

Burt Rogers chuckled, listening to them. "It keeps me awake just smelling the coffee fumes."

Maya told him that Gloria requested no resuscitation, and he entered the order.

Whit breezed through the door—he blew in like the wind before a storm, fresh and potent. He looked good, that dark hair, that sharp narrow face. She could smell his aftershave across the room. In concession to the hour, he wore a polo instead of his usual shirt and tie, his white coat crisp with starch.

"Maya." He seemed entirely too thrilled. "I'm glad you asked for me."

"Hi, Whit." Maya acted carefully offhand. It didn't happen like that, she wanted to say. He just chanced to be on call—she never asked for him, but there was no way to clarify that, not with others around. "We need your help with one of my favorite old patients."

"Absolutely. Tell me about her." He pulled up a wheeled stool, a little too close, and leaned toward the monitors. But his eyes never quit roaming, slipping subtly across her as if checking for changes.

Maya's nose twitched, overfilled with his musk fragrance. *Spill your aftershave on your head?* she felt like asking.

"A heart attack and a broken hip," she said simply.

"Broken hearts are my *specialty*," he returned, emphasizing the last word and smiling at her.

"A broken hip," Maya corrected, then glanced around. "Burt? Can you tell Dr. Thicket about Ms. Gonzalez?"

"You bet," Burt rumbled. He gave an adept summary, presenting well for a new intern. Maya made a mental note to tell him so later. Whit nodded, shifting into his resolute work mode, completely engaged in the history as he analyzed the monitor.

"Looks like a pacemaker, right?" Whit announced, rubbing his hands in anticipation.

"That's what we thought," Maya nodded. "Want me to introduce you?"

"No, just relax a few minutes. I'll go check out her ticker and tell her all about pacers. I'll be right back." He nodded and looked at her face a little too long, then went into the room.

Not surprising. Whit liked to work alone: introduce himself, set up his controlled rapport, deliver his solemn advice. He liked to make a production, calling the shots.

Whit returned, frowning. "You didn't tell me she didn't want a pacemaker."

Maya straightened, defensive. "I didn't know that."

"But you knew she was a DNR."

"Well, sure. But there's a big difference between a pacemaker and Do Not Resuscitate." Maya spoke slowly. "You get a pacemaker before you die, to keep you alive. You only get resuscitated after you die."

Whit tried to control his frustration, compressed his lips. "Why is she DNR?"

"Whit. She's ninety. She's old, not stupid." Maya stared at him. They all knew it. With advanced age, the chance of recovery after resuscitation was nearly zero. But she saw his nostrils flare, his eyes hard like marbles, and tried to soften it. "Don't take it personally."

He stared back.

"I do," he finally admitted. "When I can't talk a patient into letting me help them, when I know what a difference I can make, then I do take it personally. I've failed them. I can't help feeling that way, not when it's true."

"She's very strong-willed," Maya said, trying to ameliorate. "You're not failing her if she knows what she wants."

Whit regarded her acidly. "Do any of us really know what we want? What's really best for us in the big picture?"

That moment could have lasted a long time, neither willing to take the next step, speak the next word that would plunge them toward peace or war. Maya thought of it like a meteor hurtling toward Earth, one that might be deflected if someone knew how.

"See if you can talk her into it," Whit ordered. His face shone righteous, a general sending a good soldier into battle.

Maya felt her spine stiffen, as if it had its own reaction. "If she says she doesn't want it, then she doesn't want it."

"I don't think she understands. That this is her very life. I mean, look at that strip." He jabbed his finger at the tracing, where Gloria's line flipped and bobbed, pausing worse than before.

Maya saw she must break this momentum. "I'll go talk to her again."

The room was dim. Gloria's eyes sank deeply into her skull, nearly lost in the cobwebbed wrinkles, but they glistened at Maya as she stepped around the bed.

"Send him away," she whispered. "Send them all away."

Maya took her hand, a faint play of bones, the skin chilled.

"We can make your heart work better," Maya offered. "You don't need to die from this."

Gloria's head wagged slowly back and forth.

"I can't live like this." She seemed to understand Maya's need to be certain, returning her clasp suddenly so hard that Maya startled. "I'm ready, *mi doctorita*. It's out of our hands now."

Maya left, felt a sensation like a heavy watermelon inside her.

Whit abruptly stopped pacing, turned toward her. "Well?"

"She doesn't want it." Maya folded her arms across her chest and tried to squeeze down her watermelon heart, to give herself room to breathe.

"Are you sure she understands?" Whit too close again, making tight gestures with his hands. "Is there any family I can talk to, anyone else who could make the decision?"

"She's fully competent, Whit." Maya turned toward Burt to discuss the next orders. Burt sat at the computer, watching them with wide eyes.

"No, she's clearly not, because she'll die if we don't. That's being suicidal." His voice urgent, his eyes hot and quick. "We can make the decision ourselves—medical necessity."

"She doesn't want it," Maya snapped. "She understands everything perfectly well, and she doesn't want it."

Susan and another nurse talking by the desk turned to stare, then glanced away awkwardly when Whit glared at them.

"You don't have to shout." His teeth clenched.

"I do when you act like this," Maya replied, quiet now. He really believed in what he said. Maya touched his arm. "This is hard for us doctors, isn't it?"

Whit jerked his arm away. Maya sensed another stir by the nurses, saw Burt shift in his chair.

She felt bad for Susan and Burt, wanted to defuse this quickly. She could take the fault…it cost her nothing. "Whit. I'm so sorry we dragged you down here. I should have asked her more carefully beforehand."

He took her forearms, gripped tightly.

"This is wrong," he pronounced, now loud himself. His cheeks red, eyes too bright.

Maya leaned back, but he gripped tighter. The two nurses stared blatantly now, and Burt stood up. His bulk felt reassuring.

"Whit. You're hurting me." The words dropped from her lips like stones.

His face switched from red to ashen and he let go, backed up a step, and pointed at the monitor, stabbed it with his finger. Maya recoiled slightly, knowing he wanted to be stabbing at her instead. This wasn't only about the patient…it was about her, that she dared to reject him.

"It's wrong," he exclaimed. Then he wheeled and stalked out.

54

When Whit departed the ICU, everyone stood in uneasy silence. His anger left a vacuum, as if no one could quite breathe. The monitors peeped and sang, filling the space, sounding too cheerful.

Maya blew out a breath from deep in her chest, found a little more room inside.

"I'm really sorry about that," she murmured.

"Hey," said Susan, taking a sip of coffee.

"No problem," said the other nurse, lifting one shoulder.

Burt Rogers regarded her soberly, still standing nearby. "Everything good?"

Maya nodded and pointed at the keyboard he'd abandoned. She felt strangely matter-of-fact. "I'm good, Burt. Can you enter the orders to transfer her off the unit?"

"Of course." He sat down heavily, and she watched over his shoulder as he typed.

Discontinue cardiac monitor.

Transfer from ICU to regular medical bed.

Do not resuscitate.

"Thank you," Maya said. "And I wanted to say what a good job you did with that presentation. Very thorough, very organized."

A smile stretched across his wide face. "Thanks, Dr. Summer. I really appreciate that. I don't always get much feedback."

Maya returned to Gloria. She looked smaller, lighter, barely denting the pillow and hardly raising the sheet. But her eyes opened, dark with pain and morphine, at the small noise of Maya moving.

"Shall I stay?" Maya touched her cold hand.

"No, *mi querida*. Come tomorrow. If I'm still here." A tiny squeeze of her fingers.

"All right. Sleep well." Maya kissed her withered cheek and left.

Midnight had come and gone. Maya drove with the windows down, heat running through the car, a turbulent flow of stifling air, batting her hair and plucking at her shirt. Her head impossibly empty and overfull at once. She wanted to drive all night, slip out onto the highway and head north, swoop through the steep dry hills and crooked canyons toward Flagstaff. Find a few shreds of cooler air up there in the pines. But no— she was bound to the desert. For now.

Her phone rang as she reached home.

"She just died," Susan announced softly. "She was very peaceful."

"Thanks. Thanks for helping her. For helping me. Sorry it got so weird and ugly."

"No worries. We've seen worse. At least he didn't throw anything." Susan paused, and Maya could hear her smile. "And I'm not sure why, but nothing's ever really bad when Dr. Rogers is here."

Maya thanked her again.

She didn't go in. She sat out back and thought about Gloria Gonzalez. A long life. She had outlived her two children, both dead in their sixties. Maya wondered who would clean out her home, all those romance novels she treasured, that dragonhead cane. Things special to her. Maybe it didn't pay to know so much about your patients; you worried about odd things you could do nothing about. She thought of Burt Rogers and knew he would have those relationships with his patients. She felt good about a new generation of family docs who cared, coming along behind her.

A mosquito whined at her ear but she ignored it. *West Nile?* she thought recklessly, *bring it on.* Her mosquito report to the CDC was nearly due… she should have worked on Friday, finished that up. Damn overprotective Alex.

A coyote keened, a long quaver, then silence.

Maya stared into the night and thought about the desert surrounding her, holding its secrets, teeming with other levels of life. She thought about all the microscopic parasites and bacteria and fungi, living off larger creatures and plants—a rudimentary, unthinking survival. All the insects, the ants and spiders and termites and beetles, living their tiny realities in their tiny ecosystems, hatching and birthing and dying, utterly unaware of humans. How the nocturnal desert crawled with scorpions and snakes and mice and packrats. Coyotes loping through the darkness seeking prey, and great horned owls coasting silently, guided by their sharp hearing and huge yellow eyes. A world not designed for people. Humans lived on the fringe, supplied with their piped-in water, cowering under their coolers, waiting for relief. For change.

Maya waiting. Alex waiting. Waiting too long.

Rafael slipped into the yard. Manchado ready, alert, stretching his neck over the rails. They communed for a moment, the horse pressing his head against Rafael's chest. Then the boy climbed the fence and eased onto Manchado's back, fluid and soft. He leaned down with his face in the tousled mane, caressed the muscular neck. Rafael straightened then, fingers laced in mane, and the horse trotted off, tossed his head with glee and broke into a canter. They floated around and around the corral, the boy's small lithe body melting into the rhythm of the gait. Finally the horse slowed, and Rafael released the mane and laughed.

It was the most joyous thing Maya had ever seen.

For a long time Rafael lay back on Manchado, his legs still astride but with his head pillowed on the black-and-white rump, gazing at the moonless sky as the east lightened and dawn encroached. Manchado stood motionless. Then the boy yawned and slid off, gave a last stroke on the horse's shoulder, and stole back home.

Enough waiting.

Maya went inside and washed her face and arms, as if cleansing herself of the hospital and Whit and the complicated, peculiar life of medicine. It felt like a ritual. She changed into her favorite cotton pants and soft T-shirt.

By the time she climbed in her car, gray dawn stained the sky. By the time she reached Alex's house, the heavens shone peach and cream, those sweet hues before the heat soared and blasted the color from the sky.

She knocked twice before he opened the door, wiping his eyes. He wore drawstring shorts, his chest bare. His light brown hair mussed, half masking his eyes, not wearing his glasses.

"Um. Maya." He rubbed his eyes again, stared at her through the screen. "Did I forget something? Why are you here?"

"Alex. Do you think I can I come in? Or do you want to keep talking through this door? It's getting sort of warm out here."

He laughed and flipped the lock. "Are you at all aware of the time?"

Maya tilted her head to glance at the sky. "What is it? Four-thirty? Five?"

He peered at her. "Don't tell me you've been up all night. Not again."

"Maybe…" She shut the door and led him to his kitchen, realizing she should have drunk more fluids through the long night. "Do you have something cold to drink?"

"Is your life always like this? What is it with you and sleep?"

"It's kind of a long story. I was seeing someone in the hospital." Maya shook her head. The last person she wanted to think about was Whit, and it was impossible to relate that story without Whit inside it. "I'll tell you about it later."

"Really? It sounds kind of important."

"It is." Maya looked at him earnestly. "It's sort of why I'm here. Actually, there's a lot of reasons why I'm here."

Alex pulled a pitcher of water from the refrigerator. Puzzled but bemused, he poured her a glass, sat with her at the table. His face caring, but unsure. Maya smiled and longed to touch his chest, move her hands over him, like Rafael with Manchado, but she didn't want to startle him. Yet. She drank her water, watching him. Alex waited, gazed back. Another trait to admire, Maya thought—he was a remarkably patient man.

She put her hand on his. "Let's not wait till Thursday, all right? I've thought about this all night long. I've wasted far too much time this year. Thrown it away, like such a fool. That has to stop."

Alex blinked. "What do you mean?"

"You and me. I mean, what we're like together. Whether we're right." She wasn't certain what she should say. It had taken her an absurdly long time to recognize, but he might be the best man she knew, generous and thoughtful. Witty and tender.

"I planned to call you today," he admitted. "I almost did last night, but I knew I shouldn't. I don't want to rush things. In case you need more time."

She turned suddenly cautious. "If you're not sure, then we should wait. You should tell me now, before I make an even bigger fool of myself."

"Jesus, Maya. You must know—this is all I've wanted for months."

He stood and scooped her up from the chair, carried her to his bedroom. Maya finally relaxed, limp with relief, as he put her on the bed, kissed her once firmly on the mouth, then fluffed the pillow for her head. Arranged her arms and legs, stood back to inspect her, then rearranged them at slightly different angles. "Are you comfortable? Do you think you can sleep?"

Maya sat up, seized his arm. "No. I can sleep anytime."

"You're too tired." He eased her back down and sat beside her on the bed. His hand lingered on her shoulder, then skimmed her cheek. He toyed with her hair and his fingers brushed her ear. Once, watching her react, then again.

Maya curved into his touch, eyes closed. Her ears were exquisitely sensitive, and he somehow knew that instinctively. She turned her head and kissed his hand, looked into his sincere, hopeful face, reached up and pushed the hair from his eyes.

"Let's face it, Alex. The way things have been going, one of us could be dead by tomorrow." She rolled her eyes. "And I mean that in the least frightening way possible. I just mean that life is short."

"That's not funny," Alex scolded. He lay down alongside her, pulled aside her hair, started kissing her jaw, her neck. Nuzzled her ear. "Not at all."

"I wasn't joking. But if that's too real, then let's just say that maybe one of us could be struck by lightning. If that works better for you. You're missing my point." Her words slowed and her breath quickened as his hand drifted to her other ear. She shivered.

"Are you always so chatty when you haven't slept? Besides, there's been very few storms over the last few days, so not much chance of lightning," he reminded her, murmuring against her temple. His hand gliding down, circling her waist, slipping under her shirt against her skin. His hand warm, solid and sure. "How about being attacked by a rattlesnake? There's lots of them."

"That works," she whispered. "It could be a snake."

"Let's stop talking," he suggested.

He raised up over her and kissed her, slow and eager. Accelerated. Began searching her, moving his fingers to places he had never been before.

Maya dissolved into an overflowing dream of his hands, his mouth, of hot desert nights, of laughing horses. It might be the most right she had ever felt.

55

Alex would never admit how long he spent that morning, lying there watching Maya sleep. Eventually he padded out for a book, then returned to bed, sat reading and glancing at her as if she might disappear. He studied her short straight nose, the dark lashes against her cheeks, noticed that a few freckles sprinkled her shoulders like nutmeg. It took all his willpower not to start touching her again.

She awoke shortly before noon. Maya sat up beside him and placed her cool palm on his chest, her head on his shoulder.

"You hungry?" he asked, putting down his book.

"Mm hm. I need to get going soon, I'm afraid." The sheet fell from her. "Alex? Hello, I'm up here."

He laughed and kissed her there. "You're everywhere."

Maya smiled and tugged up the sheet. "Pay attention. I have to leave because I'm driving up to Cave Creek. To visit my parents in their retirement home. I go on Sunday afternoons."

Alex lay back, thinking what to say because he wanted to go with her. He realized he would like to meet her parents, understand them. Maya mentioned that she had disappointed them, but she was clearly close to them in a way he had never been with his parents. His distant father, his overbearing mother. While Maya's story read like a novel, his mother's disenchantment with him had been written in a different sort of book, a dry manual where the concept of love was difficult to find. You had to use the glossary. Maybe a footnote.

His impulse felt clingy, too much too soon. He said it anyway.

"Shall I go with you?"

Maya stared at him. "You want to meet my parents?"

"You haven't slept much. I don't want to barely get started in this relationship, just to have you drive off the road because you fell asleep. I could take you. Besides, I already kind of feel like I met your parents. Your other parents, at your office."

"You're being overprotective—I'm fine. And what are you talking about, my other parents?"

He recounted his trip on Friday to Arizona Public Health with the coffee mug.

Maya looked surprised but pleased. "You met Sheila and Mel?"

Alex laughed. "If you think I'm overprotective, you should see how they act. It felt like an interrogation."

"They're pretty smart. They could probably see you had devious designs on my body."

Alex waited. Maya pensive. Finally he said, "It's your move."

"You know, not everything is a chess game," she spoke sternly.

"Excuse me? Everything is absolutely a chess game. Or at least, a series of games."

"All right. Yes, sure. Come with me and meet my parents. You weirdo." Amused. "There. So now it's your move."

"Okay." He gently pushed her down, drew off the sheet. Slowly ran his hands across her, felt himself thicken. "The bishop takes the knight. Again."

56

Cryptosporidium hominus, better known as crypto. As summer progressed, the miniscule hard-shelled parasite increasingly plagued public swimming pools and splash parks. Impervious to normal chlorine levels, able to survive ten days in pool water, cryptosporidium caused profuse diarrhea that lasted two weeks. An infected child with a single small "fecal accident" or "leak," expelling less than a teaspoon of anal fluid, released many thousands of the little beasts into the water. A swimmer only need swallow a few dozen invisible organisms to be afflicted. With swimming venues in full swing, scores of cases had been reported and the numbers were rising.

On Monday morning, the health department team came to Maya with two more public pools testing positive for crypto, including WetWorks, a huge water park north of Phoenix that entertained thousands of people daily. As their ad said: *Where you can't get any wetter.* That doesn't even make sense, Maya thought crossly. Well, their patrons were now getting something extra in the water besides wetness.

So much had happened since her last day at work. She just handed Barrow's coffee mug to the lab, and she waited to hear what the toxicologist thought about her stomach symptoms. And her overfilled weekend, Gloria Gonzalez and Whit. Rafael with the horse, which she needed to tell Mel. Her parents. And Alex, so much Alex. Sunday morning, then Sunday night, too. And now they had plans for Tuesday evening.

She still digested that trip to her parents. It unexpectedly became a party, because Alex prompted her to ask Rosa and Rafael as well. They ended up cooking a big meal there and watching a soccer game—everyone had great fun, cheering and feasting. Alex sat comfortably with her parents, gentle with her mom's scattered memory. He asked embarrassing questions about her childhood and teenage years, got everyone laughing. She tried not to draw comparisons with Whit, but couldn't help herself. Did everyone look back at their trashed relationships and wonder what the hell they were thinking?

She had barely read the cryptosporidium report when Mel appeared.

"Who was that guy who came by? Reddish? What kind of a name is that?"

Maya wondered why Mel hadn't asked about Alex on Saturday morning, during Manchado's training session. Maybe because Rafael was there. She recalled Mel saying something like *I have a feeling there's a good man…* and she grasped that was after he met Alex.

"I think it's a British name," she said. "He's one of my friends from the residency clinic."

"Well, keep an eye on him." Mel's voice dropped, conspiratorial. "I think he's interested in being more than your friend."

"Mel. I'm up to my ears in cryptosporidium. I don't have time for that." Maya nearly laughed. Alex was right—Mel did act like a father.

"Ha," Mel chortled. "What can you do with those sinister little crypto parasites? Just tell people in the pool not to swallow the water, right?"

"Right. Like that's easy."

"You going to shut those pools down?"

"That's complicated. But yes. They need to hyper-chlorinate their water for at least a day or two, which means no swimming." That high level of chlorine would scorch skin, singe hair, and burn corneas.

Mel slouched out, only to be immediately replaced by Sheila.

"You've lost weight," Sheila fussed, handing Maya a cup of yogurt with a spoon. "Here, eat this. It'll help restore your healthy gut flora. You look all washed out. Maybe you should have stayed home another day. Did you see your own physician? You've never called in sick before, Maya. Never. And that doctor who came by on Friday? He was super cute in a shy sort of way. How come you never mentioned him? He's obviously crazy about you."

"Whoa, Sheila. Slow down. I'm just here to do my work, you know? Crypto's on the loose."

"Yuck. Creepy crypto, that's what I call it. You'll never catch me in a public swimming place. What did humanity do to deserve that nasty parasite?" Sheila's hands on her hips, still scrutinizing Maya.

Maya dutifully picked up her spoon and opened the yogurt, looked at Sheila with disbelief. "What has humanity done—are you kidding? Where do you want me to start?"

Finally Sheila left, satisfied that Maya would eat her yogurt. But the day did not promise productivity. Maya received two disturbing phone calls, one after the next. First from the toxicologist, who declared her symptoms last Thursday were a likely anticholinergic reaction. Anticholinergic drugs interfered with nerves and muscles in very unpleasant ways, causing dilated pupils, dry skin, flushing, and confusion. Occasionally hallucinations.

Maya squirmed with annoyance that she missed that, but Alex missed it too. The nausea didn't fit and threw them off. This was a big problem in medicine, diving too quickly into a diagnosis. Convinced it must be viral since others were sick, they looked at the symptoms in a way that made sense. This skewed mental process had a label called cognitive bias, something they fought frequently. They constantly must remind themselves to consider other diagnoses.

Possibly Maya didn't have fever after all, but dilated veins, causing the red flush. Or overheating caused by impaired perspiration, rather than an infectious fever.

"So," the tox physician said carefully. "This is *you* we're talking about, right? Not an outside patient."

"Yes." Maya understood his hesitancy.

"Well. Lots of meds can cause this, of course. Most common would be either strong antihistamines, like Benadryl, or older antidepressants like tricyclics. Have you taken either of those?"

"No…" Her mind wheeled, trying to imagine.

"And of course, there's datura. Jimsonweed." He sounded even more careful, cautiously neutral. "Been grazing on any plants lately?"

Maya fell silent. *Datura stramonium.* A common poisonous desert plant with white bell-shaped flowers, used for centuries in Native American ceremonies. Probably used for millennia. All parts of the plant carried the toxin; high doses were fatal. But how could that be possible? Reluctantly, she recalled that Jim Barrow was there all day.

Alex and oleander. Now maybe herself and datura—she felt trapped in an invisible noxious jungle. Then she remembered the bike accident, entirely different, and felt like they were all completely off base. Nothing made sense.

"I just don't see how any of this could happen," Maya said.

"Maybe I'm wrong." He spoke briskly, in a way that clearly meant he wasn't wrong. "And there must have been something else, too, because that degree of vomiting doesn't quite match."

Impossible, she thought. As a toxicologist, maybe he made mistakes too, thinking everything was a poison. Even as she entertained that notion, though, she knew better.

Maya tried to refocus, concentrate on cryptosporidium. She organized the team that would intervene with the swimming pools, spoke with those who would interview the victims. Made certain that signs got posted at every pool and waterpark, warning guests never to swim if they had diarrhea, even if recently resolved. An infected person could still shed parasites for two weeks after their diarrhea stopped. For every person diagnosed with cryptosporidiosis, there were probably fifty more undiscovered mild cases, those who never saw their doctor but remained contagious.

Then came the second phone call, this time from the lab, about Jim Barrow's abnormal coffee residue. The dry scum contained a high level of benzodiazepine. Valium or one of its cousins, for which he'd tested positive before he took his leave. The drug he denied using.

Events of the last few months tumbled into Maya's head. The nurse with the car accident after the party, the fatigue that swamped her and Alex and others who drank the punch. If Jim wanted to take a benzo for anxiety, he wouldn't dissolve it in his coffee. He would just take the pill.

Maya abandoned cryptosporidium. She sat at her desk, her thoughts grinding and screeching. She reached for her phone and saw her fingers tremble. She hardly knew where to begin.

Needless to say, she called Alex first.

57

After Maya's reports, things moved quickly and Stewart Burns redoubled surveillance. All clinic employees and physicians were interrogated, again. Water samples got analyzed, and they called in plumbers to check the waterlines. Security and police reviewed fingerprint files once more, and food catering came to an abrupt halt, except for the vending machines and the cellophane-wrapped snacks in the breakroom.

Burns instructed everyone to bring their own lunches, never to share, and he installed a bank of small lockers for their food. He insisted that no one leave a beverage unsupervised—if Burns found a drink with no one near, he promptly threw it out. No one dared complain.

They investigated the "frequent flyers," patients who came to the clinic often because of chronic physical or mental health conditions. They investigated everyone who had lodged a complaint over the last year. Most grievances came from patients who wanted antibiotics for viral cold symptoms or those who sought excessive opioids.

Two complaints originated from patients hospitalized last spring; those worried Alex the most. Maurice Banks lost his wife to lung cancer, a grim heart-wrenching death. Banks railed against the oncologist and Alex and the inpatient team for not saving her, after railing against the doctors in the clinic who failed to make her quit smoking. Alex grasped his angst and tried to talk with him but made little headway against the flood of bitterness. A small angry man with long brown teeth and a face of pure misery, Banks yelled at Alex and told him to watch his back.

The other case, June Hatter, had to have her left foot amputated when surgeons couldn't stop the rampant gangrene from a diabetic ulcer. Because the family medicine team continued caring for her and her weak kidneys long after the surgeon signed off, they became the target of Hatter's fury. Her posts on Twitter turned so vile and threatening, so profane and cruelly specific, that Stewart Burns obtained a restraining order.

That was back in April. Although neither of these patients had set foot in the clinic for months, they were scrutinized now. Any link between them and Alex's two incidents, or Barrow's coffee, remained confusing at best.

Everything felt convoluted. Alex swayed, emotionally off balance, fearful one minute about the attacks, secretly thrilled about Maya the next. The scale tipped back and forth, a dizzy sensation. Maybe it would all disappear under this intense intervention. Maybe the person would move on.

He began planning an escape with Maya. He wanted to leave town, drive to northern Arizona or maybe Colorado, flee the heat and apprehension. Find a cabin on a creek, deep in the woods, hide out. When he mentioned it to her, she lit up with delight. *Perfect*, she said. Alex floated on clouds. He took his time when they were together. He loved experimenting, inventing something new that surprised her. How to position her hip when it bothered her. He barely noticed the scars now. They were part of her landscape, arroyos left by storms.

A new phenomenon surfaced. Alex would be working at his computer, or listening to a lecture, or reading a journal—and found himself smiling. Without thinking about anything. This had never happened before.

Journal

The easiest way is putting it in drinks. No one pays attention.

Then I watch people change, start slipping away. They're all so vain and think they know everything, think they have their lives under control. They don't realize I'm controlling them.

Not one of them is worthy. I can tell Dr. Reddish wants me to be someone else, someone I'm not. I don't think Dr. Summer likes me, but she hides it well. Dr. Burns is an ignorant, angry man, and Dr. Sherman only thinks about one thing.

Their eyes go empty, they stumble. They say stupid things. I love it.

There are other ways, too, that I'm figuring out. Endless possibilities.

I get excited just thinking about it.

58

If it weren't for Alex, Maya might have begged off going to the residency that Thursday. But she could not abandon him—and besides, she had patients scheduled, so canceling would be rude and distressing to them. She simply had to be vigilant. Deal with it, she told herself sternly. She channeled the old writers and vowed not to lie down and let trouble walk over her.

She also wanted to talk with Jim Barrow.

"It's so unnerving," he admitted. He had gained a few pounds and appeared less gangly. "I mean, this may have gone on for months."

His eyes closed and a spasm crossed his face. Maya felt terrible for him.

"Can you imagine?" he asked. "Someone putting those drugs in my coffee? No wonder I felt awful, couldn't think straight." He looked at her apologetically. "Yeah, I guess you can imagine. Since it maybe happened to you."

Maya shook her head. "Just once, though, and we're still not sure. Other people got sick, too. There was an infectious pattern."

"Why? Why is this happening? I almost lost my job, my career. I thought I was going insane."

Maya smiled. "So I guess that's the bright side, right? You're not going insane."

Jim laughed and rolled his eyes. "Thanks, Dr. Summer. That makes me feel better, believe it or not." He paused. "I know you always rooted for me. I could tell. You, and Dr. Reddish, too, even though he had his doubts. But who wouldn't?"

Maya gave him a hug. She knew Alex remained cautious with Jim, but he seemed a victim more than anyone.

The clinic teemed. How could anyone figure this out? So many individuals, coming and going. Patients, families, residents, faculty, nurses, assistants, receptionists, social workers. People delivering supplies, lab workers picking up samples, laundry services bringing towels and gowns, removing the soiled ones. Now that Maya paid attention, she saw the impressive flow of human traffic. Mail delivery, couriers, a resident from surgery evaluating a patient, two medical students, two nursing students.

Someone from tech support working on computers, a janitor replacing lightbulbs. Two scribes, helping write notes. Far over a hundred people every day, often over two hundred.

She and Alex talked episodically throughout the afternoon. About Jim, about cryptosporidium, about maladjusted humans. Sometimes, when the attending office emptied out, they traded a secret smile. Maya loved his idea for escaping up north—maybe next week.

At three o'clock she grew hungry and went to the lounge.

"Bring me something," Alex called after her as he staffed a case.

Maya shuffled through the pastry drawer, a jumble of muffins. Poppy seed, blueberry, chocolate chip. She picked up one and reached for another when the cellophane on the first muffin unexpectedly split open. She put it aside and selected another, which then split as well.

She chose a third muffin gingerly, rotated it, inspecting the wrapper. It seemed fine. You're just paranoid, she scolded herself. She selected one more, handled it gently—and she saw it. A small hole in the cellophane, a little round puncture. She lightly turned another muffin until she found the same thing. Then three more wrappers without it, as far as she could tell.

Her brain halted, then flew ahead at breakneck speed.

Maya slammed the drawer shut and hurried to the attending office where she grabbed her large bag and headed back to the lounge.

"Hey," she heard Alex saying, "where's my muffin?"

"In a minute," she called, hustling down the hallway. Fortunately the lounge remained empty, so she needn't explain why she was dumping a dozen muffins into her bag.

Maya leaned against the counter. Her face felt hot, she had broken into a sweat, and she could only imagine her wild expression. The door clicked open and Veronica entered.

Veronica gave her a peculiar look. "Hi, Dr. Summer."

"Hi, V," Maya breathed, commanding her features to relax. "I haven't seen you all day."

"I was working on my admin stuff," she said briefly. Veronica rarely made small talk. Although she snagged her hair up in a ponytail, it cascaded down her back, gleaming like honey.

Veronica bent and opened the pastry drawer, then stopped short. Sent Maya a frown. "What happened to all the muffins?"

"I have no idea." Maya shrugged. She felt the bulky bag clamped under her arm.

"Well, that's just wrong. Who would do that? There were plenty a few hours ago." Veronica slid open several more drawers, as if maybe she had chosen the wrong one. As if someone might have rearranged things.

Maya shrugged again. Quit shrugging, she told herself. Veronica stood staring at her.

"Were you looking for something, too?" Veronica asked, still irritated. Her brows pulled together, her golden-brown eyes probing. A lioness, Maya thought. A sphinx.

"No. I'm just leaving." Maya twisted a little as she moved past, shifting the lumpy bag away. She slipped through the door and felt Veronica's gaze bore into the back of her head.

Maya told Alex quickly what she'd discovered, that someone may have meddled with the packaging. He would be on his own for a short time because she wanted to run back to her office and drop the pastries at the lab.

"Should I come with you?" he asked, alarmed.

"No, I'll be right back. There's still nearly two hours to go, and the clinic is so busy today. I just don't want this sitting in my car all night in the heat." She wrapped her arms lightly around her bundle, protective but careful not to squeeze it, wanting the wrappers intact until they were examined. "This might be important—we can talk about it tonight. It may also be nothing. Or I could just be crazy…it's been said before."

Alex raised one eyebrow. "You only want to talk tonight?"

"Well. We can't talk all night. We might have to find other things to do."

"I'll come up with something," he said, and they both smiled.

59

On Friday Alex looked forward to the weekend, when he and Maya would study maps and plan their escape. The world seemed completely different now. Maybe the lusty thrill of a new lover made him starry-eyed, but he didn't think so. It felt deeper; it was not like they just met. For over a year they had teased, embraced, shared stories. Shared deep flaws. They were not exactly brand new.

Maya's theory about the muffins, that someone had pierced the cellophane wrappers and maybe injected something with a needle, felt both outrageous and shrewd.

Focus, do your job. It was out of his hands now, plenty of law enforcement people on the case. His old patient Arthur Mason visited that morning, trembling with anger, incensed at his "harsh interrogation" by the police about coming to the clinic so often. Arthur's rheumy eyes leaked and his pink rabbity nose twitched and dripped. Alex kept handing him tissues and assured him there would be no more police.

Alex sent Maya an email, asking for any reports on the muffins. She responded with a single word, *Patience*, but he could feel her smile, her sharp gray eyes.

One last task, an advisory meeting with Veronica at the end of the day. Patience, he repeated to himself. In ten months, she would graduate and be out of his scope forever. She would always remind him of his mother, never a good thing. He preferred three impaired Jim Barrows over one intact Veronica Sampson, and Barrow wasn't even his personal advisee. Not that Scott Sherman did much to help Jim. Scott breezed in and out, increasingly shallow and preoccupied with everything except his work. They had hardly spoken in weeks—Scott seemed aloof, distant. Several times Alex saw him speak too brusquely with residents, and once Scott tossed a critical comment toward Alex.

"Alex." Veronica stood smiling in his doorway, holding a paper plate with three or four thick cookies. Gold earrings twinkled against her neck through her hair.

Alex made himself smile back. "Hi, V. I hope you know where those cookies came from."

She laughed. "No worries. Dr. Mercer—Agatha—was here in the attending office. You know how she loves to bake us goodies. I brought you a couple in case you were hungry. And I have to ask a quick favor."

He actually was hungry, and Agatha's cookies always tasted amazing. He noticed how Veronica did the same thing with Mercer's first name. It felt forced, an artificial privilege, but it shouldn't annoy him as much as it did.

"Of course. What's the favor?" He set the plate on his desk and took a cookie, rich and buttery as usual, studded with something sweet and crunchy, maybe toffee.

"Can we delay our meeting about twenty or thirty minutes? I just found out that a surgeon admitted one of my patients to the hospital for bowel surgery tomorrow. I'd like to run over and say hello to her, make sure she's medically stable."

"Sure." Alex suppressed his aggravation. Her impulse was correct and he should encourage such behavior, even though it meant staying later—exactly the sort of responsibility he hoped she would embrace. Since he wasn't seeing Maya tonight, not till tomorrow, he told himself to be generous. "Go see her, and then come back and we'll meet."

"Great. Thanks. Save me a cookie." She hurried down the hall, and he heard the outer door open and shut.

The clinic fell quiet. Alex usually enjoyed the late solitude, except nowadays he felt uneasy walking alone to the basement parking garage, startling at footsteps, peering down the stairwell. He should escort Veronica to her car when they were done, something that never would have occurred to him before.

He sent a few lab letters to patients, explaining their blood tests. If there were abnormalities, he always called his patients on the phone, but these were routine. Nearly thirty minutes now, and he began feeling both impatient and tired. He realized Veronica could have seen her hospital patient after their meeting, but that ship had sailed. Then Maya called.

"We're onto something here." She sounded breathless. "Many of the wrappers have clearly been altered. Punctured. And there's definitely abnormal chemicals in some of those muffins. Not all, not even half. Opioids for sure. Maybe benzos. It will take longer to check for other substances. Right now they're trying to find fingerprints."

"Besides yours, you mean," he pointed out. He could hardly believe this might be happening, right under their noses. It certainly explained Maya's symptoms—she ate a muffin on that afternoon she became so ill. It would be easy to ask if everyone with the so-called stomach virus had also consumed any. He tried to reason this out, felt he should get somewhere, but he didn't feel very sharp. No doubt because he and Maya stayed up so late last night, playing in bed. So worth it, though. He smiled to himself and bit into another cookie.

"Right," Maya said dryly. "And the fingerprints of the vending delivery person, and who knows how many other packers and distributors. Or anyone who looked through the drawer. But we've got the prints on file for everyone who works at the clinic, so that's good."

Alex explained his meeting, waiting for Veronica. Maya sympathized and said she planned to work late, too, finishing her cryptosporidium tasks. Besides, she wanted to see if the lab found more. She poked at Alex a little, saying how tired he sounded. How maybe he couldn't keep up with her and maybe she'd go easy on him next time. Alex grinned and they disconnected. He resumed his lab letters, but had lost his concentration.

Veronica appeared at last. She slid into the chair as always, like a stealth move, her hand on his wrist, searching his face and eyes.

"How have you been?" she asked warmly.

"I'm good." He felt languid, didn't want this meeting. He would keep it short. "You know, the usual. A little tired. I should get more sleep. How was your patient at the hospital?"

"Oh, she's fine. I'm just excited about my trip this weekend." She explained she was flying to visit a friend, going straight to the airport after they were done.

Alex couldn't quite track what she said. She rambled on about her trip, her friend, not completely making sense. He wanted to inquire about her rotation this month, but he couldn't remember whether it was orthopedics or ophthalmology. Something that started with O. Instead oleander came randomly to his mind. What an idiot…what was wrong with him? His face felt numb and his mouth barely worked.

She'd quit talking, sat watching him. His eyes fell shut. He forced them open, then they closed again.

"You just wait right here, Alex." She patted his hand. "I'll be back in a second."

"Hm?" He tried to focus on her.

She smiled and left.

Alex slumped over the desk in his chair, barely propped with his arms. Not good. He vaguely knew he was off in a bad way, but he couldn't think. His limbs weighed tons apiece, nearly impossible to move. Then his phone rang, right by his hand, and he managed to grasp it. Maya.

"Alex." Her voice electric. "Are you home yet? On your way home?"

"Not yet." His words like cement in his mouth.

"Are you alone?"

"Mm."

"Alex. It might possibly be Veronica. She already left, right? Her fingerprints are all over the muffins. All of them. Where are you?"

"Uh…"

"Do you understand what I just said?" Her voice turned shrill. "What's wrong? Say something."

Veronica returned. She plucked the phone from his hand and hit the button, ending the call. She looked coldly at the screen. "Is she your girlfriend, Alex? Are you fucking her now?"

A distant circuit in his brain fired, furious at what she said. He tried to react, declare his outrage, but only mumbled a few syllables. He couldn't even sit up, slouched against the desk. Veronica moved about and tidied the room. Holding a box of antiseptic wipes, she scrubbed one across his desk. Then she stepped around him and gently swiped off his face, his lips. Removed his glasses and set them on the desk. The wipes tasted terrible against his mouth, like raw chemicals.

"Just checking for cookie crumbs," she murmured, tucking the wipes in her purse.

She picked up his phone again, and a strange smile played across her face as she rapidly thumb-typed a message. Satisfied, she scrubbed the phone with another wipe and dropped the phone on the floor, nudged it away with her foot.

"That should do it, Alex." She picked up the plate with one cookie left, wrapped the cookie in a paper napkin and slid it into her purse. Observing him, she checked her watch and counted his breaths, nodded to herself. Her hair floated around her in a wide aura, honey and amber.

It seemed to fill the room. Her face suddenly right in front of his, her citrine eyes wide. "I wish I could stay, but I'm going now. Sweet dreams."

Alex slumped further, his head on the desk. In the edge of his vision he saw his phone on the floor, flashing and ringing, an incoming call. It must be Maya.

But he couldn't move. He couldn't anything.

60

"Pick up, pick up," Maya muttered. Alex's phone rang until voicemail took over. She dialed twice more, same thing.

Just give him a minute, she thought. Their connection had ended abruptly, so surely he would call right back. Some glitch in the signal, or maybe he hit the wrong key. Maybe she did.

He hadn't sounded right, his voice blurry. Again, likely a failed connection—electronics around the hospital could be temperamental. He seemed alone, still at the clinic. Maya caught her leg jittering nervously, her fingers drumming the desk. Another minute passed and her anxiety climbed. Earlier, he'd mentioned his advisory appointment with Veronica, but Maya assumed she had long gone.

A dreadful premonition swept over her. She thought of the oleander and his broken bicycle and the fear escalated. She tried again and got nothing but voicemail. She had no clue what to do, except to go there.

Maya hurried from her office, picking up speed. On a Friday evening, nearly everyone was gone. She rushed down the hall and burst through into the lobby, blundering right into Mel on the other side of the door as he headed for the exit as well. The security guard stood up at his desk as they collided and staggered, both nearly falling down.

"Whoa there," Mel said, grabbing her. "Where's the fire?"

"It's Alex," she stammered. "He won't answer his phone. He sounded strange. I think something's really wrong. I just don't know." She twisted away.

"Easy. Start over," Mel insisted. But he looked intent, believing her.

She blurted it out. How her illness last week was probably not a virus. The tainted muffins, Veronica's fingerprints. Alex's meeting with Veronica, how oddly he talked. How he'd disappeared.

"I mean, it's probably nothing. I'm sure he's fine," she spluttered, now doubting herself. If it turned out to be nothing, she would kill him for not answering, she thought irrationally.

"Crap," Mel exclaimed, pushing her forward. "Let me go with you. You got a gun in your car?"

"A gun?" Maya screeched. "Of course not."

"Well, I do—my hunting rifle. Just in case. I'll drive."

Despite her alarm, Maya nearly smiled. "Good god, Mel. We're not in Tombstone."

Still standing nearby, hearing everything, the security guard called out. Gary, a friendly middle-aged man with a heavy moustache who took his job seriously, who always looked a little bored. "Hey! Can I help?"

"Yes, please," Maya said over her shoulder. "Call hospital security. Tell them to meet us at the residency clinic." She gave him the address as Mel held open the door and overheated air leapt into the lobby like a beast that had been waiting, wanting inside. The day still ludicrously sizzling. But because Maya was not a regular clinic employee she did not have a key. She wouldn't be able to get in without help.

"Consider it done!" Gary shouted, snatching the phone. "Keep me posted."

Maya felt a moment of déjà vu as Mel unlocked his truck, the same clunky truck she'd driven to the horses that night so long ago. Whit being such a jerk. A whirling memory of battling Manchado in the dust, her frustrated breakdown, the soothing waters of the tank. It seemed years ago.

It was good that Mel drove. Too much panic gnashed in her brain. The truck bounced over a grate and into the street, and she told him where to turn.

"Now let's stay calm," Mel rumbled, deftly muscling the truck around corners, his eyes cutting over to her. The air conditioning remained pathetic, a tiny breath of air, and Maya felt sweat creep down her back. "I'm sure it's all nothing. But that's quite a story."

Maya nodded, biting her lip as Mel ran through a stop sign with barely a hesitation. At a red light, he shrugged out of his blazer.

"Too damn hot," he muttered. "Why the hell do we live here, anyway?"

"Because we're crazy?" Apparently that phrase would follow her forever. She took a long breath, then pointed. "Turn left, here."

The clinic building stood behind the hospital, the surface lot nearly empty. Maya couldn't tell if Alex's car was still there because he parked underground. Mel jerked to a stop sideways by the door, then reached behind the seat to grab his rifle.

"No, Mel." Maya halted his hand. "We've got security coming. You'll get yourself shot."

"Fine." He scowled but let go.

Two uniformed security men came walking across the street, chatting, no hurry, then altered direction and headed for Maya and Mel as they climbed from the truck.

"You the guys who called?" one asked. Older, skeptical. He squinted in the low sun that burned like acid across the glowing sky.

Maya spilled the complicated events, knew she didn't quite make sense, which made her more agitated. The harder she tried, the more outlandish it sounded.

"Long story short," Mel said with authority, "we're very worried about a colleague who might be extremely ill. Dangerously ill. We can sort out the rest later."

The guards exchanged a glance and the older one hitched his belt, laden with a pager and flashlight and revolver. Heat radiated up from the pavement and heat fell thickly from the sky, everyone perspiring and breathing hard.

"You got any identification?" The guard glanced dubiously at Mel's cowboy boots and the dilapidated truck.

Maya thanked her stars for their Arizona Public Health badges, which immediately got the guards' respect. She wanted to run up the stairs to the sixth floor, but the man fumbled through his keys and unlocked the elevator while she simmered behind him. They all rode up silently and Maya considered screaming in frustration. Mel grimaced sympathetically.

The place looked deserted, blinds drawn, down for the night. The guard made a sour face, scanning around, although his younger partner seemed more engaged and sent Maya an encouraging look. The man finally unlocked the clinic door and Maya rushed in, Mel on her heels. She flew straight to Alex's office as the guard called out after her, something about *just a minute here, slow down.*

Maya cried out.

Alex lay sprawled across the desk, half fallen from his chair, motionless. His face cyanotic and blue.

61

A frantic blur of action, time wheeling, distorted. Maya only recalled snatches of it later, too overcome and horrified. The dead weight of Alex as she and Mel dragged him from his chair to the floor. Alex limp on his back, barely breathing, her rush of elation at seeing his chest rise. Mel tipping Alex's head back, pinching his nose and sealing his mouth against Alex's, blowing a hard breath into him.

"Call 911," Maya shouted to the guards, laying her ear against his chest, thankful to hear his heartbeat. She didn't even see the stethoscope lying there on his desk.

"Who is he—" started the older guard. The young one already dialing, but Mel couldn't see him.

Mel raising his head, furious. "Call 911, goddammit!"

Mel blowing another breath, asking Maya if there was any oxygen.

Maya, running to the back, finding a heavy green oxygen tank in the procedure room and wrestling it down the hall, her bad hip catching and tripping, sprawling her across the floor, cursing. Then nearly crashing the tank into Alex.

His face lost the blue tinge, began turning pink.

The paramedic crew clattered in and swept everyone out. Mel tugged Maya from Alex's side to give them more room. Maya gulped and time slowed and became real again.

A short paramedic stood in front of her, scratching quickly on a clipboard. A smooth face, a hard expression. "You know him? Is he an addict?"

"No!" Maya aghast. "Of course not."

A jaundiced look. "Yeah. Well, he's got pinpoint pupils. Probably opioids. We'll know in a second—he's getting naloxone right now."

"Opioids," Maya whispered. She felt weak and her legs wobbled. How had Veronica done this? She straightened abruptly. "Be careful in there—there might be evidence. He's been drugged."

"Really." Disbelieving. He glanced back over his shoulder. "Hey. I think he's waking up."

Maya tried to push past him, desperate, but he shifted and blocked the door.

"Lady, please," he said roughly. "Just step back, okay?"

"Let her in," Mel commanded. "She's a goddamn doctor. If she says he was drugged, he was drugged. Listen to her."

The paramedic's eyebrows shot up and he stepped aside.

Her heart bursting, Maya knelt by Alex, who blinked and stared in amazement at the room full of people.

62

Alex sank down, deep under dark blue water. Black-blue obsidian water, heavy and cold. His bones, his organs, gripped with winter, dense as ice. A few tiny muffled sounds, inconsequential. He felt both peaceful and grim, slowly drifting lower. Sinking helplessly toward the bottom.

Something changed. Sounds grew louder and he began rising, faster and faster toward the surface, brighter. Suddenly blinding light, loud voices. Maya clutching his hand, tears on her cheeks. He'd never seen her cry.

"Maya," he said. Or maybe he only thought it. He searched her face, wanting to understand, lost and blank.

"Vitals better," someone said, helping him sit up when he struggled. "Respirations up. Oxygen up."

Another paramedic squatted beside Alex, gave Maya a sharp look. He held Alex's phone, glanced back and forth between them.

"Buddy," he said kindly to Alex, "what's going on? Why would you do this?"

"Do what?" Alex gaped, still grappling with all the people, some milling and talking, some watching him. He felt he'd been gone for months.

"It's on your phone, man. You were sending a text, saying you wanted to kill yourself. That things would never work out. Looks like…" he turned the phone, peered at it, "…you were sending it to someone named Maya. You remember her?"

"I'm Maya," Maya blurted.

Alex shook his head, more alert now, growing upset. "I never wrote that. I'm not suicidal—that's absurd. Why are you here?"

Maya grabbed the phone and stared at the text, then read it aloud, her voice savage. "I'm sorry Maya, but it will never work. I'm not good enough for you. Please don't mourn me. Eternally yours, Alex."

Maya choked, then whirled back to Alex. "It was Veronica, right? Do you remember her being here?"

Alex jolted, meeting Maya's eyes. His voice climbed, his heart pounded as his thoughts came together. "Yes. Yes. She handed me the cookies—she said Agatha Mercer baked them. But she didn't, did she? She took my phone. I couldn't move, and she left me here."

"Call the police," Maya said urgently to everyone, anyone. "Please. Right now."

Alex held up his arm to the paramedic, pointed frantically at his vein. "Draw my blood! She drugged me! Draw it right now!"

But Maya shook his other arm, speaking urgently in his ear, asking where they kept the personnel files. Asking for Veronica's address.

"Wait." Alex clutched his head, trying to think. A jumble in his mind, his memory cold sludge. Had she told him her travel destination? Why hadn't he paid more attention? "She said she was flying out tonight. She's probably at the airport. Unless she made that up…"

The young security guard took over, on the phone out in the hall, talking rapidly. Alex felt deep in a barrel, words echoing above his head, but he gestured the guard in and pointed to a framed photo of Veronica with her classmates, singled her out. Photographed Veronica smiled deadpan into the camera, her hair wild, standing slightly apart from the others. The guard nodded intently, still talking.

"Take my blood—" Alex began insisting again.

Maya held onto him. "They'll get it in the ER. That's where we're going right now. We're going to get her, Alex."

Mel stood over them, his tangled eyebrows drawn together in a terrible scowl. Alex wondered dimly why he was there.

"Damn right we will," Mel grumbled, his face stony with disgust. "We need to check all around this area—she might still be hanging out. Sometimes they do that." He threw Maya a glare. "I should've brought my rifle."

63

Maya and Alex sat arm in arm in his tenth-floor hospital room and watched the storm. They opened the blinds and pulled chairs up to the window as the tempest moved in, fuming black clouds that slung lightning at the ground, at the sky, at other clouds. Then the storm engulfed the hospital and thunder shook the thick walls, rain flowing down the glass.

"Thunder is good," Maya quoted, *"thunder is impressive; but it is lightning that does the work."*

Alex took her hand, stroked her fingers. "Who said that?"

"Mark Twain." Maya squeezed back, searched his pale face. He looked so weak. "One of my favorites."

"I'd rather be home," Alex complained. "No reason I need to stay here."

"You're a terrible patient. Just be quiet and follow your doctor's orders. What if that happened again?"

In the emergency room, Alex started slipping away once more. His words blurred and his eyes closed, respirations dropping. It took another dose of naloxone to reverse the persistent narcotic.

Alex switched his mouth and looked back out the window. "I'm sure the danger's over now."

"No one would send you home tonight after that," Maya asserted. "I'll spring you out in the morning. And you can consider this your raincheck. Now we're even."

"Maybe I'll drive myself home when no one's looking."

"You just don't like being the center of attention." Maya poked him. "You know what else Twain said?"

"Something I won't like, I'm sure."

"He said that it's better to keep your mouth closed and let people think you're a fool, than to open it and remove all doubt."

Alex made a face at her. "Since when did you become such a prophet? And why do you know so many quotes?"

Maya smiled and leaned against him.

A tap at the door and Burt Rogers ambled in, the intern from that evening with Whit and Gloria Gonzales. On call again tonight, Burt came to tell them about Alex's drug test.

"Fentanyl," he announced, wincing. He watched rain stream off the window. "Wow, look at that come down. Lots of flashfloods tonight. Stay out of the washes."

"Fentanyl? Crap," Alex exclaimed. "That's terrifying."

Maya clutched his arm, appalled. Fentanyl, the most potent opioid ever, fifty times stronger than morphine. Originally developed for anesthesia and now a huge problem in the opioid epidemic, illicit fentanyl caused thousands of deaths every year. Tens of thousands. No one had to say it aloud—Alex was fortunate to be alive.

"Pretty creepy, huh," Burt rumbled. His eyes roamed the monitors on the wall. "How're you feeling now? Your vitals look pretty good."

"I feel perfect," Alex claimed. "Ready to go home."

"Dr. Reddish." Burt looked distressed. "You could crash again."

"Thank you, Dr. Rogers." Maya flashed her eyes at Alex.

Alex groaned with frustration. Burt hooked on his stethoscope and listened to Alex's chest.

"Okay for now," Burt said. "But you'd better be here when I come check you again in an hour. No offense, sir."

Alex sighed once more while Burt left.

Another knock on the door, and here came Mel and Sheila. Sheila rushed in and threw her arms around a very surprised Alex, kissed him loudly on the cheek.

"I'm sorry, so sorry," Sheila carried on. She fussed with him, wiped lipstick off his face, straightened his gown, then formally shook his hand. "I know we don't really know each other, but we were just so worried about you. Mel told me everything. Lord love a duck, Alex."

"Mel was the hero," Maya said. "He reacted faster than anyone, including me. When he saw Alex lying there all cyanotic, he immediately leapt in and started mouth-to-mouth."

Self-conscious, Mel and Alex both rubbed their lips at the same time.

Sheila beamed and hugged Mel's arm. Then Mel sat down and turned grave.

"I thought you should know. That's why I'm here." His gaze cold. "Lucky for me, I know a few cops in high places. They apprehended Veronica—she was at the airport, just like Alex here said. About to board a plane for New York." He paused, put his hand on Alex's knee. "They'll be searching her apartment, but there was pretty incriminating evidence on her. And she had one of those damn cookies in her purse."

64

A little later, Alex was given the opportunity to read Veronica's journal. Not the original journal, but a photocopy, and he had to sit at the prosecutor's office with a legal aide. He brought Maya along.

He hesitated to go at first, queasy at the thought, unable to decide whether being inside Veronica's head would make him feel better or worse. His confidence had shattered. Alex once thought he could read people reasonably well; although wracked with doubts, he'd been fairly certain Jim Barrow would not harm him. He even understood his mother's brazen façade, which radiated from her low self-esteem. But Veronica's deception rocked him back, far back. He'd been clueless, and now felt devastated.

The cookie in her purse tested positive for fentanyl, packed with crushed bits of fentanyl lollipops, the kind used in pediatric surgery for sedation. And he'd eaten two. He remembered thinking how the tiny sweet pieces must be toffee.

An officer described her arrest. Ready to board her plane, she stood in line at the gate when they approached. She glanced quickly back and forth, then her face changed. Her eyes widened and her lips parted in surprise.

"You must be mistaken," she spoke with assurance, grasping the officer's arm. "You must be looking for someone else. I'm a physician."

He verified her name and asked her to move away from the line. She raised her head high, haughty. Alex imagined how he felt, impaled by those lion eyes.

"You are very mistaken," she repeated coldly. "Be careful. If you stop me, your life will be hell. I will absolutely sue you, and you will lose your job."

She went with them then, silent and disdainful. Her face filled with hate. She had a logic and an explanation for everything. Yes, she met with Reddish earlier that day. He seemed fine, although rather depressed. Now that she thought about it, definitely depressed. She had worried about him. But she could not explain the fentanyl in her purse. She indignantly insisted that someone must have planted it there, hinted at Jim Barrow and his problems. Or maybe someone else at the clinic. How dare they.

When they searched her apartment, they found vials of drugs, mostly opioids and benzos. Her cabinets stocked with gleaming jars of plant materials, dried leaves and flowers and stems, some minced, some ground, neatly labeled. Oleander, datura, dieffenbachia, nightshade. Others not labeled, not yet analyzed.

They found a tool, a sharp metal rasp, its tiny teeth clogged with carbon fibers.

Alex could not stop himself from researching, looking up the characteristics of serial poisoners and serial killers. Yet he found little helpful information: no clear genetic patterns, no reliable personal histories. Many suffered childhood abuse or cruelty, some did not. Most were men; only one in six were women. Many had endearing personalities, sociable and charming. Their families and neighbors expressed shock at their deeds. Many pursued careers in medicine, became nurses and doctors, where they found easy access to patients and drugs.

None felt remorse or regret. They enjoyed what they did. Their victims might be strangers or people they knew, might be perceived enemies or simply random encounters. Eventually Alex quit seeking answers, sickened by the disturbing stories.

He finally sat down with Maya to read through the journal. It seemed healthier to know since he obsessed about it anyway, imagining what Veronica wrote.

When the close-shaven young aide handed him the papers, eyes wide, he shook his head with disbelief.

"I've been reading up on this." He shook Alex's hand, then Maya's. "I couldn't find any cases implicating a female physician. And it's pretty rare with doctors anyway, even with male doctors. There are some. And nurses, yes—probably more of them. But still rare."

He kept saying *rare*, Alex noted. Almost as if reassuring himself.

"Yes, not common," Alex agreed. Clearly, the man needed comfort. Alex couldn't decide if the scarcity made him feel better or worse. Better, because he shouldn't have to be constantly vigilant in the future. Or worse, because it nevertheless happened to him. And how many times did perpetrators simply get away with it, never discovered?

The aide sat apart, watching them while trying to seem like he wasn't watching, pretending to read on a laptop.

Most of Veronica's entries were short, often mundane. A peculiar chart of her bedtimes and when she awoke, down to the minute. Patient cases, especially cancer cases, mostly those who languished in terminal states. She liked talking with them about death. Her handwriting spiked and heavy, sharp back-slanted letters full of hooks and points.

"We can quit any time," Maya said to Alex, turning a page. She leaned against him and it felt good.

"For sure," Alex agreed. Then the next two entries took his breath. Afterward, he didn't recall everything she wrote, but some of the phrases burned into his brain.

> I hoped this place would be an improvement. But they're no better here than anywhere. People always disappoint me.
>
> It's always easier than I think it will be. I worry so much ahead of time, make elaborate plans, in case someone suspects. I design excuses, escapes…but then no one ever suspects. That makes me bolder, I think.

"Jesus," said Alex. His heart stumbled and ran.

"You okay?" Maya asked.

Alex nodded. "Are you?"

"I'm pretty pissed off," she said tightly.

Alex turned the page, scanned for something revealing. He didn't have far to look.

> I like watching him struggle. Watching him fail. He's a blundering disaster and he has no idea what's wrong. Drink more coffee, my friend.

"Jim Barrow," Maya whispered.

"And now I'm pissed," Alex said, infuriated for Jim. Such a mild soul— why target him?

Only a few pages left. Alex wanted to stop, feeling empty and depressed, but he clenched his jaw and forced himself on.

> I admit I enjoy watching them. They think it's something else, make excuses. I talk to them as if nothing was happening, observing them. They don't realize that I'm taunting them. Most of them asked for it.

Alex set the pages down. How could anyone process this?

"Don't you wonder how many other incidents there have been, that no one knows about? Maybe patients, too," Maya said. A probe was underway. She shuddered slightly against him.

"Maybe we should quit reading," he suggested.

"No, we're almost done. I want to know." Maya picked up the papers.

His bicycle crashed. But it wasn't satisfying…it's better when I see it. His story went quickly through the grapevine, so I didn't even have to ask. I acted casual, surprised, like I felt so bad.

He was hurt. He suffered. Good.

This new method is working. She got sick, along with the others. It's so simple—I tell them I was sick, too, and no one suspects. I wish they knew how smart I am—it's almost too easy. It makes me want more. Much more.

Alex dropped the papers, shoved them away. Saw the aide eye him. Alex's emotions bounced around the room and off the walls, colliding and crashing, a tsunami of aftershocks. Anger, fear, bitterness, hatred. Failure, distrust. A chaotic chain of reactions. But also relief—that was there, too.

"She got too confident," Maya said quietly.

Alex looked in her eyes. That uncommon color; fewer than five percent of people had truly gray eyes. Sometimes stormy, sometimes soft, as deep as the sea. Right now troubled and bleak.

"Well." He wanted to take the papers and throw them against the wall, trample them under his feet. "I suspect we both should sign up for some counseling. If we ever hope to sleep well again." He paused and the corner of his mouth deepened. "Of course, you may be the worst sleeper I've ever known. You stay up all night when you don't even have to."

Maya unexpectedly laughed. "I still wonder why you haven't run away from me."

"Let's get out of here."

They went outside, where the furnace heat of late August struck like a blow. Alex pulled Maya hard against him until she wiggled.

"Kind of hot," Maya remarked mildly. She stretched on her toes to kiss his cheek, then shook out her arms as if shedding something.

Alex peered up, the sky a wayward mob of clouds, streaks and clumps and veils, promising rain by evening. He endured a dim memory of that deep blue chill under the glacial curtain of fentanyl, and the heat seemed good. Withering, cleansing.

The sun, brash and caustic, felt like an avenger.

"I may never want to feel cold again," he said.

65

Maya ordered pizza and salad, delivered to her house at the end of the day. They all collapsed to eat among splashed tarps and drippy buckets. Everyone had volunteered to help Maya finish her indoor painting project: Alex, Rosa and Rafael, Mel and Sheila.

Before putting on their old ragged clothes that morning, though, they all visited their polling places to vote for the helmet law. The predictions did not look favorable.

Maya carried a pail of ice into the living room for their drinks. They sprawled, tired and salty, their shirts splotched with paint. She flipped on the television to find the early returns, then dropped down by Alex and helped herself to pizza.

"I guess I might as well face it." She felt resigned, hollow. So many meetings and interviews. All those deaths last year, all the deaths to come. "It's really got no chance."

"Closer than you'd think." Mel pointed at the screen.

Maya sat up straighter and stared. "Well. That's unexpected."

"Maybe your hard work accomplished something," Mel said sagely. "We all thought that it would. If you don't get enough votes now, for sure you'll get it the next time."

Sheila refilled Alex's lemonade, put more pizza in front of him. Somewhere along the way she started mothering Alex, something everyone noticed. Maya loved it, for Alex could use a new mother.

"Thanks," Alex exclaimed, looking up at Sheila. Paint freckled his cheeks. "What did I do to deserve such attention?"

Sheila patted his shoulder and sat next to Mel. Not just by him, but snuggled against him. Maya and Rosa exchanged a glance, and Rosa smothered a smile.

Sheila went on; she never spared words. "You poor man. Someone needs to help keep an eye on you. It might as well be me. That horrible woman almost killed you—I'd like to give her a piece of my mind."

"Isn't that my job, watching out for Alex?" Maya pretended to be offended. She imagined Sheila with her short hair bristling, the errant green curl, shaking a finger at Veronica and berating her through the bars. A guard watching with alarm. Maya laughed. "Sorry, sorry. It's not funny. I just pictured you yelling at her."

She clicked off the television. The returns would take hours and it wouldn't pass anyway. Even a little hope felt cruel.

"Of course it's your job," Sheila agreed, beaming affectionately at both of them. "But since this young man seems prone to trouble, you need backup."

Mel grumbled and pointed at Maya. "There's your troublemaker. If you want my opinion."

Maya feigned innocence. She watched Alex take a helping of salad, then stir it with his fork, sifting through the greens. She bit her lip, knowing he subconsciously searched for shreds of something that didn't belong. He must have felt her eyes for he looked up at her, his mouth bent. She wondered how long it would take before they were normal again. If ever.

Mel talked with Rosa and Rafael, making plans for the weekend when Rafael would go to the ranch with Mel. Stay in the bunkhouse, start learning to ride properly, start handling a rope. "Not just jumping bareback on a horse in a pen," Mel complained, cutting Rafael a stern look. "Besides, Manchado needs to begin real work, earn his keep. It's not good for a young horse to lounge around all day. I've got plenty of other ponies you can ride."

Rosa agreed to the plan, but only if she could come cook a few meals so they wouldn't just be eating chili from cans.

"I know how men are." Rosa glared around at all the males.

Mel mumbled about interfering women while Rafael glowed, his thin face radiant, saying little. Maya interjected, pointing out that no one was getting on any horse without a helmet. A new child-sized riding helmet now hung in the shed for Rafael.

Eventually everyone went home, leaving Maya and Alex to themselves. They turned their backs on the paint and strolled outside, where late bronze light streaked the heavens and stars emerged above, distant fires. A fragile rim of moon swung near the horizon, and a few dark clouds smeared the sky.

"I think it's cooler tonight," Alex remarked.

Maya sniffed the air. "A little."

They wandered to the corral where Manchado rested. His eyes came open and he walked over, put his face to Alex and inhaled. Maya watched Alex breathe back into his nostril like she had shown him.

"Aren't you going to miss him?" Alex asked, his hand on the horse's nose.

"Yes." Maya knew it had to happen, that Manchado had a busy life ahead, but that didn't make it easier. "Mel's right, though—he needs a job, and he needs seasoning. He can't spend the next twenty years in my backyard, doing nothing. Mel says he'll bring me another, a well-broke saddle horse that both Rafael and I can use. He wants me to try riding again…he says it's in my soul." Maya contemplated the frail moon. "I don't think I can. You know, my stupid leg. It doesn't stretch that way."

Alex ran his hand down her hip. "You know, last winter I went to that big horse show in Scottsdale. I saw women riding sidesaddle…it was kind of elegant. Did you ever try that?" Before she could answer, he went on, impish. "And from what I've noticed lately, there might be more stretch in your hip than you think. I wouldn't mind being your—um—stretching coach. So to speak."

Maya's eyes widened, for sidesaddle had never occurred to her. Then his last words registered, and she smacked him. He slowly smiled, his hair in his eyes. Maya felt her heart chime like a bell…she wanted to stand there beside him all night under the soft sky, the sly smile of moon.

"We'll see." She leaned her head on him.

They hung over the rails as Jupiter materialized, a clean white burn. Doves shuffled in the tree, tiny noises.

"I don't suppose our lives will ever really be normal now, will they?" Maya said quietly, lacing her fingers in his.

Alex laughed briefly, gave her a look. "My life used to be normal."

"Your life was never normal," she scoffed. "You chess weirdo."

"Besides," he went on, turning serious. "Nothing is normal. I've got new concerns at the residency. One of the interns might be seriously obsessive, really impaired—I'm worried about her. And I think Scott Sherman has an alcohol problem…the other day he smelled like liquor. At noon." He frowned. "Well, I don't need to go into that right now, do I? Let's just say the year ahead doesn't look easy."

"Ha. You think you have problems? I mean, I know this isn't a contest, but Zika is moving up the Mexican coast, headed straight for us. And chikungunya is rising in Mexico, too. Suicide rates are higher than ever, and more people have asthma. Don't even get me started on vaping. And there's a new West Nile outbreak in Sun City." Maya closed her eyes. "Stupid mosquitoes."

"Should we foster any this year?"

"I've already submitted the paperwork. Teeny and Scratchy are waiting."

Alex slipped his arm around her, drew her off the fence. "Come on. Let's go look at the votes."

Maya lifted the hair off her neck, let the air cool her skin. She wasn't certain if she wanted to see the results yet.

Right now she felt at peace. A remarkable sensation.

Maybe she wouldn't check those returns until morning.

Acknowledgments

This novel would not have been possible without the skilled and enthusiastic support and guidance from Lisa Villarroel MD, Division of Preparedness, Medical Director, Arizona Department of Health Services.

Family physicians do everything. They do it all, all the time.

Thanks to my readers, early and late: Ted Cavallo, Cheryl Pagel MD, Kelly Luba DO, Cindy Alt RN, Patricia Cox, and Kristi Doyle.

Tremendous thanks to the patient and expert coaching of editor Margaret Dalrymple. And all the wonderful people at the University of Nevada Press for their endless support and hard work: Sara Hendricksen, JoAnne Banducci, Sara Vélez, Iris Saltus, and copyeditor Luke Torn.

Thanks to all who contributed ideas and fact-checking: Nicole Piemonte PhD, Nona Siegel NP, Sabrina Rocke DO, LeeAnne Denny MD, Stu Alt MD (about those carbon fibers), Aram Mardian MD (about controlled substances).

Deeply heartfelt thanks to Dan Klinski DVM, equine veterinarian, my hero for compassionately easing so many horses into the next world. Thanks to Brad Dirla for modeling humane horse breaking with a steady hand.

And all the valuable resources that helped inform the science:

Helmets

www.ghsa.org/issues/motorcycle-safety https://www.abc15.com/news/roads
/debate-continues-over-arizona-motorcycle-helmet-law
https://www.cdc.gov/motorvehiclesafety/calculator/factsheet/mchelmet.html
http://www.bikersrights.com/
https://www.cdc.gov/mmwr/preview/mmwrhtml/00036941.htm

Toxic plants

http://azpoison.com/
https://emedicine.medscape.com/article/154336-clinical
https://www.ncbi.nlm.nih.gov/pubmed/9322594
https://calpoison.org/news/cardiac-glycoside-poisoning
https://www.cdc.gov/mmwr/preview/mmwrhtml/00036554.htm

Fluoride

https://www.adn.com/alaska-news/2018/12/29/study-juneaus-lack-of-fluoride
-has-increased-cavities-in-children/
https://www.ncbi.nlm.nih.gov/pmc/articles/PMC5651468/

Cryptosporidium

https://www.ncbi.nlm.nih.gov/pubmed/26264893
https://www.cdc.gov/parasites/crypto/index.html
https://azdhs.gov/preparedness/epidemiology-disease-control/foodborne
/index.php#crypto
https://www.azdhs.gov/documents/preparedness/epidemiology-disease
-control/infectious-diseases-training/2017/presentations/iverson-tales-from
-crypto-web.pdf

Sporotrichosis

https://www.cdc.gov/fungal/diseases/sporotrichosis/index.html

Coccidioidomycosis

https://www.ncbi.nlm.nih.gov/pubmed/9062329
https://www.cdc.gov/mmwr/preview/mmwrhtml/mm5049a2.htm
https://www.cdc.gov/fungal/diseases/coccidioidomycosis/statistics.html

Rabies

https://www.cdc.gov/rabies/transmission/virus.html

Mosquitoes

Websites: AZDHS, MCHD, CDC
https://en.wikipedia.org/wiki/Mosquito

Palo Verde Generating Station

https://www.maricopa.gov/1659/Emergency-Planning-Zones https://en.wiki
pedia.org/wiki/Palo_Verde_Nuclear_Generating_Station
http://www.azcentral.com/arizonarepublic/news/articles/2011/08/14/20110814
palo-verde-nuclear-safety.html#ixzz5hDwljmrk

Opioids

Websites of the CDC, Arizona Department of Health Services, Maricopa County
Health Department

Marijuana

https://www.medpagetoday.org/publichealthpolicy/publichealth/78918?xid=nl
_mpt_investigative2019-04-03&eun=g1007166d0r&utm_source=Sailthru
&utm_medium=email&utm_campaign=InvestigateMD_040319&utm
_content=A&utm_term=NL_Gen_Int_InvestigateMD_Active

https://www.azdhs.gov/licensing/medical-marijuana/index.php#faqs-patients

Nutrition Action Letter, March 2019, "10 Things You Should Know About Cannabis"

Benzodiazepines

https://www.npr.org/sections/health-shots/2019/01/25/688287824/steep-climb
-in-benzodiazepine-prescribing-by-primary-care-doctors

https://www.drugabuse.gov/drugs-abuse/opioids/benzodiazepines-opioids

Serial Poisoners/Killers

https://www.psychologytoday.com/us/blog/wicked-deeds/201804/serial
-homicide-power-and-control

https://www.crimemuseum.org/crime-library/serial-killers/types-of-serial
-killers/

https://en.m.wikipedia.org/wiki/Serial_killer

https://en.wikipedia.org/wiki/Angel_of_mercy_(criminology)

https://www.theatlantic.com/magazine/archive/2019/10/are-serial-killers-more
-common-than-we-think/596647/

And for this fine work by a Pulitzer Prize–winning writer:

Stewart, James B. *Blind Eye: The Terrifying Story of a Doctor Who Got Away with Murder.* Simon & Schuster, 2000.

About the Auhtor

SANDRA CAVALLO MILLER is an author, poet, and retired academic family physician in Arizona who has helped launch hundreds of medical students and residents into their careers. She is the author of four novels, including the Dr. Abby Wilmore series books: *The Color of Rock, Where Light Comes and Goes*, and *What the River Said*. Her unlikely path to medicine includes degrees in anthropology and creative writing at the University of Illinois before attending Rush Medical College, and her essays and poetry have been published in *JAMA, PULSE-Voices from the Heart of Medicine, Under the Sun*, and *Embark*, among others. You are likely to find her hiking with a dog or riding a horse, playing piano badly, or sitting under a tree studying her latest hobby, volcanology. For more information, visit her author website at skepticalword.com.